MATE OF A ROYAL

MATE OF A ROYAL

USA TODAY & *WALL STREET JOURNAL* BESTSELLING AUTHORS

MEAGAN BRANDY
AMO JONES

This book is a work of fiction. Names, characters, places, and incidents are the product of the author's imagination or are used fictitiously. Any resemblance to actual events, locales, or persons, living or dead, is coincidental.

Entangled Publishing, LLC
644 Shrewsbury Commons Ave., STE 181
Shrewsbury, PA 17361
rights@entangledpublishing.com

Amara is an imprint of Entangled Publishing, LLC.
Visit our website at www.entangledpublishing.com.

Edited by Hoda Agharazi
Cover and Edge design by LJ Anderson
Cover images by Raspberry Floral/Creative Market, Pavel Shubin/Gettyimages, Sasha/Adobestock, and vasssaa/Gettyimages
Interior design by Toni Kerr

ISBN 978-1-68281-679-0
DIGITAL ISBN: 978-1-68281-816-9

Manufactured in the United States of America

First Edition June 2026

10 9 8 7 6 5 4 3 2 1

ALSO BY MEAGAN BRANDY AND AMO JONES

Lords of Rathe

Fate of a Royal
Fate of a Faux
Mate of a Royal

IF YOU FEEL TRIGGER WARNINGS ARE SPOILERS AND YOU DON'T NEED THEM, PLEASE SKIP THIS PAGE AND JUMP RIGHT IN.

Mate of a Royal is a dark, possessive romance featuring a reluctant pair of fated mates. However, the story includes elements that might not be suitable for all readers including, violence, gore, murder, blood, blood play, hunter / prey dynamic, bully romance, off-page discussions of massacre, and sex on the page. Please be mindful before diving in.

To the ones who feel exiled
by the same world that broke them.

Chapter One

Haide

"Run, little rabbits," I whisper, drawing back the bowstring, each step calculated against the soft forest floor.

The bow in my hands feels like an extension of my body. Exile Island pulses around me, its strange consciousness brushing against my mind like fingers through hair. It's as if no time at all has passed since I returned from Rathe and all of London's drama.

Three figures dart between the twisted trees ahead. Newcomers to the island. *Fresh meat.* They don't understand anything yet. Don't know that everything here is a game without consequences.

Distant wingbeats cut through the air above. I exhale as I tighten the bow further.

I track the first one. He's tall with panic written across his face. The arrow tip follows his frantic movements. I could pierce his throat before he takes another breath.

I smile and shift my aim.

The second target stumbles over a root and falls to her knees. Terror makes people clumsy. She looks up, somehow sensing my presence, and our eyes lock through the foliage. I wink and draw the string tighter.

"Please," she mouths.

I shift my aim again.

The third one is smarter.

He moves in a zigzag pattern, making himself a harder target. But not hard enough. I track him easily, the arrow finding his heart.

"Which one dies first?" I ask the forest. The trees don't answer, but I feel the island's hunger ripple through the soil beneath my feet.

I release the tension in the bowstring, lowering my weapon just enough to let them believe they've escaped. They'll run deeper into the island's embrace. The game is always better when they think they have a chance.

"You're toying with them again." Zevryn's voice comes from behind me, rich and deep.

I don't turn. "Took you long enough to catch up."

He steps beside me, brown skin gleaming with sweat from the hunt. "Not all of us were born part animal."

"Excuses." I nock another arrow, tracking the fleeing figures through the trees.

Zevryn grabs my wrist, forcing the bow down. "Do you

need a recap on how to pull this bow, Luda?"

"Fuck you!" I jerk away from his grip. "I'd still be able to beat your ass."

"Bullshit." His eyes narrow. "What's the matter, Haide?"

Okay, now he's pissing me off.

He sighs in clear boredom. "You had three clean shots. You didn't take any of them."

I bare my teeth. "I was savoring the moment."

"You were giving them a chance." His mouth quirks up. "The great Haide secret softie."

I swiftly draw my knife and press it to his throat. "Call me soft again."

He doesn't flinch, his mouth spreading wide. "Sof—"

My blade melts into his skin, blood spraying over my face. Life dies from the pits of his eyes, not with shock, but something else.

He smirks before his body hits the ground with a thud.

"Asshole!" I snap, cleaning my blade on my shoulder and slipping it back into the holster.

Lifting the bow again, I crack my neck and find my first target. "Looks like we're gonna have to keep this one short."

I release the bow right into her panicked face. It splits in half from the force.

I smirk, grabbing the next one and quickly finding the smartest newcomer.

He zigzags again. The moment he peers over his shoulder, I aim my arrow right into his eye.

Ten points to Haide!

I barely have the third locked in when the sound of wings beats through the air.

With a thud, boots hit gravel just as I unload the next arrow.

"Booyah!" I yell, smile wide just in time for Zev to swing at me.

I dodge his punch and swing behind him, wrapping my arm around his throat. "Nah, uh, bestie! You know you love me."

"Fuck you, Haide. You know I hate cracking through those damn fucking things."

I release my hold when I feel the tension leave his body. Only a pool of blood remains in the spot where I killed him.

"You can get me next time," I tease, the sound of large wings bashing through the air once more.

"Bullshit," Zev murmurs, plucking scales off his neck. "You damn well know I won't get one on you."

Actually, he could. He just chooses not to.

A blue dragon slams into the cliff with enough force to send rocks tumbling into the darkness below. His massive claws scrape deep grooves in the stone as he lands.

I turn over my shoulder just as the beast flings two fresh borns off his talons like they're nothing more than garbage. They hit the ground hard, rolling to a stop near the blood pool from Zev. Smoke curls from the dragon's nostrils in thick, angry streams while he stomps his foot again, making the whole cliff shake beneath us.

"Aw, come on!" I bat my lashes up at him, knowing full well he can see through my bullshit. "You know you love that I keep you guys busy! What would you do without me? Nap all day?"

If a dragon could roll his eyes, I swear this one would be giving me the most dramatic eye roll in existence. Instead, he snorts more smoke directly at my face, making me cough and wave it away.

"I've got my fair share of dragons to deal with," Zev says, brushing more scales off his shoulders with obvious irritation.

"But I still don't know how the hell you manage to test their patience like this. It's like you've got a death wish."

"You know death wishes don't work here, Zev. We just come back minutes later!"

The girl and her clever friend from earlier stumble forward. Now, with them this close, I see it. Fear. Bliss.

I pat them both on the shoulder. "Welcome to Exile Island! Try not to die."

They exchange a glance before making a run for it.

I turn, spreading my arms wide and free-fall off the cliff through humid air that rushes past my face. My stomach flips in that perfect way it always does right before I hit the water. The ocean swallows me whole, cold and dark, before I kick hard and break the surface.

Zevryn splashes down beside me seconds later, sending up a spray that hits me square in the face.

"Show off," I mutter, spitting out salt water.

"Says the woman who just murdered me for calling her soft."

We swim toward the main strip, where the real entertainment lives. The sounds hit first—screams, laughter, the crack of bone against bone. Music pounds from somewhere deeper in the chaos, drums that match the island's pulse.

Water streams off my clothes as I haul myself onto the dock. The strip sprawls before us in its usual beautiful disaster. Fires burn in metal drums, casting orange light across faces twisted in rage, ecstasy, or both. A woman slams a man's head into a stone wall repeatedly while he laughs. Two others fight over a piece of meat—that's probably not even edible—with bloody and relentless fists.

"Looks quiet tonight," Zevryn says, wringing out his shirt.

I snort. "Right. Real peaceful."

We push through the crowd, bodies pressing close in the heat and madness. Someone tries to grab my knife, and I break their fingers without looking. They curse but back off—most people here know better than to fuck with me twice.

Shouting spectators surround the main ring, cheering on the two fighters at the center. Evidence of their injuries will vanish in minutes. People here heal quick. One lunges with a makeshift spear, but his opponent manages to catch the weapon and yank it free.

He drives it through his attacker's chest.

The crowd roars.

"Place your bets!" someone shouts from the sidelines. "Next match in five!"

Welcome to Exile Island.

• • •

It's easy to spot newcomers.

You just look for the wide eyes and trembling bodies of those shaken from their first deaths. Their first stop is usually the old witch. Skin like cracked leather, eyes milky white but somehow seeing everything. The newcomers cluster around her like children, desperate for answers to make sense of this nightmare.

"Why can't we die?" asks the girl I shot earlier. She touches her cheek like she's still feeling the arrow's bite. "What is this place?"

The witch's laugh rattles in her chest, wet and knowing. She pokes the fire with a gnarled stick, sending sparks spiraling into the dark. "Death is the easy part. Quick. Clean. Over before you can scream." She leans forward, firelight carving deep shadows across her face. "It's the dying that hurts. And here? You feel every second of it."

"Exile Island doesn't let go." The witch spits into the flames. "This place was built as a prison centuries ago, when the old kingdoms needed somewhere to throw their worst. Murderers. Traitors. Those too dangerous to execute but too valuable to waste." Her fingers curl around her stick like claws. "There's plenty of folklore surrounding how this island came about." She pauses, and her white eyes land on me. Not much gives me the creeps—but she does.

Her mouth twitches. "But very few know the real truth." Her tone switches. "Like the dragons, for one. They're here to ensure we never leave. Can't leave…or are they?" she adds annoyingly. "Perhaps they serve a different purpose, only to be revealed when the time is right."

I cross my arms, and she pulls her attention back to the little pets who need a story time. Wish I could say I remember my first death here, but I don't.

"The island feeds on pain," the witch continues. "Every death, every scream, every drop of blood spilled—it eats it all. And in return, it keeps you breathing. Keeps you whole." She cackles again. "Well. Whole enough to break again. This is a place of nightmares. Not dreams."

I stiffen.

Dreams.

No one dreams on Exile Island.

Except me.

Zev casts a knowing glance my way. He's the only one who knows about the dreaming. He also knows to keep his mouth shut. Most of the time.

Before he can make a smartass remark, I spin away, calling over my shoulder, "I'm going to sharpen my knife so I can kill you with it again later."

I don't hesitate before dashing straight for the trees.

The forest grounds me when nothing else can.

The smell of dragon fire fills my nostrils as I run, skipping over cliff rocks, my boots pounding surfaces so jagged and steep they would send others tumbling to their deaths—hopefully he is one of those "others."

When I come to a halt, I can barely catch my breath as I search the ground for a suitable rock. Scooping up the first one I see, I examine it closely.

This will do.

I draw my knife and start slow, each stroke a clean scrape against the stone. My movements slow to a pause when I notice it.

The quiet.

No dragons beating through the air. No frantic footsteps of scared newbies. Not even the sounds of insects or birds.

My muscles seize and the hairs on the back of my neck rise.

Someone's behind me.

Chapter Two

Legend

She senses me before she sees me.

Her back goes stiff and those rough little hands freeze along her blade. Slowly, her head turns, eyes the color of the demented forest slamming into mine from fifty fucking feet away.

Her brows dip with confusion.

"Legend." My name leaves her lips like a wicked little prayer that claws at my insides, making my teeth ache to bite. Slowly, she turns until her body faces mine.

"How did you get here?"

I say nothing, creeping closer to the girl who thought she could run from this.

From me.

When I don't answer her ridiculous question, she asks another bullshit one. "Why are you here? You shouldn't have been able to get through the barrier."

"So that's how you want to play this?"

Haide glares, arms crossing over her chest. "I don't know what you're talking about."

A dark chuckle escapes me, and I cock my head to the side, feeling that heavy, constant fucking thrum that now beats beneath my chest. It grows louder with her nearness, driving me mad with the need to get closer. Need that's beyond my control.

"Now that's a lie if I've ever heard one."

"Go fuck yourself."

"Is that any way to talk to your king?"

"Sorry, please, *King Deveraux*, if you would kindly...go fuck yourself."

A split second after the last word leaves her mouth, she turns on her heels and runs.

"Bitch."

She's *fast*.

Faster than any chick I've seen, so I put some actual effort into my strides.

Sorry, baby girl, but no one is faster than me. I will catch you.

And when I do...

She bolts like a shot of lightning across the cliffs. I swear the earth answers her call, driving her farther from me, tearing through the blackened rock beneath her boots and throwing it back at me, like it knows I'll raze this place to the ground to get to her. Like it's trying to protect her from the sharpness of my claws.

It can't.

Nothing can.

What the little warrior princess doesn't know is I happen to like a good chase. I dart down the edge of the massive rocky cliff, thunder cracking from above, and a fire ignites in my veins. One that burns hotter than anything before it.

The girl I tore through realms for, the one whose blood sings to mine like we were carved from the same brutal stone, she thinks she has a chance. Bless her black heart.

She's doing nothing but waking the beast and leading him right to her.

Literally.

I can feel him, my Ethos, a gift from the gods given only to those with royal blood in their veins. He lives deep beneath my bones, buried in my chest—a prisoner locked away behind my ribs, only to be set free once a fated mating bond is completed.

He stirs, waking, clawing at my insides in a way I have never felt before. The pain so sharp my temples start to ache as my chest vibrates with a roar that isn't mine. But is.

This must be what my brother felt after he met his mate, London, the girl who led my little Haide to me, as fate so clearly arranged.

Haide's scent steamrolls behind her, whirling like a vortex, right into my nostrils—leather and lilac.

Wild and wicked.

Mine.

I growl, the sharp points of my teeth breaking free and puncturing my lower lip.

I don't chase her because I'm angry, though I am.

I chase her because she's mine. Because every breath she takes away from me tastes like a fucking betrayal, and everything in me says I have to.

Find her, take her, *claim* her.

That shit is on repeat in my head and I'm not sure if it's me or my Ethos who screams it. It's annoying.

She is fucking annoying. A bratty little outsider who has a lot to learn.

How dare she leave my kingdom, leave *Rathe*, the realm where magic was born, after only just storming her way into it like a demon out of hell.

Huffing, I shake my head.

Enough is enough.

My feet slam against rock, the cliffside brittle beneath years of lava rot and sea wind, but I don't slow. She's fast in a way that tells me she's made for this, for the edge of the world and the edge of a blade.

But I'm getting bored.

Her silhouette flashes between jagged rock and storm-thick mist, all wild black hair and lean muscle, untamed and unpredictable as the worthless gifted trapped on this island with her.

The stories about those who roam these grounds are true: they are completely and totally ruthless. Liars. Killers.

And not the good kind we Stygian, those born of dark magic, take part in.

But the kind that led them to the fate they dealt themselves: in Exile Island.

It's no wonder my Haide is such a fucking terror. She was born here.

Chaos is all she knows.

I watched her the day I met her.

The day my brothers and I, along with London, took the

throne that was rightfully ours. She slit a man's throat with his own teeth, then tilted her head back and *smiled.*

The beast in me wanted her and he wanted her bad. He had never been so loud. So close to the surface.

Until now.

And now she runs from me like she doesn't already belong.

The bond between us is very much alive, but it's thin, this small thread that has yet to grow into the chains that will bind us. That won't happen until we complete all the steps in the mating ritual. When I'm inside her and she screams my name like a war cry instead of a threat.

I felt it the second I heard her voice.

The moment she saved my brother's mate when she didn't have to.

The moment she dared to look me in the eye like I was the *lesser* danger.

Wrong, little pet.

Unlike my brother, who fought his bond until it damn near killed them both, I want my chains.

And I want them now.

I surge forward as the cliffs narrow, forcing her to vault over a jagged break in the rock. She lands low and rolls, dirt and ash staining her palms. Her shoulders tense like she feels me getting closer.

She's not running for safety. She's running for the thrill.

She thinks this is fun.

Haide doesn't understand the kind of game she just walked into or that the rules changed the moment the gods cursed her name into my veins.

She doesn't know I dream about her. That I smell her when there's nothing but smoke and bone around me. That her voice lives inside my skull like a brand I can't burn out.

Her head whips over her shoulder just long enough for me to catch the flicker of something feral in her grin.

"You're smiling?" I growl, gaining ground now. "Oh, so you wanna play?"

She laughs—a sharp, sharp sound that cuts through the wind like she's high on the madness of it. "Everything's a game when you live here, *Your Majesty*."

I nearly come undone at the way she spits the title like a challenge.

"Keep running then," I mutter darkly. "I want you winded when I take you down."

She veers left, a path that skirts the very edge of the cliffs, where volcanic glass juts up like spears and one wrong step means a plummet into nothing.

I follow without hesitation.

Let her try to lose me. Let her make it hard. Let her make it hurt.

The fire inside me grows with every step. Every foot of stolen distance between us. Every second she remains unclaimed.

The ground softens beneath her next step, thin and breakable, and she slips.

Just for a heartbeat, but it's enough to send panic down my spine.

I move like a shadow, like fury, like a demon drunk on the scent of his mate. My hand closes around her waist, and she twists, elbow aiming for my jaw, but I catch it midair. Her body crashes into mine with a ragged curse, both of us landing hard on the black stone as I pin her under my weight.

She thrashes like a cornered animal, breathing fire and hate and something else neither of us knows how to name.

I release her wrists and drag her upright before she can blink. My hand fists in her hair, and I tip her head back until she meets my gaze, locked and breathless and furious.

And then I throw her over my shoulder.

She screams, claws, kicks, curses me like a hellion, but I'm already walking toward the isle's edge.

My grip tightens when she wriggles, relishing the feel of her body, the scent of her sweat, salt, and blood.

"I'm going to kill you."

My grin grows. "Yes, you will."

Her brows snap together, clearly not understanding her own promise. "I hate you."

"You think you hate me now?" I chuckle lowly. "Just wait until you love me."

I throw us both over the fucking cliff.

The moment my feet leave the soil of the island grounds, my chest lurches, yanking my shoulders and head back, in an invisible yet physical tug that leaves us suspended in the air for a split moment rather than falling as we should. I grit my teeth as white-hot pain sears through my veins like fire.

And then we're free-falling again.

The ache is still there. It's like nothing I've ever known and can explain, but it must be a bond thing. I look forward to every little sting she brings me, but not as much as I look forward to giving it in return.

Hope you're ready for what comes next, little menace.

You're mine now.

Chapter Three

Haide

I wake with a gasp, flying to my feet so fast my vision blurs before catching up, adrenaline flooding through my veins like liquid fire. Sickening pink and white palette glare back at me from the walls ahead. I stumble backward until my hands collide with something solid. *What the fuck even is this?*

It's cold beneath my touch. Pristine white, with veins of marble snaking through it like arteries. A mirror stands at the center, caged by a line of bulbous lights. Delicate bottles of glass filled with mysterious liquid lurk in the corner.

"Wha—" I lose my footing, crashing onto my ass. A cascade of crystal rains down on me from above in an obscene display of wealth.

And the fucking smell.

The scent of sulfur and stone is obliterated by rose and something disgustingly expensive. But there is another smell: smoky, rich, familiar. I can't name it and that's annoying.

Whatever it is, I want to devour it.

Where the hell has he dragged me?

How did he take us off the island?

How the hell did he get *on* the fucking island?

In the four hundred years of the island's existence, not a single gifted has ever managed to make it past the magical wards that imprisoned the exiled.

Except for me.

A fact I accidentally discovered a few months ago and that I have since strived to keep hidden for my own safety.

The ease with which he came and went makes no sense.

A sharp static crackles through the air, jolting me back to the present and off the ground. My attention snaps to the frame on the wall opposite where a picture flickers to life in a glass box. I step back slightly, my senses razor-sharp.

"Have you managed to take a look around, little menace?" My fingernails carve crescents into my palms when the kidnapping king invades the frame. He's sprawled in a chair, a fire breath stick of some sort dangling from his arrogant, perfect fucking mouth.

"I have." The corner of mine curves into something wicked. "Tell me, Lord Dickship. Am I to be..." I gesture around the room with a dismissive sweep of my hand. Dirt and dried mud crust my skin, and I know my hair has never tasted the kind of luxury his has, but I don't give a damn. All I see is crimson fury. "Impressed?"

His laughter burns acid down the back of my throat as he

leans forward, bracing his elbows on his thighs. He truly is devastatingly beautiful, even if he does look a little paler than normal, with a darkness under his eyes that wasn't there before.

I wonder if these royals decay the same way we lesser gifted do. Whether their bones crumble to dust and their blood nourishes nature the same way ours does.

Or whether it just has a direct pipeline to hell.

"Here's what's going to happen, our little Haide," he starts, and my fingers carve deeper into my flesh. "You have two hours to be dressed and ready."

My arms cross over my chest, one brow lifting in challenge. "Really? Mmm, I don't know?" I saunter around the room, ensuring to take my sweet time at the small desk with all the mysterious bottles. I slide open a drawer revealing a hairbrush and creams, before using my hip to slam it shut with satisfaction. "What if I don't want to shower?"

I bat my lashes back at him with mock innocence.

His smirk is as wicked as it is threatening. "Then by all means, stay filthy." His lip twitches with dark amusement. "Prefer mine that way anyway."

"Again, should I be impressed?"

"What you should be is compliant, but river rats will do what river rats will do."

There's that smug look. It's kind of pathetic, really, that he thinks he's— What? Hurt my…

I can't even say the word.

Feelings?

Does he think I have *those?*

A laugh bubbles out of me and his stupid baby blues narrow. "Have you ever even seen a rat?" I ask. "Like a real one on the street? Not when feeding your little demon dogs or whatever people like you keep as pets, mister silk sheets?"

With his jaw clenched, he leans forward, eyes blaring into my soul while his lips part—blowing smoke into my face.

Fuck. I step back, covering my face from the assault and coughing until tears sting my eyes. It takes a moment before the haze clears and I can blink the blurriness from my vision.

Just to find Legend *right there.*

The surprise at his appearance is immediately followed by the desire to reach for him, drag him closer and…I don't know. Lick him. Maybe.

I must really want to strangle him or something; and my subconscious knows it before I do. What was that saying the Huntress of Harrowgate used to recite before allowing fallen souls to ascend? *If he made you wet, you won't forget.* The follow-on was cryptic, the book too water damaged to read further. I'm pretty sure it translated to something like: "Don't take chances. Kill him just in case."

And honestly, I love that.

Don't love that his pretty smile might have just earned me a permanent spot in the *Do Not Ascend* pile of the damned, though. That won't win me any brownie points with my ancestors. You know, assuming I have any.

Probably shouldn't kill him, though. Him being one of the four crowned kings of Rathe. That would likely end in my execution, because they wouldn't just exile me like they do with the rest of their unwanted trash. It would be a gift rather than a punishment to return me to Exile Island.

Unless Rathe's newest royal edition could save me. London does owe me one.

Hmm…no, yeah, I think if I killed him I'd still be shaved of my skin and gutter, then put in a trophy case left to float in the center of Rathe as an example.

That's what I would do if I were them.

"What is going on in that fucked-up head of yours?"

Blinking, I refocus on the man in front of me. "What?"

Legend shakes his head with a scoff, pulling his fire breath stick to his mouth again. The end burns a deep red as he fills his lungs, his wide chest expanding, and with every second that ticks by, his gaze hardens. "How are you so chill about this? You should be losing your mind. Begging by now."

His blue-black hair falls over his forehead, making his fair skin look even whiter, just as silver as his glassy blue eyes.

I nod slowly. "Yeah…not following."

"That's the fucking point!" He gnashes his teeth at me like a rabid dog. "You're a goddamn stray with no true training. I've been beaten and had my mind fried from the inside out repeatedly to manage to gain the slightest control over myself and my gifts—and I'm fucking vibrating right now being this close to you. I want to shred your artery with my claws and hold you until you're bled dry—just so I'm the first thing you see when you come back to me."

I suck my lips between my teeth, nodding. "That's…weird. But I'm not on the island, so if you bleed me dry, I'm not coming back to life out here."

His frown deepens, his gaze snapping across my features. "What?"

"If you kill me, I'm dragon meat, as in dead. No magical island to refuse to let me die."

A shadow falls over his face, and his features harden even more. "It's part of the ritual."

"Sorry to burst your bubble, but I don't know anything about a ritual, pal."

"Do not call me pal."

"Buddy."

"Stop."

"Pampered prince?"

He growls. I barely have the time to register his movement before he's shoving closer. A strange little thrill slithers up my spine at the sound. At the *nearness.*

My lips curve and he gets louder. Angrier. And I can't help it.

I laugh.

I laugh so hard tears fill my eyes and I cover my mouth with my hand, watching and wondering if he might actually—I don't know—explode into a big puff of demonic smoke or some shit.

Eventually, he's had enough of me. Long fingers wrap around my throat, and my back hits the wall.

His breath is hot against my skin and there's that smell again. Only it's stronger, richer.

Intoxicating.

What is it coming from?

"I am no prince. I am a king. Your king. And you, you infuriating little brat, are *my* queen."

I laugh, but then his words slam into me, and I freeze.

Wait, what?

My head tilts as much as it can with his fist locked around it, fracturing the strange tension and breaking my thoughts in half, but doing nothing to escape that scent. It stings slightly, the kind of smell you taste in the back of your throat. There's a coolness to it, almost slick and oily, like steel wrapped in silk. It fucking burns. It's triggering allergies.

Before I respond to his whole "my queen" lie—because I mean, be so for real——he clicks his tongue, sauntering backward until he hits the bedroom door.

"What? No hocus pocus where you vanish through the wall?" I tease.

His hand grips the frame, and if I didn't know any better, I'd say he was using it to keep his legs from buckling. "Nah. I'll save all that for my next tricks. See you soon, little hellpet. I sure hope you like chaos as much as you act like you do." The door slams shut before I can curse him out over the ridiculous nickname.

• • •

I'm not little at all.

And what did he mean I was filthy?

Tracing the footsteps toward the large tub in the center of the room, movement catches my attention from the wall that's suspended there.

What the fuck is this?

Reaching up, the girl copies my movements. Her hand is my hand. My face is her face.

I shove the small bottles on the counter aside, desperate for a closer look. My hair is dark and cascades down over slender shoulders. Beneath the grime coating my face, I can see the color of my skin, tan from the sun. I touch the two jewels embedded at the edges of my temples—one red, one blue, both having been there since I was born. Or so the island witch had said.

Is this what a mirror does? Shows you a different side of you? A weaker, softer side?

Is that who I become if I don't get out of this fancy fucking castle? Back to the dirt and decaying trenches that make my life make sense?

Panic spikes through my veins as my attention darts around the room. Scrambling through the bedroom, the soft covers of the bed brush my palms and I tear them off before hurling them over the reflection wall.

I breathe out a silent sigh. *The fuck is up with that?*

Is that girl in the mirror the one he wants me to be? Because fuck all that. I will cut off his cock and make a serpent stew out of it. Serve it to him on the coals of a dragon's nest, and laugh as I watch it burn his lips from his face.

There's a rap on the door but I don't bother turning. Anyone willing to try to kill me is either worth dying for, or worth the killing.

"Haide, hello, I'm Anaya, your handmaiden and confidant."

I turn at her announcement because she's neither of those things. But she is fucking stupid.

"I'm sorry, what?"

She blinks at me, half of her face veiled behind a thin piece of white cloth. Her eyes are as blue as mercy, her skin pristine, not at all like mine. "Your handmaiden. I am honored to be here. Before you, females were not allowed to work the royal home per the fallen Queen Cosima's orders, as her sons lived under this roof. My job is to help you—"

I take a step closer.

Her attention drops to my feet before slowly crawling back up to my face. Her fear leaves a stale smell in the air, not quite potent enough to drown out Lord Asshole's though.

"Oh really?" I ask, studying her. *What did she look like beneath the veil?* "And who sent you?"

Her legs tremble. "Ah—it, it was King Lege—"

My hands are on her cheeks in an instant and I twist until I feel the bones in her neck snap.

Tossing her body down to the floor, I don't blink, keeping my focus pinned on the small frame on the wall. A black box stares back at me.

Straightening my shoulders, I finally blink when my vision burns. "I don't speak royal." I shrug down at the dead girl. "Sorry."

I pause.

Ooooh. She's not coming back to life…'cause we're not on the island.

Shit. I could have asked her about the fucking tub before eliminating her. That would have been so much smarter.

Maybe my kill streak has gone soft and she's still breathing?

I lift the veil from her face. Flawless skin that reminds me of something I've never witnessed. It's a feeling. Nothing like her could ever exist on Exile Island. For good reason.

The veins in her neck are swollen against the newly purple shade of her skin.

"Damn. No chance of you telling me how to get clean then, is there?" I joke, pushing back to my feet just as the door creaks behind me.

"Good morning, Haide!" The first thing I notice about the new girl is the brilliant crimson shade of her hair. "I'm your new maiden," she starts, until her attention shifts to the body on the floor. For a moment, I see it. That flicker of weakness that spreads over her features.

That is why I will never see anyone for more than what they are.

Prey.

Her shoulders stiffen. She's small. Maybe smaller than the first girl, but when I take the first step, her body doesn't tremble. She doesn't cower. Her gaze burns with brown ember. She smells of something sweet that I can't place, and—

My focus sharpens. "Do you smoke?"

She hesitates. "Maybe."

My brows lift.

She crosses her arms, shrugging. "Okay whatever, yeah, I do. Why? You gonna snitch? Because let me tell you, I don't even want to be here. Honestly, I volunteered as soon as Anaya's orb turned black. Figured you might just be as foolish as we've heard and kill me too so I can ascend and—"

"Stop talking. Give me a fire breath."

She glances between my outstretched hand and my face. "A what?"

"Don't play games, girl. I'm already itching to use my hands on someone again. *Share.*"

"Share…" She blinks and then her eyes widen. "Wait, you want a cigarette."

I glare because—is that what I'm asking for?

"You're in the Royal Wing." She starts to shake her head. "I'm going to go ahead and say you shouldn't be smoking. There is a designated space for that."

"There is ?" I fake innocence. "Well, do I look like someone who gives a fuck about designated spaces…" I trail, waiting for her name.

"Sahara."

"Sahara."

Her tongue dampens her bottom lip before she rolls her eyes and dives into her pocket, whipping out a small tin.

I snatch it and flick it open. Plucking one of the skinny trunks out, I place it between my lips and light the end with a flick of my wrist. "Tell me, Sahara. How the fuck do I work this damn tub?"

The girl's fiery brows jump on her pretty face. Slowly, almost hesitantly, she looks me over for the first time.

Her nose twitches at the sight of my boots, the daggers tucked into them, and the sheath that's strapped to my upper thigh. Her gaze traces the strips of leather across my stomach, up over my chest, and then follows the length of my braided hair, settling on the two tiny stones embedded in the skin beside my temples.

Finally, her eyes come back to mine as she speaks with a low tremor. "Where did you come from?"

My chuckle is pitch-black, and I hold a hand out for the little creature of a girl. "Hell, maiden girl. Hell. Now, about this whole getting ready thing..."

• • •

The bedroom door crashes open just as I pluck another "cigarette" —weird name honestly—from the tin.

Sahara freezes, her attention darting between me and my blood-stained shirt, then down at her dead friend, who I borrowed it from. "Ah...I don't think that's quite what they had in mind when they said *make you presentable...*"

Inhaling, I allow the smoke to sear through my lungs before my mouth forms a perfect *O* and I blow smoke rings at her pale face. "Listen. I don't really want to kill you, and that's an unfamiliar feeling, so this could be fleeting. Don't ruin it by trying to tell me what to wear. I won't listen anyway, and you'll just end up...you know. Dead. Probably."

I keep the sheath at my thigh, strapped over the fishnet tights and, since there was no leather in the closet, I decided to tear mine into a makeshift skirt. "It truly is a great shirt."

"There's, like"—Sahara gestures to the front with trembling fingers—"blood splatter all over it?"

I turn, blinking innocently, and place my hands on her delicate shoulders. "Oh no. What ever will we do about that?" A burst of manic laughter spills from me as I spin around. I'm ready to roll. "So now what, little maiden?"

"Now, we wait."

Chapter Four

Legend

The moment I step into the war room, a smug grin still tugging at the edge of my mouth, the air turns heavy.

Creed stops mid-sentence. His knuckles blanch as he grips the armrest of his throne. That crown of bone-light shimmers as if it sprouted straight out of his goddamn skull, though it's merely demonic smoke suspended above his head. Just like my brothers. Just like mine.

That shit is gonna take some getting used to, but it is the war room after all, and the only way our ancestors can hear our calls.

Is our father among them yet?

I refocus on my brothers, just in time to catch Knight's

jaw tick as he leans forward, expression unreadable but eyes narrowed. Always calculating. Always quiet.

Sinner's sharp laugh cuts the air, shattering the tension. He drowns the last gulp from a gnarled black bottle, then slams it onto the stone with such force that the surface cracks beneath it.

"Where the hell did you go?" Creed fires first, voice cold and sharp as forged iron.

Knight's head cocks, like a predator sniffing out a lie. "Why are you late?"

"Did you just"—Sinner grins, teeth flashing like a blade—"fuck or something?"

I chuckle low, dragging the scent of ash and adrenaline with me as I cross the obsidian-slick floor. There's a seat waiting at the table—massive, claw-footed, carved from the remains of some long-dead Leviathan no one's seen in over a thousand years. Its surface ripples faintly as I approach, reacting to the magic bleeding off me.

Good. It remembers who I am.

I drop into the chair and kick my boots up onto the tabletop. The moment the soles hit, the Leviathan bone snarls. It pulses a muted red beneath the translucent surface, ancient veins still humming with magic that doesn't quite know if it wants to kill or obey.

"Relax," I mutter to the thing. "We've both bled enough today."

Creed exhales sharply through his nose. "Legend. You disappeared for days with no explanation. No word."

I arch a brow. "Just had to go get something of mine," I say smoothly, folding my hands behind my head. "I'm here now. Talk."

Creed shifts his attention to the center of the table. There, the runic map of the realm softly glows. Its lines of light and shadow tracing alliances, magical disturbances, and blood-signed treaties that flare when violated.

"The Argents are frantic," he finally says, his voice all steel and diplomacy, honed like a blade meant for council chambers, not battlefields. "The ascension of us four to the throne has left them feeling…imbalanced."

"As they fucking should." Sinner snaps before he can finish, swinging his leg over the arm of his throne and lounging like he's at a gods-damned tavern instead of one of the four most powerful seats in the known realm. "We don't need them. I say we kill them all. Or just wait for whoever is going around killing our people to do it for us."

Killings? That's news to me.

Creed ignores him, but I see the way his jaw tightens when my head swings his way in question. His attempt at maintaining his patience makes me want to poke harder. Sinner's wrong though: the Argents are as important for the ecosystem of Rathe as we are. You know…we gotta eat.

"We can't have the alleys of Rathe painted in blood being the first thing documented in the Archives of Aether," he goes on, voice clipped.

The Archives of Aether. I tried to read them once by breaking into the sacred lair with the help of a witch. But the moment I touched the scrolls that magically record every aspect of a king's reign, I was flung through the wall. I landed on my ass on the floor of my father's torture chambers, hellhound leashes whipping me from every direction.

My father laughed and watched. Then he poured me a drink and asked if I'd ever do it again.

I miss the king.

Creed continues. "If the scribes start recording this reign as a massacre of magic blood, we may never gain the alliances we need to solidify our rule."

I snort. "So don't start a massacre. Easy."

Sinner laughs again.

Creed doesn't blink. "Four bodies have been found as of two moons ago. All Stygian born. All savagely murdered in their own homes. Homes here in Rathe."

I sit forward, a frown pulling at my brows. "You would know this," he continues, "if you didn't run off and block us out the minute you crossed back into Rathe with that outsider." He eyes me curiously as his powers brush against my temple, attempting to enter my mind. I block him out, oddly fatigued by the effort to do so. "You are a King now; you can't disappear only to come back and hide away while waiting for your newest toy to wake the fuck up."

Sinner smirks. "Next time just don't dose her up so high."

"There won't be a next time. She is here now, as am I, so tell me what we know."

Creed frowns in my direction but gets us back on track. "Nothing. That's the problem. So far, they seem random, but we have Vicente looking deeper and checking their ancestry line for clues or connections."

"It's the Argents." I shrug. "You said it yourself: they feel threatened. They want to force doubt into the minds of our people. Make them question if we can handle taking over after Father's death."

"No." Knight glares at the table, face pinched tight in thought. "There was a scent in the air at all the scenes. Tar or lava rock. Something familiar but not Argent. And it was messy."

"Messy how?"

"Like someone lost their shit." Sinner laughs. "And blacked out in rage."

I wave dismissively. "People lose their shit every day."

"Not like this." Creed worries, looking over at Knight.

I glance between the two and sit back with a sigh. "Just say what you're thinking," I mutter, bored now. "Enough of the philosophical shit."

Knight sighs and leans back, running a hand through his hair, the scar slicing through his brow tugging slightly as he moves. "We need to keep as much normalcy as we can. We come into this reign soft. Last shit we need is people running around and treating their own kind like they're threats and making our job harder."

I stare at him.

"Again," I repeat, slower this time. "Just say it. Clearly you two talked about it already."

Creed snaps to me. "We need to go back to Rathe University."

The words hang there for a beat—just long enough for the Leviathan bone beneath my boots to pulse again, as if the ancient beast can feel the ripple of what that means.

Back to the university. Where we're forced to live on the pathetic place known as Earth, in the giftless world, yet in a school dedicated to our own. Where the next generation of magic-bloods are trained. Where politics are sharpened behind false smiles, and swords are dulled behind glamours. Where the throne was first promised to us. Where we were watched. Groomed. Tested. *Hunted*.

"We killed Magdelana, remember?" I remind them of what no one could have forgotten—of the mage who was the leader of the Argents, those of light magic, and the headmistress of

Rathe U. She and the rest of the bullshit ministry that plotted against my family are nothing but ash in the wind now. A fact that their people might not be too happy about. "Who is going to rule over Rathe U now? And what about the murders happening here?"

No one answers at first. Not because they don't have ideas—but because none of them are good.

Creed clenches his jaw while Knight expresses his irritation by sharply exhaling through his nose. Sinner, of course, just smirks, always the kind of bastard who relishes watching things spiral out of control.

"New year starts in less than a week, in giftless time," Knight adds flatly. "New blood. Freshly gifted. Half of 'em still shaking from their first vision. The other half hoping they glow in the dark or sprout wings, or whatever wild shit the Argents have been whispering into their ears since birth."

Sinner cackles and leans forward, tossing his bottle lazily from one hand to the other. "And for once, we're not the ones getting tossed into the pit with the rest of the softlings. We get to watch. We get to *choose*. We get to be the ones who tell them what this year is really gonna be like."

Knight raises a brow. "We're still being *sent* back to keep peace."

Creed nods. "Symbolic presence. Eyes on the ground. Prevent panic. Show unity and make them think we are offering protection to the most important of our kind—their untrained, precious children. That kind of thing."

"Unity," Sinner snorts. "Is that what they're calling it now? The Argents are creaming themselves over the idea. Oh, yay, let's all cohabitate. Let's be good little magelets and build bridges between good and evil. Bunch of free-spirited, happily-ever-after-loving hypocrites."

Creed narrows his eyes. "They're not all bad."

Sinner scoffs. "No, just naive. The real fun's gonna be watching the Stygian young lose their fucking minds when they find out they're expected to sit next to Argent-borns in their elemental theory classes and *smile*."

Knight leans back, arms crossed. "There will be blood. There always is."

My mouth kicks up in a grin. "Don't count out some of those Argents. They're only light magic because they can fuck you hard enough to melt the skin from your bones."

I shift slightly in my throne, the Leviathan bone beneath me pulsing with that same quiet awareness. I can feel it in the air already. The tension. The spark. The weight of a thousand new sets of footsteps crossing over the veil and stepping into the world of the giftless. Where control is tested and reality checks are served.

This is kind of perfect. Now her presence will serve an even better purpose.

"Looks like the decision's been made. We're holding an announcement ceremony," I say, voice dripping with amusement. "Today."

Creed arches a brow, slow and suspicious. "Why, dear brother…do you look so excited about that?"

I tilt my head, grin stretching wide. "Because," I murmur, kicking my boots back off the table and standing, shadows folding over my shoulders like armor. "I've got something of my own to announce."

The weight of what I'm about to do presses against my spine like a blade as I make my way back through the doors.

"And it's going to be so. Fucking. Good."

Chapter Five

Legend

Pure anticipation flows through my veins as I wait for the revelation of my little surprise, which waits outside the war room. Currently, the "future of Rathe," their parents, and a few other powerful figures, mingle among themselves. Bone stemmed glasses hover in small circles every few feet, waiting for the fingers of a gifted to wrap along the stems, and claim it for itself, their drink of choice materializing in the glass the moment they do.

Both hope and caution sit heavy in the air, and the demonic smoke, an inky black shadow of sorts that protects only those of royal blood or deemed worthy, hovers at my brothers' and my backs, and pulses in warning.

Gifted continue to pour through the portal we opened in the main courtyard of Rathe, allowing more and more to cross into the royal estate. Little by little, the space grows thick with mumbled whispers and restless bodies.

Once the maximum number allowed has been reached, the portal seals itself, leaving the rest of Rathe to listen and watch through projecting across the realm.

As it closes, a pathway carves between us and our people, and every face swivels toward the row of thrones we sit upon.

As they look at us, I'm locked on the platform at the end, the door that has yet to reveal itself.

I've purposely delayed her arrival, making her wait for a grand entrance that I know she'll wish to slay me for. I've also created a door just for her. Just for tonight. Took a fuck ton of energy to do it, too.

The music changes its tune, the room quieting only slightly and right on cue, the passageway opens with a yawn. The moment it does, every pair of eyes spins that way, landing on her.

And oh, gods.

She's wearing *that*.

Fishnet over flesh, a leather scrap that might've once been pants tied into a makeshift skirt, and a blood-stained shirt that absolutely belongs to someone else. Probably a mess that needs cleaning up.

She struts down the war hall like an angry little thing. Seconds away from turning this entire place into a battleground.

My battleground.

She doesn't flinch beneath the stares—and *everyone* is staring at my little chaos monster. The girl doesn't even hesitate as a hundred voices fall silent as she passes. A cigarette dangles from that luscious mouth of hers like she's about to break into a bar fight.

And fuck me, I don't know which one I'd rather watch.

Her entrance has an immediate effect on my brothers.

Between Creed jolting upright in his throne, Knight's narrowed eyes, and Sinner looking reluctant to even move—as if he might shatter the illusion—I don't know whose reaction I enjoy more.

None of them knew she was coming back.

And by *coming back* I mean, you know, going to Exile Island to retrieve what is mine. I bet their minds are racing right now, trying to put together why I'd want this untamed and untrained gifted mess of a girl back here.

My money is on Knight figuring out the why first.

Or Creed, mind-mirroring magic and all. If I let him in my head when his nosy ass seeks entrance, I have no doubt he'll see.

I stay seated, grinning like the feral bastard I am, and wait until Haide is nearly at the foot of the dais before I speak.

"Well, hello, my little monster," I purr, voice wrapping around the silence like a rope around a throat. "Took you long enough. Did you get lost?"

She ignores me.

Good girl.

It would be boring if she just smiled and apologized like a good little mate would.

A weak mate.

No, Haide is made different, and I can't wait to cut her open and find out just how much.

She stares up at me with a bored expression, blowing smoke straight in my face in a move made to disrespect, and I have to work hard not to laugh.

She's perfect. The air around her quite literally pulses with defiance, the war room itself recognizing a threat and making sure we've caught onto it.

Good.

Let them see what I chased. Let them see what I *caught.*

The chamber, built from obsidian and the ancient blood, begins to thrum. I can feel it under my boots, thrumming like a heartbeat as the ancient stones stir, searching for the truth of the girl before me. Above us, the lights flicker once, twice, and with a breath of old magic, it clears.

The room finally stirs, the silence replaced with whispered words of curiosity.

They want to know who stands before one of their kings.

I'm fucking humming with anticipation.

The walls begin to shift around us and Haide moves to the side, gaze flickering out across the space as I sit back in my throne.

A breath later, we turn our attention to the people of Rathe. The courtyard is full, thousands standing in the square, shoulder to shoulder, on the cracked cobbled stone, staring up at the palace as the veil between us dissolves.

Creed rises like a blade being unsheathed: sharp, cold, and carved from the kind of authority people are bred to obey.

He steps forward, but his eyes linger on Haide for a moment, a tightness teasing at his temples.

"I speak now not only as your king," he begins, his voice as steady and clean as polished steel. The courtyard stills instantly. "But as one of you."

The weight of him is different from mine. Measured. Cold. Royal in a way I've never aspired to be.

"The battle for the throne is over. The blood spilled cannot be undone, but the path forward *can* be rewritten. There will be no ministry, no share of the throne outside of the Deveraux name or split between our people."

"And while we may have walked different paths, we are all born from the magic of the grounds we walk."

"Not all of us," I murmur with a grin. My eyes trail over the masses, the Stygian roaring in awaited vengeance, and the Argents, shuffling back in silence.

Aside from the slight frown that builds along his brow, Creed ignores me. He continues flawlessly, ever the perfectly bred son. "I can sense your fear, Argents. But believe me when I say you are safer now than you were before. Trust in us as your kings, and we will not do you wrong. Cross us and die. *Disrespect us* and die. This goes for all gifted kind, friend and foe. There will be no second chances and no ministry to back you, but we will consider building a council around us that you can trust."

He waits for the news to settle before continuing.

"Now, we know there is distress in our streets. As your new leaders, we want to rule with transparency. That said, the rumors you may have heard are true. There is a murderer among Rathe."

A murmur ripples through the room, and it only grows louder when he continues.

"We have our best men on its trail and expect we are closing in." I watch the color leave their faces, feel the panic roll. "When we catch them, there will be no theater of trial—only punishment. Followed by the worst nightmare a gifted can face. Beings stripped of their powers and sent to exile."

Haide scoffs a laugh and all our heads yank toward her.

She just shrugs, rolling her wrist as if telling my dear brother to continue.

Little fucking brat.

"With that said, we have come to a decision, and that is, as of this day, Rathe University will reopen once more."

The voices sharpen and rise, men jump to their feet and woman rage from their seats.

The courtyard echoes as people push toward the barriers and against our warriors, who manage to hold them back.

I can understand their response, and this reaction is exactly what we expected.

Our people are still unsettled, and understandably so.

Their King was murdered in corruption brought by their own Queen, and more. In a matter of months, the kingdom in which they trust has been gutted and shaped anew, my brothers and I now at its helm.

They are right to throw a fit…but also, they need to fall in fucking line.

We make the rules now.

Knight kicks my foot and jerks his chin toward the crowd.

Oh, right.

This is where my gifts come in.

Leaning forward in my chair, I look out, mentally locking onto the fear, anger, uncertainty—and yes, even the hope. I breathe it in, pulling the emotions into my body and letting the shadows around my soul reshape them. I twist their emotions, bend and restructure them, creating a calm across our people. They *will* listen and believe that they are open to every word spoken by one of their kings.

Later, they can sort through how they really feel. But right now, Creed needs silence.

I push their manipulated emotions into their bodies, but just as I brush against their psyche, a sharp pain presses against my chest.

My brows snap together, but Creed has already begun to speak again.

"Do not fear for your young," Creed demands. "Your kings will be among them."

Sinner scoffs under his breath while Knight tilts his head in a calculating fashion.

"All Stygian and Argent-born over the age of eighteen are to report to the Ministry for departure. The portal will open at nightfall. Anyone attempting to remain behind" —he lets the pause stretch, a cold glint in his eye—"will be dragon food. And not the poetic kind."

Creed steps back, signaling the end of his speech. But we're not done yet.

I step forward.

"One more thing," I say casually, dragging every eye to me.

Creed's shoulders go taut. "Legend—"

"Relax," I mutter. "Just a quick note. For the people."

I walk slowly to the edge of the dais, turning my back to the brothers as I face the crowd.

"We've all lost things," I say, voice deep and calm, like I'm reading bedtime stories to a pack of wolves. "Family. Power. Maybe even a toe or two, depending on where you were standing when my brother's mate found out someone touched what belonged to her."

Sinner chuckles. Knight doesn't move.

"But I'm pleased to announce I've found something."

I gesture lazily toward Haide. "This absolute menace to sanity? She's mine."

Another chorus of murmurs explodes across the room.

"She's a gift from the gods, a threat to all structure and peace, and a constant pain in my royal ass. And I couldn't be more thrilled to introduce her. Straight from Exile Island, I give you your future Queen. Well, one of them, anyway."

The crowd *erupts.* Their emotions serve like a whip to my mind, making me grin. They hate her. They love her. They fear her.

And she hasn't even said a word.

And then a voice cuts through the chaos. Loud. Sharp.

Fucking *stupid.*

"She's...she's *unfit* for the throne—an exile? From the island? What was her crime? How did she get there? How did she get back? No one is supposed to leave those lands! You can't possibly—"

His words cut off with a wet, gurgling snap.

Haide doesn't even flinch. One moment she's standing there, the next she's sliding a blade back into the sheath on her thigh, blood misting the air like perfume.

"Hey, don't look at me. He said disrespect and die." She shrugs. "I felt disrespected so...yeah."

Sinner wheezes and doubles over with laughter. Creed covers his face with one hand. Knight says nothing—just closes his eyes and leans his head back like he's praying for death.

I beam. "As I was saying..."

Blood continues to drip on the wall Haide leans against, her expression returning to one of boredom.

"Your Queen has arrived. And as you can see, she bites."

...

Haide

I blink, head tilting slightly.

Did he just…

I look out at the room full of gifted—no the *realm* full of gifted. Hundreds upon hundreds watching from outside the castle walls.

Why are they all staring at me like I'm supposed to curtsy or blow a kiss or some shit? Like this isn't the same realm that literally throws people onto my island like trash. I mean, most are, but still.

And *King Legend* is up here, all smug and self-important, declaring me their Queen like some fool with a death wish.

Honestly, it's a terrible way to flirt if that's what he's going for.

You wanna talk about biting, Demon King? Fine.

I lunge.

The crowd gasps like one massive, useless organism as my hand fists the front of his shirt and I sink my teeth into his neck.

Not a love bite. Not a nip. But a full-on, mouth-open, flesh-tearing mouthful.

His skin gives way like sin, and the second his blood hits my tongue, I freeze.

Oh.

Oh, *fuck*.

It tastes like smoke and ruin and something so stupidly addictive I forget where I am for a second. My head reels. My spine hums.

Something behind my ribs *clicks*. Not a sound exactly. More like a pulse, like a wire deep in my chest was yanked taut. My breath snags, my blood flares, and not just with heat, but with something old, coiled, waiting.

Something *not mine.*

It crawls up my spine and hums in my brain.

I blink, dazed for half a second.

Huh.

Maybe I was a vampire in a past life.

A sexy, murderous one.

"You—" Legend chokes out a laugh, blood trickling down his throat, his hand pressed lightly to the spot where my teeth just marked him. "You actually *bit* me."

"Don't say I don't commit," I mutter, still tasting him on my tongue. He tastes annoyingly *good.* Everything about him is annoying. And hot. And now he's leaking on my shirt, which I stole off a corpse, so this feels very full-circle.

But I'm not done.

Before he can say something else stupid and smug, I draw my dagger in one smooth motion and press the tip right against his heart.

The hall erupts.

Chairs scrape, someone screams, and Sinner leaps from his throne as Knight's entire body goes taut, his shadows twitching like they're ready to pounce.

And Legend?

Legend *laughs.*

Manically, like this is the best day of his life.

I press the dagger a little harder, not enough to break skin, but enough to show I could. "Call me Queen again, and I'll crown myself with your spine."

"Gods, you're fucking perfect," he breathes.

Something coils low in my gut. It feels suspiciously like

pleasure from his pathetic little praise.

Gross.

I swallow past it, glaring up at him.

A new voice slices through the madness like a sword through fog.

"For fuck's sake, Legend. What did you do?" London, the entire reason that I ever left my island in the first place, steps out in all her white hair and black aura glory.

"London," Legend says brightly, like this is a tea party and not a blood-stained mess.

London eyes the blade still at his chest. "You planning to let her stab you and complete another step in the bond, or are we pretending this is foreplay?"

Behind me, Knight growls, low and protective.

But Legend growls back louder.

London and I sigh.

Feral. The lot of them.

Wait. My head snaps her way, eyes narrowing. "What *bond*?"

With another sigh, she turns to Legend. "Are you going to tell her, or should I?"

Legend's mouth curves upward. I'm getting real sick and tired of not being able to punch it.

He stands even taller as he looks out at his people, the humor in his voice making me murdery. "Oh, did I forget to mention?" he says. "She's not just my chosen queen. My bond thrums in her veins. Haide of exile is my *fated mate*."

I stare at him.

Then at the blood on my blade.

Then back at his dumb, perfect mouth.

Cool.

I guess I'm killing him after all.

Chapter Six

Legend

She fucking launches.

Her body wraps around mine like a murderous vine and laughter spills from my throat as my fingers knead their way up the back of her neck. I tear her off just in time for the room around us to dissolve into a splatter of colors when one of my brothers rips open a portal.

Smart. Probably not a good idea for the people of Rathe to witness one of their future Queens gut their king alive. The portal spits us onto ancient cobblestones, and I hit the ground hard.

The Royal Court spreads before us in towering stone archways draped in ivy, and gardens that have witnessed centuries of bloodshed disguised as politics and family drama.

"Let go," she snarls, but her grip tightens instead of releasing.

I roll us over, pinning her beneath me on the warmed stones. "Make me, *mate*."

Her eyes flash with something deadly, but I feel the way her pulse jumps at the name. "Stop calling me that."

"Why? It's what you are." How she manages to look sexy as hell, even while plotting my demise, is beyond my range of power. "The bond doesn't lie, my little menace. I know you feel it."

"I feel homicidal rage."

"That too." I grin down at her. "It's all connected."

Her knee comes up fast toward my ribs, but I catch it, fingers wrapping around her thigh.

"We're doing this here?" I ask, genuinely curious. She's fucking bold, I'll give her that, but of course the Gods would grace me with nothing more than a fucking menace as my mate. They know I wouldn't have it any other way. "In front of the ancestors?" I mock innocence.

Her eyes turn to slits, but with every deep breath her tits brush against my chest, and I'm suddenly aware of every fucking inch of her. Her nipples swell beneath her cotton shirt and my hips twitch into her a little.

She challenges me head-on. "I'm doing this everywhere until you're dead."

"Promise?"

Her frustrated scream echoes off the walls. Goddamn. I've never been more in love with such a fucking monster. "I swear to God, Legend, if you don't—"

"Oh for fuck's sake!" Creed snaps from somewhere in the

distance, reminding me that we're not alone. Of course they wouldn't suck me through a portal with her alone. *Wait. Did they think she could take me?* She probably could. Be willing to test it, too. "Both of you shut the fuck up."

I kick up from the ground, leaving her flat on her back.

"Why are those weird fucking things staring down at me?" Haide points to the gargoyles perched on crumbling archways.

She's right. They're watching our violent dance with stone eyes that have witnessed worse. Florals of vines crawl up the walls like grasping fingers, threading through cracks that time carved into the foundation. Beyond the gardens, there was the Royal House. The Royal House is just beyond the gardens, but I doubt we'd make it very far before Haide started throwing shit around the room.

"Okay, now everyone calm the fuck down." London extends a hand to her friend. I know she'd do nothing to hurt Haide, but I can't help the jerk reaction that claws at the back of my mind.

Mine. Don't fucking touch or I'll rip out your spleen.

Jesus.

No wonder Father made us take all those lessons in control.

"What is this mate shit he's talking about, Lon?" Haide stands, apparently ready to switch back to the topic at hand. Of course she asks London, because fuck me and what I've got to say.

The silence from Rathe's newest royal is truly amusing, but it's Haide's next words that has fire licking through my veins.

"A mate? I thought that just meant you wanted to fuck someone. Really badly. But then…that would mean I would have had multiple mates, and—"

I'm across the bed of Lilly's in a flash, my hand on her throat and her body dangling in the air like a fucking serpent looking for its next place to sink its fangs.

"I'd be very careful with your next words, *mate*." The smirk that spreads across my face drips with venom. "Or you might find yourself, I don't know..."

The color in her eyes sparkles like stars catching fire. As if my threat excites her. Mania ripples through my veins once again, and my palm heats as warmth spreads through my body in waves. I need to rip her clothes off and fuck her until she finally submits.

"Aw, little king," she all but purrs. "Don't tell me you have a jealous streak?"

I slowly lower her to the ground. Her feet don't even hit the blades of grass before I want to hurl her across the world.

"Because I'm not the kind of girl who should ever belong to a man so easily triggered by other men." She pauses. "Or women."

My jaw tightens.

"That's it!" Creed's hand flies up and a pile of bricks forms between our feet.

"Creed," I warn, fingers flexing on her throat.

He ignores me and the stones grow higher.

Haide is out of my hand in a flash. Before I can reach her, a portal opens and snaps shut, leaving nothing but a dust of smoke.

"Fuck!" I yell, glaring at them all. "What the fuck? Where did you put her?!"

Knight rolls his eyes. "Chill. We don't have time for petty mate drama—"

"Says the guy who killed his mate's best friend in a jealous fit and then felt bad later and wiped it from her memory!"

"But since you're hellbent on making your point"—he

continues like I didn't speak—"and Rathe U is reopening..." I already know what he's going to say before the words leave his mouth. Like a hit of Pixie Herb, my muscles relax.

Because this just became a game of cat and mouse.

And I'm nothing if not a thorough hunter.

Chapter Seven

Haide

I hit the hard dirt as the portal snaps closed behind me. Momentum carries me forward. I don't stop. I don't want to stop. Nothing here is good—nothing!

Don't look back.

My legs pump beneath me, blood roaring through my ears as I break into a run. I prefer to be the one doing the chasing, but this place is wrong. So fucking wrong. Too clean, too still, too…everything. It doesn't taste like salt and coal. It doesn't burn when I breathe in too deep.

I need Zev. I need the violence. The dragons screaming overhead. The constant certainty that death waits around every corner. Not this. Not whatever hell I've been forced into. Not

Legend's hands on my skin; and not the way my entire body detonates like a damn landmine when he does.

A mate.

I run harder, ignoring unfamiliar landscapes that blur past. Trees that aren't charred from an angry dragon. Grass that is actually green.

My hut. My weapons. My island where things make sense and nobody talks about queens or bonds or–

"Going somewhere, little monster?"

I duck on instinct, rolling as Legend lands directly where I'd been standing.

"Fuck off." I'm already moving again, but he's faster. Bastard. Of course he is.

His hand closes around my wrist, spinning me back against his chest.

I lash out with my free hand, aiming for his throat, but he catches my wrists while I thrash around like a pathetic animal.

"Let me go. I don't want this! I don't want you!"

"Liar." His eyes widen. "Your pulse is racing and your pupils are fucking dilated. You can taste me, huh?"

I can. It coats everything like honey mixed with something else. Something poisonous.

"I'd take the dreams," I spit at him. "The strangling ones. The drowning ones. I'd take all of them over this."

Something flickers across his face. Gone too fast to name.

"Then it's fortunate," he says, voice dropping to something dark and possessive, "that you don't get to choose."

He pulls me in close, and for a moment, I sense we're not alone.

Figures emerge between thick trees. People. Just fucking people dressed in trousers and starched shirts, their faces a mixture of confusion and fear as they stare at us both.

At me. A caged animal dragged from its filthy habitat and dropped into this ridiculous world purely for their amusement.

My blood runs cold. I need to get away. If there was ever a time that I could try, it's now.

I wrench my wrists, a feral snarl tearing from my throat. *See. Animal.* "Get your fucking hands off me."

Legend's grip loosens just enough. It's calculated, almost, but I don't stay around to test it because I pivot and sprint forward, my boots tearing up the manicured lawn. The air is thick with the scent of cut grass and unfamiliar flowers. It's so sweet it'd make me rot.

Good. I'm away. I'm—I count ten paces. Maybe twelve. Just as hope flickers—that stupid, ridiculous thing— he's there. A shadow moving at the edge of my vision and cutting me off as I veer toward a stone path.

"This is getting pathetic, Hellpet. Just stop."

"Fuck you." I dodge around him, my shoulder slamming into a student who yelps and stumbles away.

Before I can figure out my next move, he grabs the back of my shirt. The material strains as he yanks me backward. My feet leave the ground, and he spins me, slamming my back against the rough bark of a tree.

His body cages mine, one hand pinning my wrists above my head and the other tilting my chin up so my eyes meet his.

Clearly, I'd underestimated the royal douche, but that doesn't mean I'll give in easily.

His eyes burn, the amusement gone and replaced by something even hotter. Darker.

"Every step you take away from me just makes it worse," he breathes, his voice a low growl that vibrates through every bone in my body. His hips press against mine, a hard ridge that leaves no question about his intent. "I swear to the gods, Haide, I'm gonna fuck you against this tree until I forget what I was mad about."

My breath hitches. *Shit.*

It's not an empty threat. It's a promise. A future he's promising with every possessive line of his body.

Heat pools low in my belly. Traitorous fucking thing.

Fight or flight? I've always been better at the first.

"You'll have to catch me first," I whisper, letting my head fall back against the tree.

He grins, a flash of white teeth. "I already have."

Cocky. Perfect.

"No," I challenge. "You haven't."

I lift my knee up hard between his legs. His hold on my chin vanishes as he grunts, but the grip on my wrist isn't letting up. It's not enough. I swing my head forward, cracking my forehead against his. Stars explode behind my eyelids, but he stumbles back a step. It buys me just enough time. My right hand is free.

My fist connects with his jaw with a satisfying crack. His head snaps to the side. For a single, glorious second, he's just a man I hit. Not a king. Not a mate. Just a man with a broken nose, if I'm lucky.

I don't wait to find out. I spin and run, pushing through the stunned crowd of students. Their shocked faces are a blur. All I see is the path ahead. All I hear is the blood pounding in my ears. I push harder, my lungs burning as I aim toward two larger buildings connected by shrubs. A smirk spreads over my face. I'm gonna make it! I'm—

A growl ripples through the air as something dark tears through reality like a split, gaping wound.

A fucking portal!

Shit! I try to stop, heels digging into dirt, but the momentum carries me forward and the edge catches me.

"No!"

I'm sucked in deep, my stomach lurching up my throat. My skin burns, the air so tight and hot that I can barely breathe. It's like falling without landing, just floating through magic without any control.

Then solid ground slams into my knees. Pain shoots up my thighs as I crash down hard and my palms slap against polished stone. My head spins, stomach heaving as I fight the urge to vomit.

Magic. It's just death that won't rot.

I cough, splattering forward as my nails dig into the hard surface.

A pair of boots appears in front of me. Not Legend's worn leather ones. Cleaner.

I drag my gaze upward, past fitted jeans, past the black shirt, and lock eyes with none other than Creed fucking Deveraux.

Of course it's him. The oldest brother. The one who looks at me like I'm a monster in his precious bloodline.

I push myself up, ignoring the way my muscles scream. Not a fan of portals. I'm going to need to find a better way to get around these assholes.

When he stays silent, I bare my teeth in something that's definitely not a smile. "Let me guess. You're here to lecture me about my decorum? Maybe slap some handcuffs on me and drag me back to your little brother like a good boy?"

He doesn't move. Doesn't blink. Just stares at me like I'm not even worth the words that come from his mouth.

Finally, he shrugs. "I'm here to give you something you want more than anything."

I scoff. "I doubt that."

His eyes drift to mine, lazily. "Willing to bet on it?"

Chapter Eight

Haide

"What do you mean?" I seethe, but it's too late. Creed's smug face hovers too close to mine, and I can't seem to carve enough distance between us to make him evaporate.

"You will go to Rathe University." His words hang in the air like concentrated venom. "You will learn how to control your damn self." His pupils dilate like twin voids consuming light. "And you won't fucking complain."

I scoff a laugh, shaking my head. "You clearly don't know me well."

"And I have zero desire to." He steps even closer, glaring down at me with his icy blue eyes. "There is something off with you, island girl, and I do not like it."

"Good. I don't want you to. Can you pass that feeling onto your little bro because *damn*. He's a bit much, isn't he?"

Creed glares down at me, and I feel a sort of pressure roll across my forehead.

"Stop that."

"Stop what?" He smirks. "You don't even know what I'm doing, do you?"

"I know if I gut you, you won't be able to do it."

His brows snap together and he looks down at the blade pressed right against his cock. The blade that he didn't even hear me pull free from its sheath.

"Careful, Creed. Wouldn't want to lose what I'm betting is your strongest… appendage."

The man-boy sighs and gives me the space I want, but he shuffles back only a few feet.

"Do you even know what your powers are, Haide? Do you even know if you *have* any? Because I know the island blocks all magic that could threaten its purpose. You were born there, so something tells me your powers haven't even fully formed." He pauses and when I say nothing, his smirk sharpens. "That's what I thought."

"Fuck you. I could kill you with my hands before you even had time to throw your little spells, or whatever, at me."

"I'll just take your word for it," he deadpans, clearly completely unthreatened. "And you need to take mine as a royal decree. You're going to that school."

"Your royal decrees mean absolute fuck-all to me. I'm not from here. I don't want to *be* here, so just send me back and all will be better."

"That's not going to happen. I need my brother here, and

he seems to think you're more than the pain in the ass I see."

"I am not his mate."

"I'm inclined to agree."

Wait, what?

My shoulders drop. "Really?"

"Really." He doesn't blink. "I don't sense his beast stirring the way Knight's did when London came along, but it could be because you come from the island. Maybe it's blocked you from more than just your powers. Then again, maybe he's mistaken obsession for something more. I honestly don't care so long as he is safe, which means I need him near. That means keeping *you* near and making sure you can, at the very least, learn how to act like a gifted and not cause him even more problems."

"Yeah, not really selling me on this whole school situation."

"We are gifted, Haide. You might come from a place where we send the worst of our kind, but they are stunted there. Here, they are not. *We* are not. We can creep into your mind and control you. We can make you see what we want, do what we wish, and you will be none the wiser. You will be a puppet to our pleasure if that is what we see fit. Even the help could take you out without so much as an ounce of energy."

"They could try."

He glares. "The point is, whether you believe it or not, you are prey. At Rathe U, we turn prey into predator."

My mind starts to catch up to his suggestion.

It's ridiculous, honestly.

Me? Go to...*school.*

I've never been to school.

That's the point though, isn't it? Everything I learned I either taught myself or learned from the exiled on the island. Gifted who were stripped of the very thing that made them what they were—dangerously feral and unforsaken, but *powerless.* And liars, most of them.

A spark of—*something*—lights in my chest, but I snuff it out. The feeling not exactly a welcome one.

"I can see it in your eyes, Haide. You want to know what else you're capable of. What lies you've been told all your life. Learn what no one has cared to teach you. The truths and lies of the gifted world. Rathe U can give you all of that and more."

My eyes narrow, and while I can't read his damn mind, I can read his expression, as stoic as it is. "What's in it for you?"

"I told you, I need my brother here."

"No." I shake my head. "That's not it. You just want to keep me on a leash."

"If you're really Legend's mate, which I highly, *highly* doubt, then you already have one. And it's bound tight around that pretty neck of yours."

"He's not my mate."

"That's one thing we agree on." His blue eyes pierce mine, and the familiar pressure against my forehead returns. "Are you ready to make it two?"

"You're doing it again, aren't you? Trying to get inside my head?"

He smirks. "Not trying. I'm in."

My lip curls. This time, when I draw my blade, he's ready. He pins me against the wall with a thud. His chest presses against me, his mouth lowering until it's pressed against my ear.

"Nice try, brat."

"Fuck you." I look at his face the best I can from this angle. "I'm not playing into your bullshit. I don't want to be here. Send me back."

"That's not an option."

"I swear to the fucking gods—"

"Yet." He cuts me off, and with that one word, my mouth slams shut.

Creed smirks knowingly.

He widens his stance, hands folding in front of him like some privileged fuck, and I have to hold in the urge to roll my eyes.

"If you can dig deep into that empty skull of yours and find even a tiny bit of self-control, pretend you're a good little gifted girl, I will make you a deal."

"Just fucking say it already."

"Stop driving my brother into a manic state. It's weighing on him. Agree to stay where we put you."

"And what do *I* get out of that?"

"Besides the opportunity to find out if you're worth more than your skin as a gifted?" He raises a brow.

I raise one right back.

"Fine," he clips. "Agree and when the time comes, I will help send you back where you belong myself."

My head jerks back. That's unexpected. I take a step back, watching him closely. "Do you think I'm a fool?" I ask, cocking my head. "I might not know jack all about your little world, but don't underestimate me, *King Deveraux*. Because if you do, it will be a mistake you can't come back from," I warn. "Don't forget, I come from a place where there weren't just snakes in the grass but in the very air you breathe. I know a trick when I see one, and I won't be played into submission."

He hums, hands clasped behind his back as he circles around me. "There is a Royal Gateway on campus accessible only to those we let through. It is a living, breathing portal created and protected by the enchantment of desire. A safety net that allows us to get where we're needed in the event we find ourselves drained, or worse. When entered, it takes you where your heart demands. Agree, and I'll shove you through the second the time is right. Legend won't know you're gone until it's too late."

My throat runs dry. The more I study him, the less I'm convinced it's a lie. "What's the catch?"

"To enter the gateway, you have to be able to open its doors."

"And let me guess…you need power to do that?"

"Along with the blood of a royal. I can offer you one of those, but the other…well. That's up to you, isn't it?" He smirks in triumph. "So, what's it gonna be? Go back to that cesspool you call home as the girl you are now—assuming you can make it there on your own." He pauses. "Or go to Rathe U and figure out if there's anything worth a damn under this skin of yours?"

My pulse pounds widely and I glare at the bastard. "I think I hate your face more than the other one."

Creed chuckles as he steps back. "Remember that, brat. Because I can promise you this: If you're toying with my brother in some way I've yet to discover, my face will be the last thing you ever see."

And with that final anticlimactic threat, he snaps his fingers and reality bleeds into nothing.

…

My muscles shriek. Something pulses with agony. My head? My hands? My—I rocket to my feet.

The sleeping platform beneath me groans like tortured bones, and I'm caged within some sort of rectangular tomb with walls that stretch toward a ceiling painted like false galaxies.

A smaller sleeping platform crouches across from mine,

occupied by a girl with golden hair who blinks at me in annoyance.

That son of a bitch!

"Who the hell are you and where the fuck am I?" I snarl, though I'm pretty sure I already know. Instantly hunting for weapons, exits, and anything useful in this pastel hellscape. "And did he just leave?"

"Welcome to Rathe U." The girl huffs, hauling herself upright. Her head is a tangled nest of blond, cropped close to her chin, and there're some strange cuffs around her wrist. "I'm Elena and I'm guessing you're my housemate."

Housemate?!

"Creed said nothing about a housemate. I don't like people."

"Yeah, well. We don't exactly have a say here, now do we." She drives her soft square cushion down over her head and rotates to her other side. "And I wouldn't speak of our kings by name. Or get any delusional ideas about them. Royals don't talk to us ordinaries."

Ordinaries?

Ah, yes, now this I had heard of from whiny exiles. There's a little power scale those born of Rathe live by, inadvertently pitting them all against one another based on the magic that runs through their blood.

Ordinaries are considered the lesser of them because of powers so, well, *ordinary.* An exiled Fae male once said that he was an ordinary. Weird, considering his power sucked the life out of those he murdered, which led to him being sent to the island in the first place. A power bank is no joke. They literally suck the energy out of you and into themselves. If that's not a superior power, I don't know what is.

Pathetic, the weight these people put into what our minds

can do.

They forget their hands are just as much of a weapon.

Was Creed right, do I have dormant powers that the island has suppressed?

The thought makes me feel like a sheep. I allowed Creed to ship me here with the others with the promise of…what, exactly?

Knowledge I won't even need once I go back home?

Powers I may or may not have that will just disappear all over again once I step foot off the island?

Damn, girl. You really are a fucking fool, so easily played.

I don't belong here.

I belong on that island where no one can toy with me. Where no one can manipulate me to want. Or worse.

Hope.

There is no point in either.

I need to be careful here.

I need to remember that my life is one I'll live on my own.

I need to remember to have nothing is to lose nothing.

I glare at my supposed new roommate, who's clearly familiar with this place.

My eyes fall to the edge of her clothing chamber, where something revolting spins in small circles, a light purple glow swirling around it.

The crisp white blouse is embroidered with tiny silver runes down the sleeves; and the pleated skirt of black and gold looks like it'll tear in three seconds flat.

"Yours is in there." She points to another tall chamber, my name sparking through the center like flames every few moments.

"My what?"

She rolls her eyes, hands still half-buried under her pillow. “That’s the school uniform. You’ll need it to enter your classes.”

I nearly laugh. “I nearly gutted your king in a throne room two hours ago, and now I’m in a pastel coffin getting fitted for—what? Math?”

She sighs and pushes to her feet, tucking her hair behind one ear as she turns to her own uniform. “If you don’t show up, they’ll banish you to the mines and replace you with someone who actually wants to learn.”

Mines. Heh. Cute.

Also, I’m pretty sure that’s not true. I heard what the angry older brother said. Everyone has to come here.

So that means this girl is a liar.

And liars need to die.

I go to push toward her when I spot a black notebook on the edge of the bed. It’s carved from some kind of oak, and a sharp opal crystal protrudes from its center.

It stinks of witchery.

“That is your Pathway Codex,” Elana explains as she buttons her top. “It leads you where you’re required and will be your best friend while you’re here. Everything you need will be in there.”

“I don’t like being told what to do and when to do it.” I yank the crystal out and fling it at the glass wall. It clatters uselessly against the runes etched into the stone. In a blink, it’s back inside the front of the book. I glare at the stupid *Pathway Codex*. “Maybe I’ll burn it.”

“You could try and even if you figure out how, I wouldn’t.” My eyes narrow on the girl and she pushes into a sitting position. “It’s the only way out of the dorm.”

I scan the space again. Of course. No doors.

Magical books. School uniforms. Rules. Bossy brothers.

The thought of them makes me think of *him* and my breath hitches. I roll my ankle to see if I can still feel that dead girl's shirt I stuffed inside my boot before Creed tricked me into a chat. I can't bring myself to toss it, but it's not because it has *his* scent on it.

I just like it. End of fucking story.

Pursing my lips, I study the blouse and skirt again—gold and black for the Stygian bloodlines, I bet.

I tear both into strips, one for a makeshift bandolier to hold my knife. The other for a gag if some "professor" won't shut up.

Elena sighs. "Or...you could look like a half normal gifted, put on the extra uniform in your wardrobe and try to make a friend."

I pause. A friend?

She must be Argent-born. Gross.

Doesn't she know friends can leave—and then what?

Daft gifted girl.

I stare at her as the last harbinger of compromise. She looks back, unflinching, but there is an unmistakable hint of uncertainty in her eyes. Like she knows I'll bite if pushed.

Or if I get bored.

Maybe she's smarter than I thought.

Fine.

Maybe *a-not-friend but person whose name I know* can help me get back home before all hell breaks loose. And it will, but it's like the royals don't care. Odd, considering the island is a place no one is allowed to leave, but whatever.

Throwing the doors open to reveal the extra uniform, I *actually* try it on. I roll the skirt around my hips once, twice—still disgusting, but at least it's functional now and won't restrict my legs if I have to crouch or spring.

The top is a no for me. But the black jacket hanging behind it isn't so bad. I cut the bottom off just below my tits.

I smile at myself and turn to Elena.

She grimaces but nods. "I mean…better?"

I roll my shoulders, feeling the ghost of King Legend's claim tug at my bones.

Almost.

"Ready?" she asks.

At my nod, she snaps her fingers, and the wall dissolves in a pulse of magic revealing two portals.

I look to Elena. "Now what?"

She frowns and steps up to the one across from her. "Did you pay attention to nothing back home?"

My grin stretches slow, and her expression grows wearier by the second. "Do you not realize where I'm from?"

Her frown deepens and a legit giggle bubbles up my throat. "Okay, if you didn't pick up on it at that little announcement show, that's your bad. You're the one who has to sleep in the same room as me…" I cluck my tongue. "Maybe this is going to be a little more fun than I thought."

"What does that mean?" she whispers.

My smile grows and I spin around, putting my arms out. "See you later, *roomie.*"

I fall into the portal, head-fucking-first.

Chapter Nine

Haide

The world spins sideways, then inside out. Magic tears at my skin like it doesn't want me here either, which is fair—I wouldn't let me in if I were them.

But then, that's what makes it fun.

I crash to the ground like a meteor in heat.

Stone slams against my knees and palms, a shockwave of power whooshing through the lecture hall the second my body hits the floor. Gasps echo around the chamber—sweet, startled sounds—and it takes me a full second to realize I've landed right in the center of the room. Dead center. The eye of some shiny, sculpted hurricane of stunned silence.

Tables arc around me in clean concentric rings, tiered for

maximum judgment, and every seat is filled with someone who looks like they've never seen a girl drop out of hell before.

Lucky them.

I pop up with a grin.

"Well, this looks like it's going to be as boring as I assumed it would be."

No one moves. Not the professor, not the students, not the glowing board behind me with floating notes mid-lecture. The only sound is a single rune quill that clatters to the ground near the front row.

I pick it up, and flick it back to the wide-eyed boy it belongs to.

"You dropped your stick."

He doesn't catch it. It bonks off his chest and rolls across his desk.

Someone snorts behind him.

A silver-haired girl narrows her eyes at me like she's trying to determine if I'm diseased or just…uncivilized.

At the head of the class, the professor, an older male with curling bronze tattoos climbing his throat, clears his. "And you are?"

"Bored, thanks for asking."

His gaze sweeps down my ensemble, taking in the shredded skirt-turned-bandolier, the cropped jacket, the boots, and the knife strapped against my thigh. "Welcome to Introduction to Ethereal Theory."

I blink at him. "I have no idea what that is."

He doesn't look surprised. "Miss—?"

"Haide." I snap off a little bow, possibly flashing my ass on the other side. "But some people call me *holy shit, run*."

"I see," he says slowly. "Well, Miss Haide, there are no

mistakes at this school. You've been put in this class for a reason, even if it has yet to reveal itself. But something tells me I should note: here at Rathe U, we favor respectful discourse and regulated conduct. This is a school, which means you act accordingly."

I stroll forward, boots clicking against the polished black stone of the lecture floor. "Yeah well, never been to one of those before so...not sure what 'accordingly' means. Sir, professor sir."

"Take a seat," he says tightly. "Before I assign you a disciplinary rune."

"I mean you could try," I say sweetly, then plop into an open chair in the front row, throwing my feet up on the table.

The chair beside me shifts. A boy with tan skin and a jaw like sin slides his things closer to the edge of the desk, clearly hoping whatever plague I have won't touch his precious codex.

I smile at him, all teeth. "Don't worry, I only bite when asked."

He blinks rapidly.

"Though sometimes I don't wait. Ask your king. The baby one."

The silver-haired girl from earlier leans forward in her seat behind me. "You really don't know who you're sitting next to, do you?"

"Should I?"

She smirks. "That's the heir to the Sable Stone. Lord Kael."

I snort. "Sable Stone? What is that, some King Aurther shit? Because, girl, I would fight to the death for a good sword."

She gives me a weird look, probably having no idea what I'm talking about. It was a giftless book, after all. One we found on the helicopter that crashed on the island.

Lord Kael shifts uncomfortably beside me.

Professor Bronze-Throat coughs again. "Let's return to the lesson, shall we?"

"So, we just, like, sit here and listen?"

The man blinks at me and turns back to his floating fucking pictures and words.

I tune him out completely, trying to decide how to play it for when a certain royal shows up.

That little shit will show his face eventually, and when he does, I'll find a way to make him hate the sight of mine.

I just have to figure out how to piss him off. Clearly, biting him was not the answer.

He seemed to really, *really* like that. And, ever since I did it, it's like I can taste him in my throat.

I bolt upright in my chair as a thought occurs.

He loved it when I bit him.

Wonder how he'd feel if I bit someone else?

The thought coils warm and dangerous in my head, sparking a wicked grin, but the second it fully forms, something tightens in my chest. It's not panic or fear, but it's undeniable...pressure.

Weird.

I shake it off. It's probably indigestion.

Definitely not magic bond warning vibes or whatever.

Still might do it.

I roll my neck and slouch back in the chair, spinning my paper dagger between my fingers while Professor Bronze-Throat drones on about "precision of will" and "foundation of magical control." Whatever.

I've never seen anyone able to control their magic. I mean, that's why they drain you of nearly all of it when they send you to the island.

The man's voice drags on. I'm almost asleep when a ripple passes through the room, the kind that prickles at your skin and makes your bones remember you're not in charge here. A shimmer runs along the walls, pooling in the seams between the black stone tiles. Before I can even blink, everyone's clothes dissolve into shadow.

My shredded skirt, my cropped jacket, my carefully tied bandolier, all melt away in a sweep of cool darkness, reforming into a fitted, long-sleeved tunic of black so deep it drinks the light. Pants, loose enough to move in, tuck into high, armored boots. The faint glint of silver winds across my forearms in curling runes I don't recognize, and a belt hangs heavy at my hips, its clasp a snarling wolf's head.

Now this? This I can work with.

The room itself shifted into a circular chamber. Unless we were transported somewhere all together.

Every tier of desks and benches rises like a coliseum, enclosing a broad open floor of obsidian in the center. Runes, faint and dormant for now, are etched in precise circles across the surface. The ceiling arches high above us, lost in a gloom that makes it impossible to tell where stone ends and sky begins. The space is brightened by light sources that float along the walls like trapped fireflies, steady and silent.

It's the perfect time to assess the competition while everyone adjusts to their new surroundings. Frankly, they're unimpressive. A boy whose skin is an unusual gray color, nearly the exact color of rocks. Long, shimmering green hair then draws my attention to the girl next to me. Tiny sparks pop off her braid every few seconds.

I do a double-take when I catch the silver-haired girl from earlier locked on to me with such focus it's like she's waiting to see if I'll combust.

Guess she's checking out the competition, too.

I smirk at the thought, because if this outfit change tells me anything, it's that I'm about to get to use my hands.

Professor Asshole is long gone. In his place stands a beast with bright eyes and green scales along his temple. A shifter for sure, but what kind?

He lifts his chin, attention shifting across the room as he takes slow steps toward us.

"Welcome to Mastery of Warcraft. My name is Orrith, but you will call me professor," he announces, voice booming throughout the room. "This class will test and refine your mind, your command of magic, and your ability to act with precision under pressure."

"Here, you will learn to blend weapon craft with your inherent gifts. To anticipate and counter not just a strike, but an opponent's strategy. We study the battle arts of all magic, from the disciplined forms of the Stygian guard to the elemental fury of the Argent war mages. You will be broken down to your most basic abilities and rebuilt into warriors capable of defending your name, your realm, and your life. This is not sport. This is survival."

Oh, hell yes.

"We'll begin with basic warm-ups." He steps back and the floor opens up, lofting him into the air on a dais. He moves in a circular motion above us, having the perfect viewpoint to keep an eye on us all. "Foundational work. If you can't manage these with ease, you will find the rest of your training…difficult. And do not forget for a moment that today is assessment day. So don't slack off. It will only hurt you in the end."

He lifts his hand and a rack of throwing daggers appears

at the center of the circle. Each one gleams with its own faint aura: storm blue, molten gold, or rich violet. "Summoning," he says simply.

One by one, the students take turns. Rock Boy doesn't move a muscle—just narrows his eyes, and a dagger launches from the rack straight into his palm. Spark-Hair flicks her braid and a blade spirals toward her in a neat corkscrew. A dragon-blood girl with bronze scales along her cheekbone exhales a thin ribbon of smoke, and a dagger drifts to her hand like it's afraid to keep her waiting.

Then it's my turn.

I lift my chin at the rack, trying to imagine the dagger flying to me.

Nothing happens.

I lean forward a little, glaring at it harder. Still nothing.

"Focus, Miss Haide," the professor says in that tone adults use right before they decide you're hopeless.

"Oh, I'm focusing," I say. "Maybe it's shy."

A ripple of laughter runs through the room. Someone coughs "giftless" into their sleeve.

I lean back in my chair, folding my arms. "Next."

The professor's mouth pinches, but he moves on. The rest of the warm-up is more of the same: light a practice torch with a spark; shift a pebble with telekinesis; balance a rune in your palm without frying it. All the little tricks they've clearly been doing since they could toddle around in mage diapers.

I fail every single one, because *hello*—born on exile fucking island where magic literally goes to die.

Finally, the professor claps his hands once, sharp. "Form up. Now we fight and you will give it your all."

Now we're talking.

Pairs are called. Students slide down to the central ring, the floor's runes flaring faintly to life under their boots. The magic here is thick, like the air is holding its breath, waiting to see who bleeds first.

When my name is called, my opponent is a tall, narrow-shouldered boy with pale hair and the kind of smug face that makes you want to break it just to see if he can still smirk afterward.

"No magic for you either, Caelum," Professor Orrith says, his voice like gravel ground against steel.

Caelum smirks and rolls his shoulders as if limbering up for a workout he's already bored of. "Guess I'll keep it light, then. Wouldn't want to break her on her first day."

My mouth curls slowly. "Aw, that's adorable."

The second the professor calls "begin," he starts circling me. His posture loose, like this is a warm-up for him and a lesson for me. His eyes flicker over my hands, my boots, my stance, judging everything he sees.

I move before he finishes that little assessment.

One step inside his guard, my hand catches his wrist and twists. Not enough to snap it, just enough to lock him in place.

My palm drives up into his jaw in the same breath, forcing his head back hard enough to make bone crack. Before the sound's even finished, my other hand's already drawn the dagger from my thigh.

The blade flashes once. Quick and clean across his throat.

Three seconds.

He collapses to the floor with a wet, choking gasp, blood blooming bright against the black stone. His wide eyes fixate on me but quickly lose focus.

I crouch beside him and tap his cheek. "What was that now?"

Gasps erupt around the room, sharp and panicked. A chair screeches back, someone shouts for a healer, and the faint metallic tang of blood floods the air. The runes on the floor flare to life in a blaze of gold, binding my arms to my sides in a cage of light.

I glance down at them and smirk. "Cute trick. Are these magical bars?"

The heavy doors at the far end of the chamber slam open.

And what do you fucking know. It's the bossy big brother himself.

Creed walks in like the room was built to make an entrance for him.

Honestly, it might have been. What do I know about royal rituals and whatnot? Never had one of those on the island before.

His long coat sweeps behind him as he moves with the kind of stillness that makes everyone else feel like they're fidgeting too much. The ropes pinning me don't disappear, but they yank my arms back out of his way.

His eyes find me instantly. "Of course it's you."

I grin at him, leaning forward just enough to make the chains hum. "You're a real dick, you know that?"

The entire room gasps, an actual wave of sound rolling through the students. I'm confused until I remember this is one of their kings.

I'm guessing kings don't get talked to like this. At least not in public or without repercussion anyway.

Creed doesn't react in the slightest, his gaze never breaking from mine as he speaks to the rest of the room. "Class dismissed. This little thing is coming with me." Without another word, he turns on his heel and stalks toward the door. He must just assume I'll follow because he doesn't check to see if I'm behind him.

The ropes vanish with a hiss, and I roll my shoulders. "If I had known you were the school's new babysitter, I would have tried harder to kill the guy. Make your little trip down here worthwhile."

That earns me a ripple of horrified whispers from the stragglers who haven't scurried out yet. Creed doesn't so much as twitch.

We step into the corridor, the heavy doors sealing behind us with a solid thud. Out here, the air is cooler, and the sound of the class vanishes into a silence thick enough to chew. The hall stretches long and vaulted, ribbed with black stone arches and lit by braziers that burn with slow green fire. Every step echoes like the building's judging me.

Creed's pace is measured, unhurried, each stride a study in control. I match it out of pure spite, refusing to jog just to keep up.

"Is this the part where you lecture me about playing nice with the other kids?" I ask, dragging my fingertips along the rough stone wall. It hums faintly under my skin, old magic prickling like static.

"This is the part," he says without looking at me, "where I decide if you're worth the trouble of keeping you alive."

I grin. "Aw, that's practically a compliment. You must really like me."

"I don't," he says flatly, and gods, it's so dry I almost laugh. "But my brother does because he's not in his right mind."

That digs under my ribs in a way I don't like. I mask it by sighing dramatically. "Oh, so this is about Legend. You're jealous."

That gets me the faintest flicker of his eyes in my direction, cool as winter steel. "Jealous implies wanting something he has."

"Right," I say. "You just wish you could pull off black leather like I do."

His mouth twitches. It's tiny, but it's there. Victory.

We pass through an archway into a side hall, this one lined with narrow windows that leak pale light onto the floor in broken stripes. Creed stops without warning, turning to face me. "You will not kill another student."

I tip my head. "Even if they deserve it?"

"Especially if they deserve it." His voice is calm, but there's a razor under it. "This place is held together by politics and the illusion of civility. If you shatter either, you make my life harder. Make my life harder, and I will ruin yours. You agreed to behave. We had a deal and you are not holding up your end."

I pretend his words don't draw a hint of panic, tapping my chin. "So what you're saying is…kill them where no one can see."

"Haide."

"Creed." I mirror his tone exactly, mocking him with a straight face.

For a heartbeat, we just stare at each other: the cold, immovable king and the chaos he probably wishes he could catapult back to Exile. Then he exhales through his nose like he's had enough of me for one lifetime.

"I don't have to tell you that you don't belong here. You know it as well as I do. Don't fool yourself into thinking you're the one in control. There is something going on and you are at the center of it. I will find out what it is, what you did or the part you've played, and I will end you if that's what it takes to fix—"

He cuts himself off, his chin lifting as his eyes harden.

He's clearly said more than he wants to.

Not that I've got any fucking clue what he's trying to say, but whatever.

I just need to pee. "Are you almost done?"

His mouth thins into a hard line. "You've got classes again tomorrow," he says. "Be on time. Wear the uniform. Try not to cause chaos in the first five minutes."

"Okay, in my defense, the professor said fight. He didn't tell me not to kill him and back home, *fight* means *kill*...because you know we can't die there."

His expression grows thoughtful. After a moment, he gives a small nod. "Okay. Fine. That's fair. Still, I am telling you now and my word overrules anything you *think* your professors want you to do. Or what you're used to. If you're not sure about something, ask. Trust your Pathway Codex. It won't lead you astray. It's incapable."

He watches me closely, and then his head tips slightly. I feel a brush of something against my temple. No, it's in my mind.

He's in my fucking head!

"Dude!" I jolt, shaking myself as if that will change anything. I think of that one time back home when Zevryn and I hid in the trees and threw animal bones at a couple getting down in the mud until they spotted us. One of them slipped trying to get to us and broke his wrist. Zev laughed so hard he fell out of the branches. He dislocated his shoulder. I reset it with a rock.

I force the image into my head on repeat like a war drum. *Bones. Blood. Zev's unhinged cackle.* Anything to keep Creed from sniffing around in places he doesn't belong. Not that I have anything to hide.

Creed's brows snap together and he takes a step forward.

"Who is he?"

My smile is slow. "Ahh…so that's the part that stuck. Does everyone know your gift is Mind Mirroring? Pretty fucking wild to be able to see inside someone as if you're them."

"Who. Is. He?"

I chuckle lowly. "You'd have to take a trip to the isle to find out."

Creed huffs, shaking his head. "There is no mating bond within you, is there?"

Something annoying inside of me heats at the reference to the little king.

Aches a little.

But I'm not about to tell him that.

"I told you. I'm not his mate and even if I were, which I'm not, I don't even know what a mating bond is." Not really, anyway.

He steps up to me, toe to freaking toe, though he is a whole ass head taller. "Bond or no bond, Legend believes a bond pulses within him, but I *know* something is twisted. So you need to behave, or he will lose his shit."

"What makes you think I care?"

Creed's features harden, his eyes glowing white as he pulls his power to the surface. "He watches, because the so-called bond demands it, but he's yet to arrive. Don't give him a reason to abandon his current task until it's done."

Okay, that is basically an invitation.

I grin to myself, already thinking of ways to piss off my—

No not *my*.

Just Legend.

He's just Legend.

Right?

Chapter Ten

Haide

The next morning, campus is already a fucking zoo.

Students swarm from the dorms, every single one of them moving like they know exactly where they're going. Fucking sheep. I just let the current pull me along, trying to map it all out.

I stumble out to the main courtyard, a huge open space paved in dark stone that looks slick in the morning light. Archways branch off everywhere, with runes twisting over them. Laughing students cluster around a black obsidian fountain that spits out water with weird blue shimmer. They trade looks that probably mean something. Something I don't give a shit about.

I veer left, heading toward what I'm pretty sure is the

lecture hall from yesterday. The path winds through a covered colonnade, the ceiling arched high above and carved with images of battles I don't recognize. Creatures with too many limbs clash against warriors wreathed in fire, their faces frozen in silent screams.

Cheerful.

A group of girls pass me, their voices high and sharp, laughter spilling out like broken glass. One of them glances my way, her eyes flicking over me with the kind of casual dismissal that makes my fingers itch for a blade.

I smile at her. Teeth and all.

She looks away fast.

Good girl.

The lecture hall looms ahead, its entrance marked by twin statues of Sirens, their jaws open in eternal snarls. I slip through the doors and find a seat near the back. If I'm going to be stuck here, I'm at least going to have a clear exit.

The room fills quickly, bodies sliding into seats with practiced ease. The boy from yesterday—Lord Kael of the Sable Stone or whatever—takes a spot two rows ahead, his posture perfect, his expression bored. Spark-Hair sits near the front, her braid coiled around her wrist like a living thing. Silver-Hair girl is here, too, perched on the edge of her seat like she's waiting for something to happen.

The professor sweeps in a moment later. A woman this time. Tall and sharp-edged, with skin the color of burned amber and eyes that glow faintly violet. She doesn't introduce herself, and with a wave of a hand, the floating board behind her flares to life with symbols.

"Today," she says, her voice cutting through the murmur of conversation, "we discuss mating bonds."

Oh, for fuck's sake.

A ripple of interest runs through the room. Students sit up straight and lean closer.

I slouch lower in my chair.

The professor taps the board, and the symbols rearrange themselves into three distinct sections. "There are stages to a mating bond," she explains. "Recognition. Claiming. Completion. Each one deepens the connection, and each one makes separation more...difficult."

She lets the word hang in the air like a threat.

"Now, while those are the three words that sum it up, it is far more complex and a bit different for all fated pairings." She looks around the room. "Recognition," she continues, pointing to the first section, "is the initial pull. A soul-deep awareness of another being. It's instinctual, primal, and often inconvenient. It's been known to arrive with dreams and hallucinations of each other. But they're not hallucinations at all. They're very real. The soul splits from the physical form to hunt its other half and, during those moments, they are able to be together."

A few students laugh. I don't.

"This stage can occur without warning. A scent. A glance. A brush of skin. The bond recognizes its match before the conscious mind does, and once it begins, it cannot be ignored." Her eyes sweep the room, landing on me for just a second too long. "Those who try to resist recognition often find themselves...distracted. Fatigued, or borderline insane."

Distracted. Sure.

"The second stage," she says, moving to the next section, "is the claiming. This is a conscious choice. An acknowledgment of the bond and an agreement to pursue it. It requires intent, often marked by a physical or magical act—a bite, a vow, an exchange of blood. The claiming solidifies the connection and makes it known to others."

Her hand moves to the third section, and the symbols pulse with a faint golden light.

"Completion"—her voice drops, quiet and heavy—"is the final binding. A ritual that fuses two souls together permanently. Once completed, the bond cannot be broken. Upon death of both mates, they are reborn within each other. Life forces synchronize. Your powers will grow significantly and separation becomes unbearable. If you are lucky enough to be born of royal blood, or find yourself fated to a royal, not only will your own powers grow in strength, but a second will rise from within."

"Their Ethos," a girl up front shouts. "I saw it in King Knight and his new mate the day the Queen Cosima was exiled!"

"That is correct. Royals and their fated are born with their Ethos within them, but the demon within can and will only be freed by their fated."

"Gifted who complete a bond without true compatibility," she continues, "often go mad. The magic tears at them, seeking balance that cannot be found. It's rare, but not unheard of, for a completed bond to end in mutual destruction."

Fucking hell. That's bleak even for me.

"Questions?" she asks, turning back to the room.

A hand shoots up near the front. A boy with bronze skin and sharp cheekbones. "What happens if one half of the bond dies?"

"The surviving half usually follows," she says simply. "The bond doesn't release easily. It clings, even in death."

Another hand. Silver-Hair this time. "Can you break a bond before completion?"

"Theoretically, yes. But the damage is severe. The magic doesn't let go without taking pieces of you with it. Most who attempt it are left…diminished."

I tap my fingers against the desk, mind churning. *Recognition. Claiming. Completion.* Three steps to tie yourself to someone for the rest of your life, with the promise of agony if it goes sideways.

Sounds like a trap.

The professor moves on, diving into the mechanics of bond magic, the way it alters brain chemistry, the hormonal shifts, the heightened senses. I tune most of it out, already bored, but one thing sticks.

"The bond demands proximity," she says. "Especially in the early stages. The longer the separation, the more intense the pull becomes. It's not uncommon for newly bonded pairs to become volatile when kept apart."

Volatile. Another fun word.

I think about the ache in my chest when Creed mentioned Legend. The weird tightness that flared up when I thought about biting someone else in spite. The way my skin prickled when I landed on this campus, like it was a living, breathing thing, waiting for me to arrive. Only once I was locked away inside could I finally breathe that sigh of relief.

Fuck.

The lecture drags on for another hour, and by the time it ends, I'm ready to claw my way out of my own skin. I shove from my seat and head for the door, ignoring the curious stares that follow me.

If these people tuned into the little show when the Royal assholes announced reopening the school, they would have heard Legend's little declaration.

Did that part get shared across the realm?

Did they hear him stake his ridiculous claim?

Do I want them to have?

I sigh, annoyed with my damn self. No. No, I don't.

Because it's not true.

Outside, the air is cooler, and I suck it in like I've been drowning.

I need to move. Need to do something that doesn't involve sitting still and listening to people explain how screwed I might be. I don't understand this place, and the worst part of it all?

There's this pestering in the back of my mind, warning me that the longer I'm here, the more I might want to.

That would be a terrible fucking idea.

Chapter Eleven

Legend

The rot's denser here.

It hangs in the air like it's got nowhere else to go, bleeding into the bark, curling through the spaces between ancient stone. Sulfur stings my nose, but there's something underneath it. Something heavier. Death, maybe. Or whatever the fuck lingers after.

The river cutting along the shifter quadrant looks all kinds of wrong—less silver, more like the color of a bruise that hasn't quite healed. Clouded and murky.

Sick.

Knight's crouched by the tree line, fingers trailing over something half-swallowed by moss. "This one didn't even make it far enough to run," he says, voice flat, detached.

I step over a body twisted at an unnatural angle, my eyes catching on the mark burned into the ground next to it. Some crude emblem smeared in ash and blood—a moon split clean through by jagged lines. I've never seen a sigil like this. Not on this side of the realm, anyway.

The message painted across the house wall behind us is almost poetic in how fucked-up it is.

Am I being too subtle?

Blood drips from each letter, mixing with something tar-like that makes the whole thing look like it's crying black tears. Still wet enough to catch the dim light.

Yeah, real fucking *subtle*.

A family lived here. Shifter-blooded. *Stygian* born. Now they're scattered across their own doorway, throats opened wide, eyes vacant and glassy.

Then I feel it.

The bond slams into me like a punch to the ribs, flooding me with her terror in waves that make my jaw clench. She's here. Close. Too damn close to all this carnage.

I spin, scanning the tree line, and there—

Haide.

On her knees at the edge of the clearing, hands pressed into the moss, blood streaked across her throat, her arms, soaking through her clothes. Her eyes are feral—more animal than girl—chest rising and falling with ragged breaths.

"Fuck," I mutter, already moving.

My chest detonates. The bond screams *mine* so violently it feels like my ribs are splitting apart. Like something feral is clawing its way out of my skin to get to her, to bite, protect.

My vision tunnels, heat flooding my veins, instincts crashing over reason in a brutal, blind demand to destroy first and think later.

She's hurt. She's bleeding. You fucking failed her.

"What happened? Who did this?" Panic closes around my throat, but as I reach out to her, the scent hits me and it's wrong.

Not her blood.

I blink, and just like that, the haze clears. "I thought…"

For a moment, her features seem to soften before she forces a frown.

Creed appears beside me a second later, his expression going hard at her presence.

Knight straightens from where he's crouched. "What the hell—"

"I don't—" Her voice cracks, raw and wrecked. She stares at her hands, at the blood coating them, trembling. "I was in my room reading over what Professor Astra said today about—" Her lips clamp shut, and her eyes slide to me. "Never mind. It's not important. I was reading and then I was here."

"Wow. She knows how to read." Sinner smirks.

I make a mental note to figure out what professor Astra is teaching her, because it must be good if she's being tight-lipped—my girl loves to speak her mind.

I move closer, and the bond hums between us, confirming what I already know in my bones. She's telling the truth. I can feel it, absolute.

But Creed's not convinced. His jaw tightens as he stalks toward her, hands raised like he's dealing with something wild. "You're portalling."

"I sure as fuck would be…if I knew how!" She snarls, shoving to her feet. Blood drips from her fingers, and the sight of it makes something primal twist in my chest. "I can't even make a fucking feather float! It's like I said, I was doing what you asked—stupid school shit—and then I woke up in a goddamn murder scene!"

"You're a lying little—"

"Enough, brother," I cut in. "She said she doesn't know how she got here and she's telling the truth."

Creed glares my way but remains silent. I know my brother. He's biting his tongue, and he's never been very good at that.

Knight circles the body closest to us, a frown building over his brows.

"What is it?"

"What it isn't is random." Knight frowns. "This feels targeted."

"Feels personal," Silver, Knight's best friend and our newly appointed Grand Healer, adds. His duty above all is to keep us alive when we fail to do so ourselves, which makes him our happy little shadow. "Could be revenge. A lover's vendetta, maybe."

"Against an entire bloodline?" Knight raises a brow.

Silver shrugs. "You've seen what grief can do."

Vicente shakes his head. "No. This wasn't rage. This was deliberate. Calculated."

Vicente is Silver's father and was our father's most trusted and number one warrior. His dedication earned him the coveted spot as the King's Guardian. Now, he serves as ours.

I glance back at the bodies and the way they're positioned—almost staged. "Then whoever did this wanted the scene found. But what the hell does that mean?" I jerk my chin toward the scribble on the wall.

"Too subtle?" Silver scoffs. "And I thought we were fucked-up."

"Family dispute?" Knight suggests, jaw tight as he stares at the message, trying to work it out.

"Doesn't make sense, they're all here."

"Not all of them," Vicente mutters, momentarily lost in his own thoughts before his eyes lock on mine. "I remember this pack. They had a third mate, but the third mate only shared a bond with one of them and it eventually drove him mad with jealousy."

Damn, that blows, but why's he looking at me? "Where is he now?"

"He was banished," Vicente says quietly. "A decade ago… to Exile Island."

The words hang there like a noose.

Creed turns back to Haide, expression dark though he says nothing, likely searching her mind for the truth.

"I didn't do this," she says, but there's less fire behind it now. Just exhaustion and something that looks too close to fear. The bond feeds it to me, her terror bleeding into my own rage until I can't tell where hers stops and mine starts.

Creed's anger only grows. "Portalling without knowing how? That's not normal, even for the gifted. If you can even call yourself one."

"Tell me, oh mighty King Creed, what part of this *is* normal?" Haide snaps defiantly. "And you forget, I never wanted to come here in the first fucking place!"

"Sure you fucking did. You want power just as much as the next, but I doubt you're even worthy enough."

"So which is? I have power, or I don't?"

His eyes flash in warning. "*Behave.*"

"You," I warn, my lip curled.

His features stiffen, but you'd have to be watching to see it, and I am fucking watching.

Yeah, he doesn't want Legend to pick up on his subtle reminder of our deal but he wants to make sure I don't forget it. As if I fucking could.

I've been thinking about that little conversation we had that day, and something isn't quite adding up.

I open my mouth to ask him something.

"Enough." Knight's voice slices through the tension before I can speak. "We need to look at this closer, and outsiders are not welcome while we do."

I snarl. "She's not a fucking—"

"Yes, I am! Stop trying to come to my damn rescue. I don't need nor want it!" she snaps, burning me with her glare. "You can all fuck off now."

Then she moves, stalking toward the tree line with that lethal grace that makes every instinct in me scream to follow, to drag her back, to chain her somewhere safe where nothing can touch her.

But I don't.

I watch her disappear into the shadows, the bond stretching tight between us, and force myself to stay still.

For now.

"She's gonna end up dead if she keeps this shit up," Creed mutters.

"No," I say, voice cold and certain. "She won't."

"People will start to talk."

"Let them."

I'll burn this whole fucking realm down before I let anything happen to her.

I should stop her as she walks away, but I don't. Because she can throw a fucking tantrum loud enough for the Gods to hear, but that ain't gonna change shit.

"You think she's gonna behave?" Knight asks, brow curved. We both know she isn't, but it's what makes her Haide. My little fucking monster.

"Focus," Creed demands, turning his attention back to the task at hand. The dead fucking shifters at our feet.

"We need to stay vigilant, explore every angle as Dad would. And do not, under any circumstance, allow yourselves to be -distracted. Our own mother betrayed us not long ago. Let that be your reminder." His words settle over us, but the only response he gets from me is a single shoulder shrug.

Sinner's the first to move, circling around to my left like a wolf testing weakness. "So, we're just gonna ignore that the most likely suspect is also the one person Legend won't let us interrogate?"

"She's not a suspect," I growl. I can't wait for Sinner to land ass first on his mate.

"Everyone's a suspect," Creed corrects, stepping closer. "That's how investigations work. Or did you forget that part when you became obsessed?"

Knight puts a hand on Creed's chest. "Creed. Settle."

Creed shoves it away. "Don't defend him. He's not thinking straight."

"I'm thinking clearer than all of you." Creed's always been a pain in my fucking ass, but lately, even he's pushing it. "The bond—"

"The bond is the problem!" Creed's shout echoes across the clearing. "It's clouding your judgment, making you see innocence where there's only convenient coincidence."

Silver stands, holding a vial of ash from the symbol. "It's not just convenient." He throws the vial to me. I catch it instinctively.

The contents hum against my palm, familiar and wrong. "That's from her hut. Her ashes, Legend. Someone burned her old life and painted it here."

My fist closes around the vial. Glass cracks.

"Could be a message," Knight says quietly. "Someone saying 'I know where you came from.' A lot of people aren't happy about her being here."

"Could be a trophy," Sinner counters. "Someone bringing their work home."

Creed's eyes never leave mine. "Could be a confession."

I move. I don't remember deciding to, but suddenly I'm in Creed's space, chest to chest, magic sparking between us. "Say it again."

"She's either the killer, the target, or the trigger." He doesn't back down. "And I won't let your dick destroy this kingdom."

Knight and Silver grab my arms, pulling me back. I let them, but only because I'm calculating how many bones I can break before they subdue me.

Vicente's quiet voice slices through the rage, veering us back on track. "What if, whoever this is, is using her as a way to get to Rathe from Exile. Like a portal."

The word *portal* freezes everyone.

"Go on," Knight says.

"If this person is somehow linked to her—through the bond, through Exile magic or whatever the hell you want to call it, he could be using her as an anchor. She appears at the scene because he's pulling her here. Or the magic is."

"That's diabolical," Sinner scoffs.

"So is appearing at a murder scene you didn't commit," Vicente shoots back. "The question isn't whether she's guilty. It's whether she's the weapon or the target."

The bond in my chest twists. Haide's fear floods through, clean and sharp, cutting through my anger. Fear? Haide isn't scared of shit. But I understand it. She's like a wild animal that's been placed in a home with rules. Her fear may not look like others', but it's there.

"Fuck," I breathe, the fight draining out of me. "Fuck."

Creed sees the change. "What now?"

"She's scared." I look at my brothers, really look at them. "Not of us." Because I want to make that very fucking clear. "Of *this*. Of being among a world she's not sure of."

"Then," Knight hesitates, "we keep an eye on her."

Sinner rolls his eyes. "Poetic."

"Practical," Creed corrects. "If she's being used, we need to find the hand moving her. If she's using us, we need to know before the body count rises."

They drift away, back to the bodies. I stay, staring at the symbol.

My palm still burns from the vial. Her ash. Her past. Her ghost. Her home.

• • •

Thirty minutes later, there's still nothing else we can find. We call in a trainee mage to clean the scene. Knight's fingers fly over his phone as he mutters orders to Silver and Vicente about everyone meeting in the war room at eight to announce the curfew. Creed took off a while ago for some school bullshit—I think he secretly likes playing the sophisticated man in charge.

I'm fucking sick of whoever this bastard is already. My muscles ache with fatigue, as if demanding her touch.

Fucking moody bastard. I get the bond and my mate, but

damn. I'll at least string her out for as long as I can take it. So, when I get to her, she's going to be desperate for me. Exactly the way I want her.

A tiny little tendril of her emotions bleeds into mine, but my mind is too slow to catch onto what it is.

I turn to leave.

"Legend," Knight warns. "You good?"

But I'm already throwing up a portal, the air splitting in a burst of black light. I step through without another word.

Chapter Twelve

Legend

The corridor splits open around me, shadow peeling back from stone, and the first thing I see is her. She's got blood on her throat like a necklace, jacket hacked off and riding the top of her ribs, eyes full of knives, and Creed beside her looking like the world's most exhausted executioner.

The bond slams into me the second I'm through, vicious and greedy, a hot hook under the breastbone yanking me forward like I belong in her orbit and nowhere else. I hate it. I love it. And I'm already smiling.

"Who did this?" I ask, voice low enough to rattle the floors.

She doesn't flinch, just tips her chin like she's daring me to step closer. "Relax, Your Majesty. Warcraft just keeps getting more interesting."

Creed's gaze cuts to me, a warning so sharp it could gut a god. "You should not be here."

"Go take attendance somewhere else," I snap.

I step in and she doesn't step back.

Good girl.

There's a smear of red at the corner of her mouth that isn't hers or mine, and something feral slides through my chest like a blade unsheathed. I lift my thumb, slow, and drag it across her lower lip. She watches me the whole time, eyes bright and unbothered, like I'm a knife trick at a street fair.

The growl crawls up my throat before I let it die in my teeth. "Say it."

She blinks. "Say what?"

"That you're mine."

She smiles, sweet as poison. "Buy me dinner first."

Creed exhales in that very special way that says he's actively choosing not to murder either of us. "Mastery of SpellChemy at dawn," he says, like we're not vibrating the mortar out of the walls. "She bails or is even a moment late, I will personally see to what follows. I expect both of you to pretend to understand what consequences means."

"Consequences?" she echoes, eyes never leaving mine. "I don't know if you even understand the meaning of the word, big king."

"Don't call him king. *I* am your only king, little monster." I lean in so the edge of her breath is in my mouth and my ribs ache from being this close without breaking something. The bond is a storm under my skin. Static clawing at bone, heat licking vertebrae. That black lace thrum that says take, mark, bite, keep. And I know she has to feel some of it. How could she not?

The gods didn't wire me to burn alone. There's a fire in me and it's alive and thriving—stealing my energy and demanding I bind it to hers.

"You feel this," I murmur, letting the words curl against the soft part of her ear. "Don't lie to me, monster."

She laughs, bright and terrible. "I feel…bored."

It hits harder than a dragon's tail to the fucking face.

The smile stays on my face because I made it to last through wars and funerals, but something ugly rakes along the inside of my ribs. I test the bond. Just a pulse. Just a little snap of heat. Nothing she can name. And *there*, the smallest falter in her breath. The tiniest catch like a wire drawn too tight.

"There you are," I breathe, triumphant and mean.

She smooths it into a grin like it never happened. "You're hallucinating, King Gaslight."

I want to bite her hard enough the pain blinds her.

"Enough," Creed says, and the corridor obeys, the braziers guttering to a sterner flame. He plants himself in the middle without quite getting between us, older-brother arrogance wrapped in a funeral coat. "You're forcing something you're not ready for."

"Don't make me kill you, brother."

"Legend, take a fucking beat before you create a shitstorm that can't be undone. Trust me on this."

"She is mine."

"So you keep saying."

My eyes slide to his, holding.

Big brother grits his teeth. "Fine. But do not start a war in my hall because you can't manage your teeth."

"My teeth are perfectly managed," I say, and then I look back at her mouth and decide that statement is a fucking tragedy.

She's close enough to kiss. Close enough to kill. Close enough that if I breathe deeper, we'll share a heartbeat. It's a miracle I'm even pretending to be civilized. "You smell like detergent," I tell her, because it offends me on a cellular level. "Fix it."

"Aw," she says. "Does it mask your cologne? Smoldering ego? Notes of petrol and delusion?"

"Gasoline," I correct softly. "And hunger."

The bond drags a claw down my spine. I swear I feel her flinch though she attempts to mask it. She's stone. She's smoke. She's the first thing I've wanted to worship and ruin in equal measure. The calm that used to live in my hands is a ghost.

"Run, then," I murmur, stepping back half a breath because I'm either going to kiss her or break the wall with her spine. "I'll give you a head start."

"I don't run," she says.

I grin. "I know."

Creed tips his chin at her. "Dorm. Now. And if you see a blade on your way, don't pick it up."

"Terrible advice," she says, brushing past him like a storm in a stolen jacket.

I let her shoulder hit mine as she goes. Let the bond yank. Let the heat rip. Let the hunger kick my ribs open from the inside. I don't follow, because I want her to feel the space I leave behind like a hand at her throat. She doesn't look back, of course, but rounds the arch and vanishes from sight.

I stand there, smile still cutting my face, and hate how empty the corridor gets without her.

Creed watches with an expression I can't quite place, but when he speaks, it's not full of anger like a moment ago. It's lower, laced with something that sounds a lot like concern.

"You keep pushing like that and she'll tear the campus apart just to spite you. That is drama we do not fucking need right now."

"I know," I say softly, thinking of blood on black stone, of a smear at the corner of her mouth that wasn't mine. "I'm just teaching her to enjoy it."

He shakes his head as if at a loss. "Dawn. Don't be late."

He turns away, coat whispering secrets to the floor.

I'm left with the taste of someone else's blood and the certainty that the next time I touch her, I won't stop until the whole damn university wears my fingerprints.

She thinks she's not affected.

She thinks she can starve the bond out.

Sweet little liar.

Keep pretending, baby.

I can wait an hour.

Maybe two.

The silence stretches thin as wire, and I realize I'm still standing here like some lovesick fool, breathing the air she left behind. Pathetic. I rake a hand through my hair and turn toward the east wing, where my room waits with its four walls and the kind of quiet that used to feel like peace.

Now it just feels like waiting.

My footsteps echo wrong in the empty corridor, and the bond writhes under my skin like a Lycan who hasn't had a meal in weeks.

I know sleep won't come easily tonight. It hasn't since I brought her back. My mind is weighted, like a cloud of demonic smoke settled there, pressing against my conscience.

Suddenly too tired to call a portal, I reach the tapestry that hides one to my chambers. I press my palm against the woven threads, recognizing the royal blood that flows in my veins.

The portal opens, a mouth of darkness that tastes like home, but now there's this pit of emptiness that follows.

I step through, let the magic fold around me like a familiar coat, and emerge into my bedroom where moonlight cuts silver bars across the floor. The portal seals behind me with a whisper that sounds almost like her laugh.

I strip off my jacket, let it fall where it wants, and sink onto the edge of my bed. The mattress dips under my weight, and I can still taste her defiance on my tongue, still feel the ghost of her shoulder against mine.

Dawn is hours away.

Too many hours.

I lie back and stare at the ceiling, where shadows dance like memories of what I almost had. What I will have. What she can't run from forever.

The bond purrs in my chest, patient as a lion for once.

Let her sleep.

Let her dream.

Let her pretend she doesn't feel this thing between us clawing at her ribs the way it claws at mine. That it doesn't leave an absence in her she can't name even when she's near.

Chapter Thirteen

Haide

Roomie doesn't stop fucking talking.

As if waking into a horror scene this week wasn't enough, I'm stuck with a roommate who won't shut the fuck up.

Roomie stares at me, eyes wide, mouth slightly parted. Did she ask me something?

"What?"

She rolls her eyes and goes back to applying the color over her lips. "I said, you're coming to a party."

Part of me wants to throw her against the wall to see if her head splits on impact for thinking she can tell me what I'm going to do. But the other…

I swing up onto my bed, legs dangling over the edge. "What

kind?" Hesitation has me asking questions first, because if there's one thing I've learned when it comes to these *students* it's that they're disappointing. Honestly. Send me back to Exile.

The clasp of her makeup case snaps closed as she meets my gaze in the mirror. "The kind where we can get messed up on Fae party favors and you can pretend you're not going to fail. No offense."

She meant offense.

I slide off the bed, bare feet hitting cold stone. "Where?"

"The Depths," she says, like that means something to me. When I stare at her blankly, she sighs. "Underwater caverns beneath the campus. Magic keeps the air breathable, the pressure from crushing us, and all that fun stuff." She waves her hand dismissively. "It's where they hold all the good parties because the professors can't hear us scream. Plus, after the explosion of the Dragon Lair just before the school closed last time, it's one of the few places we're left with."

Yeah, that's too much information for me. I focus on the important stuff.

Underwater. Magic. Screaming.

"Sold."

I quickly change into one of the outfits I found in the trunk that appeared at the foot of my bed after my first set of classes. I lace up my boots and sit back, fingers brushing over the edges of my codex, still lying open on my bed. "Hey, you said this place is waterproof, right?" Not that I think water could ruin a magical book, but still.

"Yep," she confirms, not looking back as she finishes putting her own shoes on.

Nodding, I stuff it in the back waistband of my leather pants, just in case.

An hour later, I'm following Roomie down a spiral staircase. The walls grow damper with each step, leaving the taste of salt in my mouth. Students brush past us, their laughter echoing off wet stone. I catch glimpses of scales that shimmer and disappear, gills that flutter shut, eyes that reflect light. Predatory, hungry, low-key playful.

"Don't stare," Roomie hisses. "Some of them get bitchy as fuck when they're nervous."

The staircase ends at a pool of black water that stretches into darkness. Students dive in like it's the most natural thing in the world. Their bodies shift mid-dive—legs fusing into tails, lungs adapting, skin growing translucent. The magic hits me as soon as my toes touch the water, a rush of power that rewrites my biology in seconds.

I don't wait. I dive.

The transformation tears through me like liquid lightning. My lungs seal and reopen, gills carving themselves along my neck. My legs stay legs, but my skin takes on a pearl-like sheen that makes the water feel like silk. I can breathe. I can see. I can move like I was born for this.

The party sprawls across the sea floor in a cavern that defies physics. Soundwaves thrum from bioluminescent coral. Students dance in three dimensions, some sprout fins while others grow tentacles. Some fully shift, but all of them strange and drunk on magic. This is the kind of weird party shit that happens in Rathe U? I mean, I ain't mad at it.

The cavern pulses with more than just music. Sirens weave through the water graciously, their voices layering harmonies that make my bones vibrate. Some students wear plugs in their ears, but others let the songs wash over them, faces slack. The longer I listen, the more I feel my body relax to every tune, as if their singing itself is intoxicating me with every second. One siren drifts past me, scales shifting from silver to deep blue, her song pulling at something primal in my chest before she moves on to easier prey.

I'm floating near what might be a bar—carved from living coral that serves drinks in shells—when someone bumps into me.

"Shit, sorry—" He turns, and I'm looking at eyes the color of storm clouds, hair that floats like dark silk, and a mouth that screams trouble in all the right ways. "I'm not used to the currents down here yet."

"Zeke," he says, extending a hand. "You new here? I don't recall seeing you around."

"Haide," I say, taking his hand and letting my fingers linger longer than necessary. His skin is warm despite the water, and when he smiles, something hungry unfurls in my stomach. Not love. Not even like. But he's hot and he'll do. "And I probably won't be here long, since I'm pretty sure I'm failing already."

He's pretty enough to break. Probably soft under all that university polish. I like breaking pretty things. I'm suddenly very interested in petting him.

He laughs, and the sound makes me want to bite his throat. "Want to fail together? I was about to explore the outer caverns." He hands me a drink. Or shell. Or both. Whatever. They complicate shit here. "Apparently, there are things down here that predate the university."

A siren's song crescendos nearby, and a group of students sway dangerously close to the cavern walls where jagged rocks wait like teeth. Zeke leans into me. "The sirens here aren't students—they're older, wilder things that the university keeps as controlled chaos. Their scales bear scars from centuries of hunting, and their smiles promise beautiful deaths."

"They're perfect." I wasn't just meaning the sirens, though they are. Zeke is the exact kind of distraction I need. Pretty, willing, and completely unaware that I'm already planning how to use him. "Lead the way."

As soon as we enter the tombs, massive rib cages of fallen sirens arch overhead like cathedral bones. Ancient runes carve spirals down every surface. Dark. Unpowered, yet make the water taste like copper and ancient rage. Skulls larger than houses hide in alcoves, allowing privacy for those who seek it.

This place should terrify me. Instead, it feels like coming home.

Death has always been my most honest companion. These bones understand what I am—what I've done, what I'm still capable of doing—in ways the living world refuses to. Zeke babbles about how the university uses this place for "advanced studies in aquatic necromancy" while I trail my fingers along a spine that could double as a bridge. Something dark in my chest purrs with satisfaction.

"You're not afraid," Zeke observes, swimming closer. There's heat in his voice now, the kind that comes from magic and proximity to danger.

"Should I be?" I ask, because the water here tastes like violence, and I'm drunk on it.

Other students have followed us deeper into the tombs, but they're not here for the history lesson. Bodies press against bone walls in the shadowed spaces between ribs. I watch as hands explore skin that shimmers with magic and clearly drunk with sweat. Damn. This how the folk around here fuck?

The power here is thick enough to choke on, making everyone desperate and reckless. A girl with gills fluttering along her throat has someone pinned against a siren's femur, their movements making the water around them pulse with bioluminescent light.

The magic hits me like liquid fire, making my skin hypersensitive, with every brush of current feeling like fingers trailing lightning.

Zeke floats closer, close enough that I can see the same hunger burning in his storm-gray eyes.

"The magic here," he murmurs, hands finding my waist and pulling me against him, "it makes you want to do terrible things."

"Does it?" I let him drag me into his orbit, magic wrapping around us like silk laced with poison. "Or does it just make you honest about what you already wanted?" I'm not sure I can tell the difference, and I don't hate it.

We claim our own alcove carved deep between cages of ribs, where ancient binding runes pulse like dying heartbeats. Zeke's back hits bone and I settle onto his lap, intoxicated by the thrum of power that hums around me. I've never felt the high of magic like this.

His hands tangle in my hair when I lean down to kiss him, and he tastes like salt and secrets and exactly the kind of mistake I want to make. Unease crawls up my throat, but before I can overthink it, my teeth sink into his lower lip, marking him the way I mark everything that's temporarily mine.

The water around us turns black.

Zeke's eyes go wide with terror just before darkness devours us whole.

The sensation is like being turned inside out and fed through a needle made of midnight. Water becomes void—turns into something that tastes like old magic and...rage. Pure, undiluted rage.

My lungs scream, my vision shattering into a thousand pieces, and then—

Stone replaces water. Dry air burns my modified lungs as the magic slowly dies off and the gills evaporate.

I open my eyes to Zeke. He held me through whatever that was and didn't let go?

Impressive. I wonder how flexible he is in bed. Eager to test that theory asap, but before I can voice it, storm-gray is replaced by something infinitely more dangerous.

Blue. Not like the ocean, but like the color of a corpse right before it hits rigor mortis. He's smiling like he's just won a war.

Or about to start one.

Fuck.

"Had fun?"

Chapter Fourteen

Legend

The scent hits me before the sight does. Not her blood, thank the gods, but the sharp tang of another male too close. Too *interested*. My vision rims in black as the bond snaps taut, burning like a brand in the center of my chest.

And then I see her.

My little menace. Straddling that wide-eyed pretty boy like he's a throne she means to desecrate. His hands on her hips, *my* hips, his mouth close to hers. Her pulse stutters with want. *Zeke.*

He must have a death wish, or a need for revenge. I mean, we did murder his mother when she dared cross our king.

Yet another example why Argents shouldn't be mistaken

for pure and good. Light magic is as dark as our magic, only where ours turns you to rot, theirs fucking blinds you.

Purely fucking pathetic.

A sound rips from my throat—half snarl, half laugh. "Had fun?"

The boy jolts like prey hearing the predator's pawstep, but Haide doesn't even flinch. She turns her head, slow as death, those wild island eyes locking on mine. Defiant. Like she doesn't know the bond is screaming in both our veins. Like she doesn't feel it.

It makes me want to set the entire cavern on fire just to remind her who she belongs to.

The pretty one swallows hard. "I…Legend?"

I bare my teeth. "King Legend," I correct him. "You're lucky you still breathe, now run along, little Argent," I purr. "Before I send you to meet your mother."

The little fuck, Zeke, dares to glare at me. But I can't focus on him right now, as much as I want to rip him to shreds on principle alone.

With a flick of my hand I send him flying, my attention now on her face.

My mate's hand presses to her temple, just as a thin line of blood spills from her nose, bright red against the pearl sheen of her skin. My body moves before my brain can think, crossing the distance, hauling her into me like she'll vanish if I don't.

"What the fuck is that?" she mutters, swiping at the blood, but I feel it. Gods, I feel it. The bond convulsing, spinning and shredding, tearing at the edges like reality itself is unraveling.

Like *she* is unraveling.

The sight of her blood makes my teeth ache. My chest claws inward, heat searing straight through the tether. She thinks it's just magic, some side effect of her power, as latent as it is at the moment. Maybe even the Argent.

But I know what I'm feeling, and she must be too.

Starvation.

Our bond is starving. She doesn't understand the pull between us so she mistakes it for nothing at all. She mistakes need for weakness.

And now it makes her bleed, just like it's been eating away at my energy.

I mean, what else could it be?

My lips curl. "Careful, little monster. You keep fighting the bond, it'll rip you apart."

Her laugh is brittle, defiant. "I'd have to feel it for that to happen. Which I don't."

"You feel me."

"I feel...*nothing* for you."

The thought makes me unhinged.

I drag my thumb across her jaw, smearing the blood. "Keep saying that. But your body knows. Your bones know. And when you break—because you will—I'll be right there to bear witness. And when you reach for me, begging me to put you out of your misery, I will do it without hesitation," I promise.

There's a flicker of something in her gaze but it fades far too quickly, and then she jerks back. "Fuck off."

And I grin, wide, feral, manic. "Oh, I plan to. All over you."

Her pulse thrashes against me, furious. She claws at my chest, shoving hard, but it only makes me laugh. "Go ahead. Fight me. Bite me. Wonder how I'd feel if you bit someone else..."

Her nostrils flare, her teeth flashing like she might do it.

My cocky grin sharpens into something darker. "Pull some

shit again, and I'll show you exactly what it means to be mine."

Behind me, the cavern begins to groan—sirens scattering as runes flare bright along the bones overhead, warning wards screaming of breach.

My head snaps over my shoulder, seeking out the threat, but I spot nothing, and when I face forward again, Haide is gone.

That same smell from before burns my nostrils.

Rot, hot and fuming.

"Damn that little brat."

Every one of my senses sharpen instantly, and I whip around, prepared to tear through every single person in this crowd to get to her.

Then I hear the screams.

I follow, shoving past the crowd. Haide stands in the center of the hall, over a body crumpled on the ground, head twisted, eyes glassy.

"It was her!" someone spits, finger stabbing at Haide like a blade.

"She hated her!" another voice snarls.

"Look what you did!"

"What?" Haide throws her hands up, half laughing, half snapping. "You think I, what, strangled her in the middle of a crowd? That's so boring."

The boy nearest her surges forward, jaw tight with fury. "It was you."

I step in before he can touch her, my presence slamming like a wall between them. "Don't." My voice cuts, sharper than steel.

The students recoil. Haide glances back at me, throat working, but I don't let anyone close. Not one step.

This is fucking bad. A murderer right under our noses, on

university grounds.

I close my eyes for a moment, linking with my brothers through our royal bloodline.

Another body.

The air warps a heartbeat later. Knight's shadow. Vicente's power. London's scowl as the portal snaps open behind me with Creed the last to charge through.

He examines me before turning his attention to the body, studying the scene before taking in the chaos around us.

"A student," Vicente rasps, kneeling by the body. His hand gently brushed the girl's jaw. "Name?"

"Elena something," someone whispers. "Fae. Argent born."

Vicente is already pulling through threads of record. His magic cold and efficient. "Elena Darrow." His gaze cuts to me. "And her roommate…" His jaw tenses.

My head jerks to Haide. "Really?"

Haide tips her head with a smirk, voice cutting through the tension. "Oh, what's the verdict? You think I snapped her neck clean in front of all of you? Please. If I wanted her gone, you wouldn't find a body." She twirls her hand toward the crumpled girl like she's presenting a piece of bad theater. "There would be ash. Or teeth. Something to make it interesting."

Gasps ripple through the students. A professor pushes forward. "Do you hear yourself? That is a life at your feet—"

Haide interrupts, laughter bright and edged. "Yes, Professor, I'm very observant. Thank you for the lesson."

He takes a step closer. My body reacts before my mind does—A low hiss escapes me, dangerous, primal. My power flares and the professor freezes where he stands. "Think very carefully before your next move," I warn.

His throat bobs, and wisely, he holds.

Vicente doesn't so much as glance up at the commotion as he continues his examination of the body. His tone is a rasp, rough with certainty. "Cervical fracture. Snapped clean. Not magic or poison. *Force*."

I look at Creed waiting for his verdict, but he only glares at Haide, a look I can't decipher on his face. He's probably digging around in her head for answers.

I kind of want to deck him for it. I don't want anyone touching her, and that includes her mind. But he had a hard time reading London's mind before she and Knight bonded, and it was due to her powers. I've got a feeling it's the same with Haide.

Haide spreads her arms, mock-offended. "Oh, come on. If I were going to start murdering roommates, do you think I'd pick now? Middle of the hall, mid-panic, no theatrics at all? Where's the fun?"

"London," Vicente calls gently and then a barrier is thrown up around us, even Haide is stuck on the outside.

They can see us, but they can't hear.

"What is it, Vicente?" Creed pushes, keeping an eye on those around us.

Vicente finally rises, his gaze locking on me, then sliding to Knight. His words scrape the cavern like bone dragged across stone. "Darrow's mother had a partner before she found her fated mate. Once she did, it was game over for the partner and so he tried to kill her. The fated stepped in, saved her life, and the jaded Fae was dealt with."

Heat curls sharp in my chest. "What are you saying?"

Vicente's stare hardens. "You know what."

The crowd screams again, the sound breaking through our private conversation, and London lets the barrier drop.

The crowd parts and we slip through, finding yet another message. This time in a smear across the floor, blood undercut with the scent of gasoline.

My patience is running out.

"Shit," Creed hisses.

"What is it?" The words fly from me with urgency, because I know that fucking face.

He knows something.

And it's bad.

Chapter Fifteen

Haide

I'd be lying if I said I slept well last night which is annoying because one, I didn't even care for my roommate—she spoke too much—and two, what do I care that these assholes immediately blame me for someone dying?

So my track record isn't that great.

So *maybe* I did threaten to kill people as soon as I got here.

And okay, there was that one guy in Warcraft class. But that was a misunderstanding—even if he did need to be knocked down a couple steps. Also, I am sort of hardwired to forget when you die off the island, you're actually dead and it's really hard to rewire your brain from that.

But the second Creed mentioned the potential of any

unknown powers, I've found myself more intrigued.

Which brings me to the issue at hand: People keep staring. Any other day, I wouldn't give a fuck. I'd wink, but I'm about one bad decision from being torn away from learning more about myself. Since I don't know anything outside of the fact that I was born on an island that was created for evil, magical beings. It's a dangerous game, to...hope for something. A game I do not fucking play on principle.

And yet, here the fuck I am.

Rounding the corner to one of the many identical gothic buildings around campus, I pull out my Pathway Codex and flip through the pages. Before Elena died, she told me this book would be everything I needed. That the pages are bound specifically for its owner and will do everything to ensure said owner gets exactly what is destined for them.

I call bullshit, but right now, it's doing a good job at directing me to where my next class is.

SpellChemy 101. Great. Another fancy class I can suck at so everyone can once again point fingers at the weird feral girl Legend dragged off a prison island.

Thirty faces turn at once, hungry. I bare my teeth, a little. Just enough to say, try me.

The book creaks in my grip, my fingers leaving dents in the leather, but I keep my game face on.

The professor's silver braid coils around her neck like something venomous as she turns. Her eyes flick over me for half a heartbeat before continuing as if I'm just another desk.

Her chalk scrapes against the board without her doing it. "SpellChemy. The art of twisting what should not be twisted," she says. I know women like her. There are plenty on the island. They may be small, petite, and charming, but one step and they'd drop you.

I think I like her.

Using the edge of her nail, she cleans the rim of her lipstick while staring at her reflection in a compact mirror. "The science of violence." She snaps the mirror closed with a forced smile that shows all her teeth. "If you're clever enough to survive it."

Someone behind me coughs. The sound wet and desperate, but nobody acknowledges them. I think of the pit back home. The way the weak ones coughed right before blood started coming up.

I miss the island. I miss the rogue nature of my people. How they didn't give a single fuck for the prim and perfect because Exile was where shit like that went to die.

This place is where people like us do.

I stare at the board. Floating chalk writes symbols in a language that isn't mine and draws shapes that look like they'd crawl under your eyelids. I can't read it. Not yet. Maybe never.

My face gets hot, and I want to break something.

I can't do this. Spell casting? Hell no. The only thing I know how to cast is my fist.

I don't even think I've ever *heard* a spell before.

"Haide?" The teacher calls. I lift a brow in answer. Her lips twitch. Not a smile. A dare. "Since you're so eager to *participate*, why don't you demonstrate?"

My lips roll beneath my teeth. "Um, at what point between"—I point to the door and back to myself—"did I give that impression?"

A few snickers ripple through the room. Fuckers.

I stand, slow, deliberate. The book presses against my thigh as I make my way to the front of the class.

"What's the spell?" I ask, voice rough. As if I know shit about spells.

"Something simple." Professor Astra flicks her fingers. The

chalk scribbles out a sigil consisting of three jagged lines that intersect like a broken star. "Light a candle."

I stare at it. Then at her.

She doesn't blink, and I swear I see a hue of purple swim through her blue eyes. "Magic isn't just about power, Haide. It's about *precision.*"

My eyes snap toward hers, narrowing slightly.

Precision?

Excitement, or something close to it, unfurls low in my stomach. A hum of promise I've never felt. *Precision,* I understand, and the idea that magic might answer to that makes the air taste suddenly stupidly sweet.

Because I *know* precision.

Instinctively, *intimately.*

I mean, no shit, right? It wasn't a choice, but a requirement when you come from where I do. Especially when you're born there as the witch of the isle informed me I was. I am nothing if not the picture of survival. And survival comes from instinct and instincts are a product of precision. If not the other way around. Either way, I'm made up of both. Back home, there was no better fighter, no better hunter or builder.

Precision.

Professor Astra's lips twitch and I swear she can see it, but she's no longer the object of my attention.

I reach out, fingers hovering over the sigil. The air hums, but it's not for me. It's laughing.

Fine. Let's see what happens when I *improvise.*

Chalk dust powders my fingertips. I exhale through my nose, slow, before pressing my palm flat against the sigil.

The class holds its breath. I hope they fucking choke on it.

I don't whisper the incantation. I *growl* it, like a curse. A promise. The sigil *twists* under my hand, the lines moving off the board. My palms begin to warm, and heat spreads through my arm. It's warm and...*right*, somehow. Like the fire isn't rising in me but waking *for* me.

A low thrum rolls beneath my skin. It's primal and hungry, as if something buried in my bones has been waiting for this exact spark. The heat curls up my wrist, as comforting as a wood flame fire on the beaches of my home. It tingles like recognition, like my body is remembering something my mind has never even learned.

Is this what magic feels like?

I focus harder.

A pillar of black flame erupts, skating the ceiling, casting the room in eerie, flickering light.

My smile splits my face.

I fucking did it!

The professor's braid unravels a fraction, just enough to see the pulse in her throat jump.

I turn my head, just slightly. Thirty pairs of eyes stare back, wide and white-rimmed. One girl snatches the grin off my face. Seated in the front row with blond hair and wearing the same prissy face that most Argents carry. Her hand's covering her mouth, a pearl—fucking pearl—choker around her neck.

The professor's voice cuts through the white noise ringing in my head. "Well. That's...*one* way to do it."

I smirk at the girl, slow and feral, before blowing out the flame. "I might like this class after all."

Professor Astra clears her throat. "It appears you may have found your niche, Ms. Haide."

Twenty minutes later, I jump up to hurry out with the rest of the class, but a barrier pops up before me, trapping me.

My brows furrow. I search for the source of the spell and find the professor staring right at me.

She puts her palm up, curling her fingers as if to call me to her in the creepiest, unnecessary witchy way I've ever seen. The barrier falls and I head right for her.

She smiles at someone behind me then seals us off once again. "That was good work today."

"I know."

Professor Astra chuckles, dipping her chin, but then her expression turns serious. "As soon as you depart today's lesson, crossing the threshold from class to hall, your codex will grow in knowledge." She points to the book in my hand. "Inside, you'll find many spells you may practice outside of class. The grounds surrounding the university are protected, so stay within the wards. You may use the Casting Fields or Flying Grounds should you wish to practice. And something tells me that you will."

"Something tells you right." This is the first thing I've been successful at here, and I need to know if there is anything more to it.

I need to know if Creed was right.

Professor Astra nods lightly, holding my gaze, and my spine prickles in alert.

I cock my head. "Now that you got that out, what is it that you truly wanted to say?"

"Be careful when calling on fire," she says without pause.

"Why?"

"Because you are no Fae, which means you do not possess elemental magic, and yet the element was eager to answer your demand. Dare I say, it was compelled to."

Her words loop in my mind, and even by the third pass,

still make little sense. "You know, for being a school, all you people in charge could really benefit from a speaking class or something."

Professor Astra's brows raise in surprise, but I just pop a shoulder and head out. For the first time, I'm not rushing to avoid the failure, a feeling I didn't even know before this fucking place, but the opposite.

Today, I did something a real gifted can do.

Legend is going to—

My feet freeze mid-step.

No. We don't run to royals to…ew. Share accomplishments?

"I swear to the gods, Haide," I murmur to myself. "Keep your head fucking straight. You don't want to impress him. The opposite, in fact." *He would smirk and say he couldn't wait to see more, and he'd mean it.*

More of that warmth stretches across my chest and I scrape my nails across it, annoyed.

Ugh! Stop.

Pushing through the sea of gifted, I can't help but stiffen. My mind might be high on magical fumes, if that's a thing, but my body feels wound tight, just waiting for one or more to prove themselves a threat. Or attempt to come off as one, anyway.

A few hundred steps later I'm crossing paths with others.

I mean, damn, how many fucking students does this place have?

The good thing, if there is one, is I don't have to shove people out of the way, since every whisper on my trek is pointed directly at me. *Did you hear about what happened in Professor Astra's class? She almost burned it down. Bet she did kill Elena…*

Bunch of softies is what they are. Their whispers are

irrelevant to me.

I'm not here to make friends or be their entertainment. Hell, I never asked to be here in the first place, but after today's class, I don't know. There's this nasty little nagging of optimism building in the back of my skull. A slow-burning fire created by the flame of my own making, telling me to dig deeper.

If speaking specific words that were scripted by some ancient witch or what the fuck ever can give me fire…then what, if anything, can I do my damn self? With my own words, actions, or whatever else it is that the gifted draw from?

I have no idea, but I'm going to find out. And when the time comes, Creed will help me get away. I'll leave with whatever it is I've learned.

Hopefully the island, greedy bitch that she is, doesn't take it right back when I return home for good.

Can you really go home and leave him *here?*

I shake the thought away.

I wander the campus, letting my feet take me deeper into the campus grounds. The paths twist and branch, leading through courtyards and gardens, past training yards where students clash with staffs and swords, their movements sharp and controlled. I watch for a while, leaning against a stone pillar, and feel a pang of something I don't want to name.

Zev would love this place.

He'd take one look at these pristine little warriors and their perfect forms and laugh himself sick. Then he'd probably challenge the biggest one to a fight and win through sheer audacity and a willingness to fight dirty.

Gods, I miss him, and I hate missing things.

Miss the way he'd sprawl across my bed whenever I'd want him to, all long limbs and easy grins, bitching about the heat.

Or the shit we had for food. Or whatever else. Miss the way we'd spar until we were both bruised and breathless, then collapse in a heap and let the adrenaline bleed into something else entirely.

No strings. No expectations. Just…easy.

Nothing about this place is easy.

I push off the pillar and keep walking, following a path that winds upward, climbing toward a section of campus I haven't seen yet, my codex held tight in my hands. The air changes as I go, growing cooler, sharper, like the magic here is older somehow.

The path ends at a small hut.

Thatched roof sagging, walls patched with moss and crumbling stone, and beyond its crooked doorframe, vines choke what might've once been a garden, now swallowed by shadow. The door hangs ajar, no lock, nothing keeping me out—but my pulse kicks up anyway, some animal instinct whispering *back away.*

I step closer.

The pull slams into me, chest-deep.

Not pain. Weight. Like whatever's inside has hooked into my ribs and started reeling me in, hand over hand.

I reach for the doorframe, fingertips grazing splintered wood, and then everything goes black.

• • •

I wake up in blood.

It's everywhere. Pooled beneath me, soaking into my clothes, slick and warm against my skin. The smell hits me next, copper and iron, thick enough to choke on.

I jolt upright, heart slamming against my ribs, and scan my surroundings.

Some kind of house. It's tiny, packed with stuff, and feels way too close—shelves everywhere stuffed with books and jars and weird things I can't even identify. The labels are either worn away or in an unfamiliar language. There's just one window that leaks grayish light, which still fails to illuminate the room in any helpful way. Through the dirty glass, I can see trees with their naked, twisted branches scratching at a dull sky like bony fingers.

The blood isn't mine.

Blood *coats* the room. A man—forties, maybe, though it's hard to say for the giftless—lies sprawled near the center. His throat is torn so deep the jagged edges of muscle and cartilage gape open, bone glinting like a knife left in the dark. His fingers claw the air, frozen mid-reach, eyes wide and glassy with whatever final terror he saw. The walls wear his death in streaks, the shelves drowned in it, books and jars slick with crimson. A slow dripping of it hits the ground.

Then there's *her*.

The woman in the corner sits slumped, her chest split open like a butcher's prize, ribs splayed wide as petals. Her face tilts toward me, mouth slack, horror still etched into every line. Blood soaks her dress, turns her hair to clotted ropes, and seeps into the floorboards in a stain that's already crusting at the edges.

My boots skid in the mess as I jerk back, breath sawing in and out—too loud, too raw—in the suffocating quiet.

What the fuck. What the fuck. What the—

My hands are clean. No blood under my nails, no cuts, nothing bruised. My knife's still strapped to my thigh, sheathed and dry, with the leather strap undone but not messed with. I frantically check myself over, looking for wounds, for proof, for *anything*, but there's nothing. Nothing on me. Nothing that explains why I'm standing in this slaughterhouse surrounded by death and gore and that overwhelming copper smell.

But here I am.

In this house.

Surrounded by corpses.

With zero memory of how I got here other than touching a damn door handle. Not even THIS door handle.

This looks fucking bad. I need to leave.

I stumble backward, fingers groping blindly for the door handle, but it vanishes when the door tears open from the other side.

I tumble into blinding sunlight, squinting as I throw up a hand to block the glare, and there, blocking my escape, stand the four royal assholes.

Legend's eyes snap to mine. "What the *fuck* are you doing here?"

I spread my arms out, the blood-splattered walls surrounding me like some twisted picture frame. "You think I know? I touched a door and next thing, I'm waking up in the middle of this shit show."

"Bullshit." Creed moves forward, jaw clenched, gaze sweeping over the carnage at my back. "You actually expect us to buy—"

"I don't give a shit what you believe. I just got here, same as you. So don't even try to pin this shit on me. I'd have no problem admitting it if it were."

Silver, the one nonroyal who seems to get a pass into their little royal squad, moves past Legend. He observes the scene with clinical detachment. He crouches near the doorway, fingers hovering over a smear of blood without touching it. "The blood's borderline cold. If she did just arrive as she claims, this would have happened before she got here."

"Like I said." I cross my arms.

"Or maybe she's standing right in front of us and knows a good cooling spell." Knight's voice cuts through the tension. He leans against the doorframe, his eyes as cold as his words. "Convenient timing, don't you think?"

The rage flares hot and immediate. "Convenient? You think I *wanted* to wake up covered in—" I bite off the words, swallow them down. Getting angry won't help. These assholes have already made up their minds.

Legend pushes past his brothers, stalking toward me with that predatory grace that makes my pulse kick up for all the wrong reasons. "How did you get here?"

"I told you. The door—"

"What door?" He's close now, too close, and the heat rolling off him makes the air between us shimmer. "There are wards all over this campus. You can't just *appear* somewhere without triggering them."

"Then maybe your wards are shit." I meet his glare with one of my own, refusing to back down even though every instinct screams at me to run. "I was walking. Found some old hut I was planning to practice this candle thing. Touched the door. Then this."

Creed's eyes fall to my codex and he frowns, muttering something under his breath before turning to Silver. "Check the perimeter. See if there's any residual magic."

Silver nods and disappears around the side of the house, his footsteps crunching through dead leaves.

Knight straightens, his attention shifting from me to the interior. "We need to figure out who they were and why the fuck someone is feeling so bold."

"Whoever did this—" My words die as something catches my eye. A photo frame hanging on the wall, half-obscured by a spray of blood. The glass is cracked, but I can still make out the image beneath.

A boy. Maybe fourteen, with dark hair and eyes that look too old for his face.

He's standing between the two corpses, the man's hand on his shoulder, the woman's smile strained.

I know that face.

"Wait." I push past Legend, ignoring his growl of protest, and move closer to the frame. The blood makes my boots stick to the floor with each step, the sound wet and obscene. "I know him."

"What?" Legend's voice hits my back like a fist.

I tap the glass, leaving a smudge. "This kid. He's on Exile Island."

The silence that follows is absolute.

Then Creed's there, shoving me aside to get a better look. His breath catches, and something shifts in his expression—something raw and dangerous. "What did you just say?"

"I said he's on Exile." I step back, giving them space as Knight and Legend crowd in too. "Just arrived a few weeks ago. I put an arrow through his eye."

"So, they have a son on Exile Island..." Creed turns to me over his shoulder. "Another connection to you, I see..."

"The thing about seeing, Creed, is I can rip your eyes out so you don't have that problem anymore." I flash him a wide smile before shrugging. "It wasn't me. So I don't know what else to tell you."

I turn on my heel, done with this shit, done with their

accusations, and done with the way Legend's stare burns holes into my back. I'm halfway to the tree line when a hand clamps around my arm, yanking me to a stop. The grip is iron, and I don't need to look to know it's him.

"Get the fuck off me," I snarl, spinning around, expecting another round of blame to spew from his mouth. My fist is already moving, pure instinct, and it connects with his nose in a satisfying crunch. Blood sprays, hot and wet, splattering across his face as he stumbles back a step.

Legend doesn't flinch. Doesn't even curse. He just laughs—a low, feral sound that vibrates through the air and hits me somewhere deep and dangerous. He throws his head back for a moment, something feral flashing in his eyes, before he lunges at me. My spine crashes against the tree bark, the hit knocking the air from my lungs, and suddenly he's right there, his body boxing me in completely. Blood's leaking from his nose, running down over his mouth, but he doesn't give a shit about cleaning it up. No—instead, he drags his face across my cheek, painting me with his warm, iron-scented mess. I read about this last night. They called it scent marking.

My breathing catches, and goddamn it, I hate how my stupid body responds. My nipples tighten under my shirt, hard and aching, and heat pools low in my belly. I'm pissed, frustrated, and yeah, maybe it's been too damn long since I've had a good, hard fuck—but the urge to grab him and drag him down so he can take out all this tension on me is strong.

I blame the dry spell.

I blame the way he presses into me, the way his blood feels like a fucked-up claim on my skin.

His tongue darts out, sliding along my jawline as he tastes his own blood. It's dirty and raw and has my thighs clenching together. I can feel him getting hard, pushing against me, rocking into my clit with this slow, agonizing rhythm that makes me gasp for air. "Fuck, you feel that?" Legend rumbles, his voice scratchy and low right by my ear. "Tell me you don't want this, my little monster." My hands bunch up his shirt, caught between pushing him away and yanking him closer. My body throws away every bit of self-control I've got left.

I'm not some helpless girl he can fuck with.

I grab his hair, twisting my fingers in tight and pulling hard enough that he hisses. It hits me like a jolt of electricity, and I use my grip to shove him downward.

"On your knees, Royal," I smirk, my voice light but edged.

I'm finished being the one backed against this tree, finished letting him think he's running this show.

He resists for half a second, those feral eyes flashing with defiance. Then he drops, hitting the dirt with a thud that makes my pulse spike.

He grips my hips, fingers digging into my flesh through the fabric of my pants, and I don't give him a chance to take back control. I shove his face forward, guiding him exactly where I want him, my other hand fumbling with the waistband of my pants to shove them down just enough.

"Fuck, Haide," he mutters, voice muffled as his mouth finds me, hot and hungry. His tongue rips through my pussy, rough and hungry, lapping up my wetness with this growl that fucking buzzes right against my clit.

My head slams back into the tree trunk, and I can't stop the gasp that tears out of me when pleasure hits like a fucking hammer. I yank his hair harder, keeping him locked in place, making him earn every second, my hips grinding against his face while he eats me like he's been starving for days.

Every dirty swipe of his tongue is desperate as hell, and I can feel everything winding up inside me, my body already about to fucking snap. My nails rake through his hair, holding him exactly where I need him as heat explodes through my core. The orgasm hits like a fucking lightning strike—white-hot and devastating—and I cry out as pleasure shatters through every nerve.

Before I can catch my breath, Legend surges up, his hand clamping around my throat and slamming me back against the tree. His eyes are pure heat, lips glistening with me.

"Listen the fuck up," he growls, fingers tightening just enough to make my pulse jump. "That pussy? Mine. No one else's mouth gets near it. Ever." His thumb presses harder against my racing pulse. "And you don't come for anyone but me from now on. Understood?"

"Hilarious—"

His grip tightens, cutting off my words before I can argue.

I slap his arm but he doesn't relent.

"Agreed?" He pushes, brows raised.

"Fine," I snap, and when he finally lets go, I shrug. "But only because I'm needy and I don't see any better options for good dick."

I shove past him, yanking my pants back up with shaking hands. My legs feel like they're made of water, but I force them to move, one foot in front of the other, refusing to look back.

"Hey, monster."

I freeze, jaw clenching.

"You know you can come to me anytime you *need*? I will never deny you."

I flip him off without turning around, the gesture sharp and definitive. His laugh follows me through the trees, low and satisfied, like he just won something I didn't know we were competing for.

Asshole.

There's no way I killed those people.

The path back to campus blurs as I move on autopilot, my mind still spinning from everything—the blood, the bodies, the way Legend's tongue felt against my clit. I shake my head, trying to clear it, but the images stick like tar.

By the time I reach my dorm, the sun's starting to dip, casting long shadows across the stone walls. I lock the door behind me, and lean against it, finally letting myself breathe.

My reflection catches in the small mirror by the basin. Blood still streaks my cheek where Legend smeared it, rust-brown now and dried. I look like I've been through a war.

Maybe I have.

I strip off my clothes, toss them in a heap, and turn on the water. It runs cold at first, then scalding, and I don't care. I scrub until my skin's raw, until every trace of blood and dirt and him are gone.

Chapter Sixteen

Haide

It's just after sunrise when the world splits apart in a surge of black smoke and crackling power, and when I blink next, I'm standing in the War Room. Torches flare along the walls, casting shadows that lick and twist across the floor. With the absence of the long table, it's just high wing-backed chairs that look more like thrones than seats.

Every single one is occupied.

Creed sits at the head, arms crossed, jaw tight. Knight lounges to his right, one leg thrown over the armrest, eyes cold and assessing. Sinner sprawls across from him, grinning like he knows something the rest of us don't. London perches beside Knight, spine straight, fingers drumming against the table in a rhythm that sets my teeth on edge.

And Legend. Legend stands behind me, close enough that I can feel the heat rolling off him in waves.

I glance around, cataloging exits, counting faces, assessing threats. Standard protocol. But there's no empty chair. No spot for me.

Good.

I take a step toward the edge of the dais, ready to disappear into the shadows where I belong, when a hand clamps around the back of my neck.

"Where do you think you're going?"

Legend's voice is a low rumble against my ear, dangerous and possessive. His fingers tighten, not enough to hurt but enough to hold, and before I can spit out a retort, he's yanking me backward.

I stumble, off-balance, and then I'm falling—straight into his lap.

"What the hell—"

"Sit." His arm locks around my waist, pinning me against him. His thighs are solid beneath me, heat seeping through the thin fabric of my uniform. I try to twist free, but his grip doesn't budge.

"Let me go, you fucking—"

"Sinner." Legend's voice is smooth and controlled, which only annoys me more.

I snap my head toward Sinner, whose grin only widens, something wicked and gleeful sparking in his eyes. He lifts one hand, fingers curling in a lazy gesture.

Fuck.

My body locks. Every muscle seizes, frozen mid-struggle. I can't move. Can't even twitch. My arms hang limp at my sides, my legs useless, my spine relaxing against Legend's chest like I'm some docile fucking pet.

Panic flares hot and immediate, but I shove it down, bury it deep. *Breathe. Think.*

I can still feel everything. The scratch of his coat against my shoulder blades. The steady rise and fall of his chest behind me. The hard ridge of his cock pressing against my ass.

And I can still talk.

"I'm going to fucking stab you," I hiss, voice low and venomous.

Legend leans in, lips brushing the shell of my ear. "Behave yourself like a good girl," he murmurs, dark and threatening, "and Sinner won't cause you any embarrassment." His hand slides up my thigh, fingers splaying possessively. "Like, I don't know, making you suck my dick in front of the whole school."

Heat floods my face—rage or arousal, I can't tell anymore. Maybe both. His breath ghosts across my neck, and I want to sink my teeth into his throat until he bleeds.

But I can't move.

Can he really make me, or would it be an illusion?

A very vivid illusion?

No. Bad thoughts.

Definitely don't tell them you'd do it in front of all of them without being forced if the mood was right.

Sinner's magic holds me in place, limp and pliant, like a puppet with cut strings.

"Sad how you have to ask big brother for help, Legend. How very *prince*-like of you," I damn near sing the taunt, waiting for him to get pissy and do the whole "Baby, I'm a King" bullshit. He doesn't.

He just chuckles, low and dark. "I see you still have much

to learn in that little codex of yours, though this might work in my favor if you continue to be as clueless as you are…or are pretending to be. Not sure which it is quite yet. Maybe a bit of both."

"Fuck you," I manage, voice tight.

"Later." He laughs. "Promise."

The doors to the War Room groan open, and the sound of footsteps echoes through the chamber. Students file in, professors trailing behind them, their faces pale and drawn. Chairs materialize along the walls, stacking upward in tiers so everyone gets a view of the dais.

The room fills quickly. Whispers ripple through the crowd, eyes flicking toward me, toward Legend.

They think you killed your roommate.

They see you on their King's lap.

I almost tense, annoyed that a single thread of someone else's thought could affect me enough to almost gain a reaction.

They can think I killed the girl, I don't really care. But if they run their mouths about where my ass is planted because the man beneath me is a complete pain in the fucking ass, we're going to have problems.

Once the last student settles into their seat, Knight stands. His movements are smooth, unhurried, but there's a tension in his shoulders that sets my nerves on edge. He scans the crowd, gaze sharp and assessing, before he speaks.

"Effective immediately, there is a curfew." His voice carries through the chamber, cold and commanding. "No one leaves their quarters after sundown. Anyone caught roaming the halls will spend the remainder of their time in The Cellar."

Silence. Heavy and suffocating.

And then—

"What if I'm supposed to be getting my dick touched tonight?"

Laughter erupts, sharp and nervous. I glance toward the voice, spotting a lanky boy with messy blond hair and a cocky grin. Kael, I think. Son of some minor Argent lord.

"I guess he has a point," I murmur, half to myself.

Legend's hips buck upward, grinding his hardening cock against my ass. I bite back a gasp, heat pooling low in my stomach.

"The only dick you're being fed is mine," he whispers, voice rough and dark. "And trust me, you won't be going anywhere else during this curfew."

My throat tightens. My pulse thrums in my ears. I hate that my body reacts. Hate the way heat coils between my thighs. Hate that he's the only one who can make me feel like this.

I think it's time I took a little walk to check out this *gateway of desire.* I know it's here; it was the first thing I searched for when I saw the little map page in my codex. Maybe Creed lied. Maybe I don't need him the way he says I do.

Knight's voice cuts through the noise again, sharp and unyielding, and I tune back in. "The murder you witnessed wasn't the first."

The laughter dies. The room goes deathly still.

"We've had others," Knight continues. "And the brutality is growing."

Chaos erupts. Voices rise, overlapping, frantic and accusing. Students jump to their feet, pointing fingers, shouting over one another. Professors try to restore order, but their voices drown in the tide of panic.

Creed leans forward, jaw tight. "Legend," he murmurs, voice low enough that only those on the dais can hear. "Calm them down."

Legend shifts beneath me, his grip on my waist tightening. I feel the tension in his body, the way his muscles coil like he's bracing for something.

But nothing happens.

Creed's head snaps toward him. "What's wrong?"

Legend's jaw clenches, frustration bleeding through his carefully controlled mask. "It's not working."

Silence stretches between them.

"What do you mean, it's not working?" Creed's voice is low, dangerous.

Legend's chest heaves against my back, his breathing ragged. "Chill." He stops talking, and I've never heard him sound so unsure before. "Barely slept last night, must be that."

Creed's face twists into something ugly, lips curling back to show teeth.

My heart hammers. Everything inside me is screaming to bolt, to get the hell out, to throw punches. But I'm stuck here by Sinner's little game, completely fucking helpless, trapped on Legend's lap by an invisible string, like I'm some trophy he won.

Creed leans back in his chair, gaze never leaving mine. The weight of his stare is suffocating, like he's dissecting me, peeling back layers to find something rotten underneath.

That's one thing he's right about. I am rotten.

But if they think they can pin this on me, they're in for a fucking surprise.

The mob keeps screaming, a mess of scared and pissed-off yelling. Knight opens his mouth again, but nobody can hear a damn thing he's saying over all the noise.

And all I can do is sit here, trapped in Legend's arms, feeling his heartbeat thunder against my spine.

This is going to end badly.

• • •

The next morning, I wake to the weight of eyes on me.

My lids crack open, and sure enough, Legend's swinging lazily on a chair too close to my bed, one boot propped on the edge of my mattress. Watching me. Like some kind of stalker with a death wish.

"You're being creepy," I grumble, voice thick with sleep.

The corner of his mouth tips, the expression one that makes my pulse kick despite the fog still clinging to my brain. "You haven't seen anything yet."

I groan, grabbing fistfuls of the sheets—best part about being off the island, if you ask me—and yanking them up over my face. Maybe if I pretend hard enough, he'll vanish. Or combust. Either works.

The sheets stop moving.

I blink into the fabric, confused, then I feel his weight. His fists press into the mattress on either side of me, caging me in. The heat of him bleeds through the thin barrier as he leans down, and suddenly the sheets are pulled away, his face hovering inches above mine.

His nose brushes over mine, and while it's barely a touch, it's enough to make my breath hitch.

"Get out of this bed," he warns, voice low and rough, "before I end up in it."

My lips twitch. "That won't be so bad."

The words slip out before I can stop them, playful and testing.

His eyes darken instantly. Heat floods them, molten and hungry, and I feel the answering pull low in my belly. My nipples tighten beneath my shirt, and from the way his gaze flicks down, he notices.

For a second, I think he's going to kiss me. Or do something far more dangerous.

Instead, he pushes off the bed, standing abruptly. "Your first task today requires you all worked up and tense."

I blink at him, thrown by the sudden shift. "What?"

"Get up."

"I don't want to get up," I grumble, rolling onto my side and pulling the pillow closer. "Five more minutes."

His hand moves before I can process it.

A press. Right against my clit through the thin fabric of my sleep shorts.

Electricity ignites through me, sharp and immediate. My hips lift slightly, involuntarily, and a gasp catches in my throat.

"Later." His voice is gravel and promise. "We can get back to this shit later. But right now, you need to be worked nice and tight."

He releases me, and the loss of contact is almost painful.

I grab the nearest pillow and hurl it at his head. He catches it mid-air, laughing—actually laughing—as he backs toward the door.

"Five minutes," he warns, still grinning like the smug bastard he is. "Downstairs. Don't make me come back up here."

He leaves and I stare at the ceiling, pulse racing, body still humming from that single, devastating touch. "Asshole," I mutter to the empty room.

But I'm already swinging my legs out of bed.

Eight minutes later, I'm dressed. My body's still buzzing, nerves alive and skin too sensitive, and I know that's exactly what he wanted.

Worked up. Tense.

Bastard.

I hit the bottom of the foyer and freeze.

His eyes rake over me, slow and deliberate, and that smirk returns.

Only he's not alone.

There's a girl, blond, pretty, all prim and demure, standing too close.

Is that the fucking girl from Spellcaster 101?

Something vicious coils in my chest.

Hot. Sharp. Teeth bared beneath my skin.

Mine.

The word slams through me before I can stop it. What the fuck? He's not mine. I don't want him to be mine. I don't even fucking *like him*. Not really, anyway.

But watching her touch him makes me want to rip her hand off at the wrist.

Legend's gaze flicks to me over her shoulder, and the corner of his mouth lifts. He sees it.

Smug bastard.

He says something low to the girl, and she glances back at me, eyes widening slightly. Then Legend nudges his head toward the hall, a silent dismissal.

The girl scatters.

My pulse hammers as Legend straightens, pushing off the wall. He crosses the space between us in three long strides, and before I can snarl, snap, or do something stupid, his hand wraps around mine.

"Jealous?"

"Fuck off."

His grin widens. "You're cute when you lie."

I yank my hand back, but his grip tightens, fingers lacing

through mine with a possessiveness that mirrors the rage still simmering under my ribs. He tugs me forward, and the air around us ripples, magic crackling to life.

"Wait—"

Too late.

Everything lurches sideways, reality collapsing into itself, and suddenly we're tumbling through nothingness. The portal coils around us, freezing and charged, dragging us through space in a stomach-turning blur.

My boots hit stone hard when we land, scraping across the surface, but Legend's hand catches me, keeping me upright through the dizzying spin.

When my vision clears, we're somewhere else entirely.

The scent hits first—salt and iron and something ancient. Stone walls rise around us, slick with moisture, and torchlight flickers against surfaces carved with runes I don't recognize.

"Where—"

"Your first task." Legend releases my hand, stepping back to watch me with that same infuriating smirk, though I can't help but notice the way he forces it to stay in place, a hand shooting out to steady himself when he starts to sway.

Before I can make fun of him, he speaks. "Hope you're ready."

The room shifts.

No—shifts isn't the right word. The room *becomes.*

One second, damp stone walls. The next, darkness so thick it eats the torchlight whole. Then color detonates everywhere—shades I can't name, colors that shouldn't fucking exist. Purple spilling into gold, electric blue cracking into something that tastes like metal on my tongue.

My breath snags.

Under my boots, the ground shifts. Stone turns to sand—hot, loose—and I stagger as desert explodes into existence. Dunes rolling out forever in every direction. Air rippling with heat that crawls over my skin. The sun sits low and vicious, a ruthless eye searing against a sky that's too fucking red to be anything but wrong.

Then it vanishes.

City lights explode into existence, glass and steel towers shooting up from nowhere. The desert's gone, swallowed by concrete and neon, sounds slamming into me—horns screaming, voices yelling, music pounding from places I can't see. The air goes cold, sharp, tasting like exhaust and rain that hasn't hit yet.

My pulse kicks hard. Sweat dots my temples even though the air's freezing now.

Something's fucking wrong.

The dread wraps tighter, winding around my ribs like it wants to crush them. Every shift—desert to city to whatever the fuck comes next—drags it with me. This suffocating wrongness that makes every instinct I've got scream *run*.

"What the fuck is this?" The words rip out, sharp enough to cut.

Legend stands a few paces off, completely unbothered while everything around us warps and twists. His face gives me nothing. Just those dark eyes tracking every move I make, every flinch.

"Your task," he says again.

The city blinks out. Night slams down like someone dropped a curtain. Stars explode overhead, way too many of them, burning way too bright, arranged in patterns that don't exist anywhere I've ever been.

My hands ball into fists.

"Legend—"

The ground shakes.

I drop, instincts kicking in before thought does, weight shifting as the ground rumbles under me. The stars blink out. Darkness floods everything and the cold hits like a punch.

Silence.

No city noise. No wind. Nothing but my own breathing.

Just the dread, heavy and suffocating, filling my chest like smoke.

Then Legend's voice, slicing through the black.

"Find your way out."

The maze *explodes* around me.

One second, there's nothing. Next second, jagged concrete walls shoot up around me, black ivy crawling up the surfaces like it's alive—pulsing, *breathing.* The air goes thick. Humid. Cloying. Tasting like wet stone and something way older. Something that's been rotting for centuries.

I slam down on my ass, the impact punching all the air from my lungs. "Fucking *Royal.*"

Legend's laugh rolls through the space somewhere behind me, but when I spin, he's gone. Disappeared like he was never standing there at all. Just the maze. Just me. Just these new walls pressing in on all sides.

Perfect.

I push to my feet, dusting off my palms. The ivy *twitches* as I near it, tendrils recoiling slightly before creeping forward again, testing. Like it's alive. Like it's *hungry.*

"Real mature, Deveraux," I mutter, stepping closer to the entrance.

The maze doesn't just *stand* there. It *waits.*

Darkness yawns at the mouth of the first path, a black so

deep it looks like it's *drinking* the light. The ivy here is thicker, glistening with something that isn't water. My boots stick slightly as I step forward, the soles making a wet, tearing sound when I lift them.

Perfect. Blood-ivy. Because why the fuck not.

I exhale through my nose, rolling my shoulders. Fine. If this is some twisted game, I'll play. But I'm not playing *nice.*

As soon as I step inside, my movements stop as darkness swallows me whole. I spin around, but the entrance is gone.

"Dammit," I whisper, cracking my neck. I take the first step through the narrow maze toward the distant echoing of crashing waves. Where is it coming from? My feet pick up, but the faster I go, the farther away it sounds. Frustration coils around my forehead as I halt, heaving in deep breaths.

I lean over my knees, when the ground gives way beneath me.

I hit water.

Cold. Fucking *freezing.* The shock steals my breath, lungs seizing as I plunge under, darkness pressing in from all sides. My limbs flail, seeking purchase, finding nothing but endless liquid void.

Up. I need *up.*

I kick hard, breaking the surface with a gasp that scrapes my throat raw. Water streams down my face, blurring my vision as I tread frantically, spinning to get my bearings.

Stone walls rise around me, slick and ancient, forming a circular chamber. No exit. No ledge. Just water that tastes like salt and copper, and walls too smooth to climb.

"Legend!" My voice echoes back, mocking. "This isn't fucking funny!"

Silence answers.

The water shifts.

Not a current. Something *deliberate.* The surface ripples outward from a point behind me, and I whirl, heart slamming against my ribs.

Legend materializes on a platform that wasn't there before—dry stone jutting from the water's edge, high enough that I'd need to haul myself up. He crouches at the edge, forearms resting on his knees, watching me with an expression I can't read.

"Get me out of here." My teeth chatter despite my best effort to keep my voice steady.

"No."

The word lands like a fist to my gut.

I swim closer, reaching for the platform's edge. "Legend, I swear to fuck—"

He stands. Steps back. Away from me.

The distance between us stretches, impossible and wrong, and something hot and terrible claws up my throat.

"What are you doing?"

"What I should've done from the start." His voice is flat. Empty. "Letting you go."

The water feels colder suddenly. My fingers slip on the stone as I try to grip it, pull myself up. "Stop fucking around."

"I'm not." He crosses his arms, and the gesture—so casual, so *dismissive*—makes my pulse stutter. "This was a mistake. *You* were a mistake."

I stiffen.

No.

The word screams through my head, but my mouth won't form it. My hands shake as I grip the platform harder, nails scraping stone.

"You don't mean that." Why the fuck do I care? It's not like I wanted him to begin with. So he's hot, can kind of be funny, and is annoying enough to make me want to fuck him into submission, but I didn't really want him.

"Don't I?" His lips curve, but there's nothing warm in it. Nothing *Legend* in it. "You're worthless. You were never fit enough for a royal."

My heart clenches, squeezing so tight I can't breathe. Can't *think*.

Fingernails bite into my palms. "Fuck you."

"You're not my mate." The words carve through me. "You never were. Just convenient. Just *there*. But I don't need convenient anymore."

The platform shifts, rising higher, pulling away. Legend's figure grows smaller, more distant, and I'm still in the water, still drowning in this impossible space.

"Don't." The word breaks on my lips, raw and desperate. "Don't leave me."

He turns his back.

Just…*turns away*. Like I'm nothing. Like I never mattered.

The walls start closing in.

Slow at first, then faster. Stone grinding against stone, the chamber shrinking, water rising as the space compresses. My pulse hammers in my ears, too fast, too erratic, each beat stuttering like it might stop altogether.

I can't breathe.

Can't *move*.

My limbs turn heavy, leaden, and the water drags at me, pulling me under. I kick weakly, but my body won't respond right. Won't *fight*.

Because what's the point?

He left. He walked away. He doesn't want—

My vision tunnels, darkness creeping in at the edges. My heart skips. Falters.

Flatlines.

I take a deep breath, flying off the floor with a rush of pain I never knew existed. I fucking hate this place. I hate everything about it.

"Well, I guess you don't hate me as much as you thought, huh?"

Legend sprawls on his back like he owns this gods-forsaken void, grinning up at me with that infuriating smirk that makes me want to carve it off his face.

"Stay the fuck out of my head." The words rip from my throat, raw and vicious. My chest heaves, lungs still burning from the phantom drowning, heart hammering against my ribs like it's trying to escape. "You manipulated me."

His eyes roll—actually fucking *roll*—and he props himself up on his elbows. "I can't do that. That's more Sinner's specialty and it's more an illusion than a manipulation."

"Bullshit."

"Not bullshit." He tilts his head, studying me with an intensity that makes my skin prickle. "It was real, Hellpet. Your first task was to see if you hold the same power as me. Calm." His gaze darkens, something almost like disappointment flickering across his features. "Which you clearly don't."

The words land like a slap.

Heat floods my face—rage, humiliation, something uglier I don't want to name. My fists clench so hard my nails bite crescents into my palms.

"Fuck you."

I spin on my heel, boots scraping against stone—or whatever

the hell this dark void is made of—and stalk away. Doesn't matter where. Just *away.* Away from him, from his stupid grin, from the way my chest still aches like something vital got ripped out and stomped on.

His hand catches mine before I make it three steps.

The touch jolts through me, electric and unwanted. He tugs, and despite every instinct screaming to yank free, my body obeys. I stumble back, landing hard beside him on the cold ground.

"Don't." My voice comes out sharper than intended, brittle at the edges.

Legend doesn't let go. His fingers lace through mine, thumb brushing over my knuckles in a gesture so unexpectedly gentle it makes my throat tighten.

"I'm sorry."

The words hang between us, foreign and strange coming from his mouth. Legend Deveraux doesn't apologize. He commands, he teases, he threatens—but he doesn't *apologize.*

I stare at our joined hands, pulse still racing, body still trembling from whatever fucked-up illusion he put me through. The memory of his voice—*you're worthless, you were never fit enough for a royal*—echoes in my skull, sharp and cutting.

"For what?" My tone stays flat, guarded. "For making me think you were abandoning me? For being a manipulative bastard?"

His jaw tightens, a muscle ticking near his temple. "For all of it."

The admission surprises me more than it should. I chance a glance at his face, expecting that cocky smirk, that arrogant glint that says he's already three moves ahead and enjoying every second of my discomfort.

But his expression is serious. Almost vulnerable, if Legend Deveraux is even capable of vulnerability.

"You needed to be tested," he continues. "We needed to know if you carried the same Ethos. If you could calm the masses like I can." His grip tightens slightly. "But I didn't expect—"

"Didn't expect what?" I cut him off, a bitter laugh escaping.

His eyes lock onto mine, dark and intense. "That you'd flatline."

The words steal my breath.

"Did I fucking die?" I ask, brow raised.

He snickers. "Fuck no, like I'd let that happen."

I notice it for the first time. The dark rings around his eyes. Not obvious, but there. I wince a little. "Don't do it again."

"Can't promise that, little monster." He flashes me a smirk that shouldn't look so sexy on a man who looks so fucking exhausted. "Since tomorrow, you have Knight."

"Knight?" I ask, folding my arms around myself. "And what exactly is his royal gift?"

He sprawls back against his hands, bending his head to look up at me. "One I think you'll like, but in the meantime, want me to show you a trick?"

Legend pushes to his feet, swaying slightly before catching himself. The movement's so subtle I almost miss it—would've missed it if I wasn't already cataloging every exhausted line of his body.

"Come on." He extends his hand, that cocky grin firmly back in place. "Time to learn something useful."

I eye his hand warily. "Like what?"

"Portalling."

My brows shoot up. "You're going to teach me how to portal?"

"Unless you want to keep relying on me to drag your ass everywhere." He wiggles his fingers impatiently. "Though I'm sure you'd love that, being at my beck and call—"

"Shut up." I grab his hand and let him haul me up. The motion brings me too close, our chests nearly touching, and heat floods my face before I can stop it.

His eyes darken, tracking the flush spreading across my cheeks. "You make it too easy, little monster."

I shove him. Not hard—just enough to create distance. "So how does this work?"

"Close your eyes."

"Why?"

"Because I said so." He moves behind me, his presence overwhelming even without touching. "You need to feel the magic first. Visualize where you want to go."

I close my eyes, trying to ignore how aware I am of him standing there. The warmth radiating from his body. The faint scent of cedar and something darker, more primal.

"Picture it," he murmurs, voice dropping lower. "Every detail. The stone beneath your feet. The air temperature. The sounds."

I focus on the War Room—the massive table carved from Leviathan bone. The high-backed chairs. The torch-lit walls covered in ancient tapestries. My magic stirs, sluggish and uncertain, like trying to wake something that doesn't want to move. Lazy bitch. No wonder we don't get along.

"Now reach for it."

I do. Pushing my will outward, grasping for that mental image—

Nothing happens.

"Fuck." My eyes snap open. "This is stupid."

"Try again."

"I am trying—"

"Then try harder." His hands land on my shoulders, steadying. The touch sends electricity racing down my spine, but his voice stays firm. "You're overthinking it. Just *want* it. Demand it."

Right. Because demanding things always works so well for me.

I close my eyes again, jaw clenching. This time I don't picture—I *command*. The War Room. Now. Take me there.

Magic flares hot and wild, ripping through me like lightning. The air shimmers, reality bending—

Then collapses into nothing.

I stumble forward, catching myself on my knees. "What the hell?"

"Better." Legend sounds amused. Also exhausted. "You almost had it."

"Almost doesn't count."

"Again."

We go through it three more times. Each attempt gets closer—the air ripples, space starts folding—but nothing *holds*. By the fourth try, sweat beads at my temples and my magic feels scraped raw, like I've been running it against sandpaper.

"Why don't you just portal us?" I snap, frustration bleeding through. "You're right there. You could do this in half a second—"

"Where's the fun in that?"

"Legend—"

"Again."

"No." I flop down on my back beside him, limbs sprawling across the cold stone. "I'm done. This is pointless."

He doesn't argue. Just lowers himself down next to me with a carefulness that makes my chest tighten. His breathing's slightly labored, those dark circles more pronounced up close.

Silence stretches between us, heavy but not uncomfortable.

"You look like shit," I finally say.

His laugh sounds rougher than usual. "Flattery will get you everywhere."

"I'm serious." I turn my head, studying his profile. "When's the last time you actually slept?"

The pause before he answers tells me everything.

"Yeah, didn't get much of that last night."

Images of the blond girl flicker through my memories and now I don't care if he drops dead in this very spot.

My head whips to the side, finding him already watching me. My stomach roils and electricity prickles down my spine.

"Come here," he murmurs, soft and lazy. When I don't respond, his arm wraps around my back and he pulls me down.

"Legend."

"Mmm?" he asks, his tone sleepy.

"This friends with benefits thing doesn't include cuddling."

His chest vibrates when he chuckles, before his hand slips over my lower back and cups my ass. "Wasn't thinking about cuddling."

"Necrophilia isn't really my thing…" I muse, giving in and resting my head against his chest. Muscles tighten beneath my cheek before finally relaxing.

His breathing evens out first—deep, steady pulls that make his chest rise and fall beneath my cheek. The arm around me goes slack, heavy with sudden sleep, fingers still curved possessively over my hip.

Legend's asleep.

Actually fucking asleep.

I should move. Should shove him off and portal myself back—or try to, anyway, since apparently I'm shit at that particular skill. But his heartbeat thuds against my ear, strong and rhythmic, and something in my chest unclenches at the sound.

Proof he's alive. Proof he's here.

Proof he didn't actually mean those words in the water.

My jaw clenches. I'm not some clingy female who needs reassurance. I don't *care* what Legend Deveraux thinks of me. Don't care if he finds me worthless or convenient or—

His arm tightens reflexively, pulling me closer even in sleep.

The gesture does something terrible to my insides. Makes them twist and ache in ways that are foreign to me but slowly, frustratingly, becoming more and more obvious. More and more…welcome.

Because I do care what he thinks and how he sees me and if you ask me on a good day, I might even say I want to stay here. Flip the bird to Creed Devereaux and tell him thanks for the idea, but the helping hand back to the island won't be necessary.

But that would be wild, wouldn't it? If I just…stayed?

His warm breath tickles my exposed skin and a frown pulls at my brows.

"Stupid Royal," I mutter against his shirt.

He doesn't respond. Just keeps breathing, keeps holding me like I'm something precious instead of the volatile disaster everyone knows I am.

My fingers curl into his shirt without permission.

Fine. Five minutes. Then I'm waking him. Clearly, he needs sleep.

His breathing stutters, then deepens again.

I close my eyes.

Just five minutes.

Chapter Seventeen

Legend

I hit the floor on a half-bent knee and bite back the sway. Portals are clean when I'm sharp. Surgical. Now they punch like a cheap uppercut and leave the room bending at the edges, walls rolling before they snap into place.

My royal room at Rathe U drags itself out of the blur, and the first thing that comes into view is the black bed with ironhead posts. The walls are racked with weapons like art, and there's a nasty little window view of the inner quad where all the hopefuls parade their new coats and masks. It's a sad little place that can't hold a candle to the Royal House at the edge of campus that I *should* be staying in alongside my brothers and London. Can't bring myself to be that far from my little mate, though, so meager living quarters it is.

Haide steps out of the ripple like she's walking off a stage. No stumble. No tell. Like the world moves to make room for her. As it fucking should for a future queen of Rathe.

Her gaze flicks to the Leviathan tooth mounted over my desk, the knives lined spine-out above the hearth, and finally to the couch nobody sits on because I don't invite people here. Her chin tilts toward me. That look can strip paint.

"That was a nice power nap." She crosses her arms, her eyes rolling over me. "So why do you still look like shit?"

"You're adorable when you're concerned." I shrug off the throb behind my left eye and the iced-iron drag in my limbs. "Just need more sleep." I knock my knuckles against my thigh. Stay upright. Stay present. "You survived and got out of the maze."

"You set me up to drown." She glares. "Literally."

"You set yourself up to fight back." I let the grin slip out. "You did."

Her mouth wants to smile. She doesn't let it. "You're full of shit."

"Consistently."

The door swings without a knock and I know who it is without looking or using my damn senses.

Sinner never knocks because manners bore him. He leans on the jamb with one hand, black shirt open at the throat, an unlit cigarette teasing his lip, eyes bright with the kind of humor that usually ends with someone bleeding.

"Family meeting," he says, like it's a joke. "Creed and Knight in the bone room. Bring your crown and the stick up your ass."

Haide lifts a brow at him. "You let your pets talk to you

like that?"

"The ones with teeth," I say. "Wait here."

She snorts. "Make me."

I take two steps like I'll indulge the argument. I don't. I don't have the time to burn my temper down into something soft and warm and useless.

"Stay." I meet her stare. My voice drops. "I'm not asking."

She bares her teeth. Pretty. Dangerous. "Go fuck yourself, Royal."

"Charming," Sinner murmurs, amused.

I shoulder past him and, when my mouth is near his ear, pitch the words low. "Bind the room."

He does so discreetly as he follows me out, flashing his teeth in a grin. "You sure you want me to collar your little monster? As you said, she bites."

"She'll try."

"What's the matter?" He laughs against his cig. "You forgetting your knots? Bind it yourself."

I keep walking, voice level. "Something's wrong with my magic."

The humor tilts, curiosity sliding in. "Since when?"

"Since it started fucking choking on me."

"The calm not hitting?"

"Among other things..." I grumble, picturing Haide's protests already as she tries to break out of the royal room.

We move through the hall. Old stone eats sound. It's almost quiet, but really, it's just the sound of everyone listening. Banners crawl with their own faint magic, old colors and older grudges stitched into them in gold, black, and purple. Students watch us from doorways yet pretend they aren't. They're amusing, to say the least. Every year, we have a new load dropped, but this is the first year that the school is entirely run by us Deveraux Brothers. I'm certain that's the single most terrifying thing to them. As it should be.

Sinner whistles under his breath. "You look like death fucked you. How was the wild animal with her first train?"

"Fine," I mutter, cracking my neck. "She doesn't hold the same gift, though, if that's what you're asking." It would be. Nosy bastard.

His laugh cackles through the air. "You really had to test that? That girl is fucking chaos. Ain't nothing calm about that." He taps ash from a cigarette that isn't lit. Habit. Tell.

"She's not a girl."

He nods in agreement. "She's a bomb."

"Then we can all watch her explode." My eyes flicker with something I'd assume looks like mania. "Because she's going nowhere."

He shakes his head, grin deepening. "You know you're gonna need to send her to Arabella. With whatever magic manifests within her, and if she really is your mate—

"She is."

"Her Ethos will start to rise within her at some point, and she's gonna need Arabella to"—his hands wave around the place—"control all that chaos."

I know he's right, but the thought of Haide being anywhere near Arabella has the hairs on the back of my neck rising. Not because I give a fuck about the soft little lamb, but because Arabella is basically the fucking princess of the Argents. Since we've eradicated the council, I'm gonna go ahead and assume that if we bring any more heat by harming yet another Argent, it'll just give their people more of a reason to stir.

Bone Room doors swing open with a shove. Without

everyone in here, its emptiness feels…just that.

Empty.

Knight sits slouched in his chair, lazy on purpose, all coiled lines and deadpan eyes, but it's Creed who concerns me. For whatever reason, which I'm no doubt about to hear right now, he hates Haide. His finger taps against the table but his eyes follow me. I love our big brother, but he's the most like Father. I used to think all his good parts…but recently, I've seen a lot of the bad, too.

Knight's nose scrunches an inch. "Shit, Lege. You smell like burnout."

"Nice to see you too."

Creed is going through a mixture of emotions with his eyes alone. First, assessment. The second is annoyance. The third is something like worry, which I hate on him because it means it's real.

"Sit."

"I'll stand."

He ignores it.

Sinner sprawls into a chair, boots kicking up like he can't wait for the family drama to spill out of everyone's mouths. Like we don't have whole fucking murders happening on our streets.

Sinner points with the cigarette. "Legend's magic's acting like a drunk trying to pick up a girl way out of his league."

Traitor. He winks like he just lit the fuse for fun.

Creed's mouth flattens. "How long?"

"I don't know. Recent enough." I finally take the chair, knowing that I won't be able to escape this conversation. Brothers. They're basically extensions of your parents. We can't escape one another ever.

Knight's gaze is steady. "Define 'recent.'"

I roll my shoulders to shift the ache. "Since the Island, I think. Since I got back."

Creed leans forward. "Your principal powers don't 'slip' unless something knocks it out of you."

"Thanks for the primer," I say. The laugh chokes in my throat and comes out a rasp. "I didn't study."

Knight's eyes cut to my face. He inhales, that little flare that means he's not just smelling with his nose. Bonds. Oaths. The weft we all carry. "You smell wrong."

"Appreciate it. I'll take a shower later."

"Like you've been hollowed," he continues, ignoring my hiss. "Like something is picking bits away."

Sinner makes a low noise. "Sexy."

Creed's gaze slices like he wants to cut what he sees out of me with a knife. "We need to name the cause if we're going to cauterize the wound."

The word cauterize makes me twitch. "We?"

"We." He gestures a hand at the table. "And, since you're already lying to yourself, I'll do the knife work." He holds my gaze. "*She* isn't your mate."

My hands curl on nothing. The room drops a degree. Even Sinner doesn't crack a joke.

"I know what bonds feel like," Knight goes on. Calm. Reasonable. Hammer to the skull. "I know what they do, what they give." He studies me with critical eyes. "They fuel, stabilize. They don't drain. That girl, she is emptying your reserves."

Sinner shifts, attempting to save some of the argument. "It isn't a normal bond we're familiar with, I'll give you that," he says to Knight.

"Shut up," I snap.

Knight's words land heavy in my chest, but only because

I want to knock him out for trying to make sense of Creed's bullshit. There is no sense to be made.

She is mine, period.

Knight leans an inch into the table, and the bone doesn't dare creak. "London binds sanity to me, not madness. She doesn't leave me a cracked vessel. She is not a leak. She doesn't take. Haide"—He lets the name hang. My jaw tightens—"does. You want to pretend that isn't true because she makes you feel things you didn't before, something about her demands your attention and loyalty. But it isn't love. It's compulsion; and compulsion feels like drowning when it's not fed."

"You done?" I say, brows raised, unfazed.

"No. You're off. You're dangerous when you're off. Not just to you. To everyone who depends on your calm—"

"I am not off." I step into the words. "And don't you dare put London in your mouth when you're trying to teach me what a mate is. We all know the bond isn't one size fits all. It arrives exactly as it should depending on the people who are connected."

Knight's brows lift. Sinner snorts a laugh that almost goes ugly.

Creed's eyes flatten. "She is not your mate, Legend."

"How do you know, Creed, hm?" I press. "Because her head isn't just a pretty little buffet for you to feed on the way you wish, but instead a god damn maze you can't see your way out of?"

His features harden and I scoff. "That's what I thought. You don't trust her because you can't find the truth in her mind and you, dear brother, have wrapped yourself in your gift so tight you abandoned observation, inference, instinct. Hell, you've abandoned *everything*, except the one shortcut that keeps you comfortable."

His nostrils flare and I shake my head. "You don't know how to find truth anymore, Creed, only how to *extract* it."

My brothers don't even blink. "She is a leech. She's not your mate, Legend."

"What the fuck do you know about a mate, brother? Hmmm?" I challenge. "Got one of these we're not aware of?"

"Legend." Knight's tone is so quiet and I look his way.

"What?"

"Breathe."

I do. In. Out. It burns like I inhaled razors.

Fuck. I don't know what to do with rage when I can't calm myself. Heat prickles down my throat, enough to make me almost choke.

Creed watches. He always watches. "Your magic is failing because something is yoking it. That isn't an accusation or something that needs...*extraction*." Yeah, knew I burnt his ass with that. Good. "It's a diagnosis. And that something is her. She's from Exile Island, Legend, and you've been weakening since she got here. Meanwhile, how was her training yesterday? Good? How is she doing under Professor Astras's instruction? What is she gaining, Legend?"

"It's not." My nostrils flare. "Her. She's gaining strength only because she's fucking amazing."

He remains unmoved. "She doesn't mirror your calm. She doesn't steady. She accelerates. Every time she's near, your pulse spikes and your power warps around it trying to ride the storm. You both share nothing of similarities outside of affection, obsession...and this strange conception you have that she's your mate."

"Say it again," I whisper.

"Legend," Knight warns.

"Say it again," I repeat, louder. "Look me in the face, without fucking blinking, and tell me she isn't mine."

Creed exhales, all long-suffering king. "She isn't yours."

I want to tear his head off, feed it to a feral Lycan and burn what's left of him for all to see as a warning to any who dare speak against the gift the gods gave me. That fate gave me.

If he weren't my brother, I just might, and now I'm too fucking tired to fight.

"Go fuck yourself," I say. "And you—" I jab a finger at Knight. "I expected more from you. You know what it becomes, how it mutates you."

He doesn't even flinch. "You want my truth? Here." He bares his teeth without humor. "You smell like her even when she isn't in the room. Like copper and knives and bad weather. She's in your blood. But the magic's wrong. Her weight on you is wrong. It isn't a match, Legend. If it was, why are you weakening?"

Silence.

I can't argue with that point, because that is the one consistent theme in terms of bonds.

Creed's jaw sets. Clearly I've pissed off big brother as much as he has me. "You also don't get to drag his real mating bond to compare to your fake one."

"Look at that," Sinner drawls. "We're all a family of dysfunction."

I laugh, once. Ugly. "You can all go fuck yourself. I thought we were here to talk about the murders. Why am I hearing each of you bitch about my mate?" I seethe, allowing my eyes to rest on all of them before settling back on Knight. "If you're quite fucking done, I've got some place to be—

"The opening ball tonight." Knight's words hit me.

"We're still doing that? Despite the fact that there's a murderer on the loose?" Now they've all lost their fucking minds.

Sinner shrugs. "It's an easy way to pluck him out. Put everyone in the same place, you know, old school techniques that the humans used to play to find the guilty one. If another murder happens during the ball, we can rule out all those who attended."

"And the curfew?" I ask, anger still simmering beneath my skin.

Creed's voice only heightens that. "It's still on school grounds."

I kick out my foot, spreading my legs wide. "Now I have to try to put her in a dress."

"You're not taking her to the ball," Creed says. "There's too much at stake. We have press. We have higher Argents who will be attending and just *waiting* for us to fuck up. Haide? She gives that to them easily."

I grind my teeth, the snarl deep. "She's coming, and she's coming with me. And there ain't shit any of you can do about that."

Creed studies me a moment, and for a second, I see his hardness soften. I almost see the big brother beneath the hate he has for my mate. "What happened yesterday? When she saw you with Arabella?"

My lip twitches. "Get the fuck out of my head."

Creed's brows lift, as if waiting for me to answer.

"She won't start shit. You can't expect her to blend in and at the same time keep her exiled." I shake my head, running my hand down the side of my face. "And besides that, why don't any of you fuckers give a fuck about my happiness?"

"Happiness?" Creed actually chokes on a laugh. "You aren't happy. You're high."

"Same difference." I step back from the bone, finally pushing back to my feet. "Bring in mages if it'll make you feel better. Drug the students. Do whatever the fuck you want, but she's coming."

"Legend—"

The door's already opening for me again. Sinner rises with me out of habit. I ignore Knight's clear desire to continue the conversation and the way Creed's fingers twitch like he's fighting the urge to drag me back. I give them nothing. Because if I sit in there for a second longer, I know I'll say some shit I can't take back.

The long halls swallow my movements as I move faster than I should with how my lungs burn. Faster than I should with my energy levels, a sure tell that I used too much portal and not enough food. Students scatter. Good. Wise.

My door looks like every other heavy wood door in this hall, except it isn't. There's a hairline of burning embers around the hinges that says Sinner put his toys on it. I can feel the bindings hum—slick, smirking magic that tastes like violence.

Knuckles hit my face and I stumble back, slamming the door closed. The back of my skull hits wood and the taste of copper instantly fills my mouth.

Haide flexes and shakes her hand out. Doesn't apologize. Doesn't look sorry.

"You locked me in," she says, almost pouting.

I brace a palm against the door and push off as a mixture of laughter and a growl escapes me. "I told you to wait. The fact that you tried to leave proves why I needed to fucking lock you in."

"So you had your brother tie the leash!"

"I prefer cages," I say, and then my hand is around the back of her neck, forcing her back. I've moved without thinking and she's moved to meet me.

This is the part of us that makes more sense than breathing. The part where skin is the argument and our mouths are the only weapons we need.

Her forearms land on my chest, not to push away, but to brace herself. Her spine hits the old stone behind her with a thud.

I growl as my hands land on either side of her head, caging her in. I like her like this. Defiant with nowhere to run.

Her chin tips up like a challenge. "Don't," she says.

"Say it," I breathe. My forehead touches hers, and her pulse beats like a hard drum. Mine matches. "Say it. *Mean it.*"

Her breath rubs my mouth. "Fuck you."

I shove my knee between her thighs and pin her. Her gasp burns steady now.

Be careful. *Be cruel.* Be what she wants.

"You lock your jaw, throw a punch and think that's a no?" My voice drops. Carefully. This is the wire we live on. "You want me to stop—say it." The corner of my mouth twitches. "See if I listen."

Her hand slides into my hair and tightens. Pain prickles like an honesty that no one has ever given me before. A second of silence. "I—"

I crush my mouth to hers.

It's not sweet. It's a collision. Teeth-clash kind of collision. She punishes me back with the kind of violence she most likely fights with.

Hands. Where? Everywhere. Her shirt is soft—fucking

wrong. I want her in knives and leather. I grab the hem and bunch it, not kind, not gentle. She slaps my wrist and drags it lower, greedy as I am. A silent fuck you and a fuck me in one cruel little tug.

I grin against her mouth because I can't help it. She tastes like salt and something that could be an addiction if I let it.

"I should leave you locked in here," I murmur into her, words against tongue. "See what kind of carnage you unleash when you don't get what you want."

"Do it," she says, kissing me between the words. "And I'll leave claw marks over every single thing you touch."

My hand finds the line of her throat. Not squeezing. Not yet. Just feeling the slick beat under my thumb. *Mine.* The word lights up my nerves like a current. My brothers are fucking liars. Whatever bullshit they're thinking, they're wrong. This time, they're wrong.

I drag my mouth to her jaw. To her ear. "Mine."

"I am not your–" It comes ragged. Stops when I circle my tongue beneath her ear. She shakes, her fight giving out. "Legend."

I hiss, circling my hips into her. "Say that again."

"Legend."

Fire races down my spine, burning the ache and fatigue. My magic that's been sulking for so fucking long leans toward her like a pet.

I kiss her again and this time I take my time. Not slower. Just precise. She squeezes the back of my neck and my cock hardens as I slowly grind against her.

She bites my lip and then sucks the hurt back like she can't decide if she wants to punish me or soothe me. Good. Same.

My hand slides under her shirt and I hiss through my teeth

at the heat of her skin. She's fever-sweat hot, like a forge. Like a blade fresh from the quench. She bows into my palm like she wants closer and then shoves me like she wants distance. The friction of both is perfect.

"You hit like you mean it," I murmur against her throat, licking the pulse, my energy tingling from the high of having her in my arms like this. "Next time don't telegraph the right."

"You deserved it," she says, breath chopping on the last word.

"Probably." I scrape my teeth down the tendon. "Do it again and I'll bend you over the desk to teach you why we don't throw hands at kings."

"Try it," she says. The half laugh breaks. Her fingers fist in my shirt. "Don't stop."

Yes. That. The plea that pretends it isn't. I anchor a hand at her hip and push her higher up the wall. She's strength and heat and mean—and I love her for all of it.

My other hand slides down, rough and claiming, yanking her thigh up to hook around my waist. I grind into her, hard and deliberate, the friction a fucking inferno. Her gasp claws the air, and I swallow it, thrusting against her with a rhythm that's all dominance, all need, her body arching into every brutal press.

I hook a finger in the soaked strip of lace and yank—fabric snaps, elastic bites, then nothing but bare skin under my palm. She's already on me, hand sliding down my abs, fingers closing around my cock like she owns it. One thumb swipes the slick crown, spreads the bead of pre-cum, paints me with it while her eyes dare me to breathe.

I don't. I haul her up, thighs clamping my hips, slamming her back into the stone. One thrust and I'm buried, her cunt warm, milking every inch.

She groans into my mouth, dirty, desperate, the kind that I feel charged beneath my skin.

My eyes roll back as I ride her against the wall, then her hand lands on my throat, nails pinching crescents into my neck as she matches my pace.

Fuck.

"Take it," I growl, grinding harder while sucking on her lip. "Take every fucking inch, little monster."

She squeezes, both around my cock and at my windpipe. Stars explode. I answer by claiming her mouth, tongue fucking her the way my dick fucks her pussy. Ruthless, raw praise spilled filthy between breaths.

"Good girl," I snarl when she clenches, "so fucking perfect for me."

Her answering moan sounds like more ragged worship, and we're nothing but wet skin, bruising thrusts, and the filthy fucking whispers of *yes* and *more* and *mine.*

The fatigue hums there. The ache. The weird empty ringing that has followed me since the Island. *They're wrong.*

I pin her there, thighs locked around me, her heat searing into my skin as I slow my pace. Each thrust is deliberate now, a deep, grinding drag that pulls a shudder from her core. My cock slides in and out, slick and heavy, every inch of her cunt gripping me like a vise, like she's trying to keep me there forever. I'm not fucking her to finish fast—I'm fucking her to *feel* her, to watch her unravel under me.

Her dark green eyes lock on mine, sharp and unyielding, even as her breath hitches. There's no hiding in this. No fucking expectations. Just raw, brutal intimacy, the kind that cuts deeper than any blade she's ever wielded. Her nails dig into my shoulders, carving half-moons into my flesh that match the ones on my throat. The sting grounds me. Keeps me from losing myself in the haze of her.

"Legend," she rasps, voice breaking on my name, a plea wrapped in a snarl. Her gaze doesn't waver, burning into me like she's seeing every fucked-up piece of my soul and daring me to look away.

I don't. I can't. I lean in, forehead pressing to hers, sweat mingling, breaths tangling. "I've got you," I growl, low and rough, my hips rolling slow, torturous, dragging out every pulse of pleasure. "Every fucking inch of you."

Her lips part, a silent gasp, and her body arches into me, trembling on the edge. I keep the rhythm brutal but measured, each thrust a claim, a promise, driving her closer to that shattering point. Her walls flutter around me, tight and desperate, and I know she's close—fuck, I'm close too, the heat coiling tight at the base of my spine.

"Give it to me," I murmur against her mouth, teeth grazing her lip. "Come for me, little monster. Let me see it."

Her eyes flare, wild and defiant, but her body betrays her, clenching hard as she teeters on the brink. I grind deeper, slower, drawing it out, making her feel every brutal second of the build until she's shaking, pinned between me and the stone, ready to break.

I growl low, teeth grazing her collarbone. "Mine."

Haide's breath catches, a sharp, broken sound, and then she shatters. Her orgasm rips through her, a violent wave that has her clenching around me so tight I nearly lose it.

Her body convulses, thighs trembling around my hips, nails raking down my back as she cries out—a raw, feral sound that's half-snarl, half-scream. Her dark green eyes glaze over, lost in the storm of it, and fuck—she's beautiful like this. Completely undone. Every wall she's ever built crumbling under the force of her release.

I can't hold back. The heat of her, the way she milks my cock with every shudder, drags me over the edge.

My own climax hits like a fucking weighted blow, hot and brutal, spilling into her as I growl her name against her throat.

My hips jerk, driving deep one last time, every muscle locking as I empty myself inside her, the pleasure so intense it borders on pain. My vision blurs, the world narrowing to the slick heat of her body and the ragged sound of our breathing.

We collapse, a mess of sweaty bodies, hitting the ground hard, her weight crashing against my chest as we land in a heap on the cold stone floor. Her hair sticks to my face, her breath hot and uneven against my neck, and I can still feel the aftershocks of her trembling through every inch of her body pressed to mine. My own chest heaves, lungs burning, the ache and fatigue from earlier creeping back in, but I don't give a fuck. Not right now. Not with her here, wrecked and perfect, sprawled half on top of me like she owns every broken piece of me.

Creed's words still carve lines into my skull.

She isn't yours.

She drains you.

I wrap her body closer and imagine carving those words out of my brain with the edge of a knife.

"Stop thinking." Her voice brushes my sweaty chest, her finger trailing after. "You're loud."

"You're bossy," I murmur, yawning, cock still inside where it's supposed to be.

"You like it."

I smirk against her head, arching my hips. "Unfortunately."

Her laugh vibrates over me.

I can pretend there's no world beyond this. That my brothers accept her the way I'd always imagined them accepting my mate. That she's welcome to the opening ball tonight just like everyone else. That their words don't affect me.

"Legend," she says. Quiet. The word isn't a plea this time. It's a touch. "What did your brothers want?"

"They don't believe you're my mate."

She tenses.

I squeeze. "They're wrong."

She relaxes.

She fucking relaxes? Since when? The thought that I'm working my way into the stubborn shell of hers shouldn't feel as triumphant as it does.

"I told you I wasn't." She tries to roll off me but I lock her in place.

"Shut the fuck up." I kiss her head. "They don't know shit. I have always been the smarter brother. I've known you're mine since the second I smelled you from across the room."

She laughs, but I feel her pain against my chest.

"Another thing. You might not like this one."

"Yay," she mocks, resting her chin on her hand and looking up at me from below.

"You have to wear a dress."

Her face falls. "What?"

"It's for a party." I shrug, as if that should soften the blow. "Last I checked, you happened to like those? Huh?"

"Okay, grumpy." She smirks. "Let me guess. Ball gowns and crowns and a lot of fragile egos pretending they're not terrified I'll tear out their hearts."

I curl a lock of her hair around my finger. "Something like that."

"And you're taking me." Her voice is low, as if she needs reassurance.

"I'm taking you," I say. "Unless you'd rather I take someone else…"

"Not unless the other side of your face would like to meet my knuckles?" She says casually, breaking out in a fit of laughter as I roll her onto her back.

I settle between her thighs. Fuck, she looks beautiful. Dark hair sprawled out around her, skin slick with our sex, and eyes dark.

She touches my cheek, the gesture unnatural for her, and pulls at something in my chest. "Don't lock me in like that again."

I smirk. "Am I to let you run?"

Her smile dies slowly. The part of her that's always half on a cliff looks at me. "I run only when I'm chased."

"So don't make me chase you…" I nip at her bottom lip.

"I want you to chase me." The honesty delivers yet another harsh slice to the chest. "I just don't want you to lock me away."

I cup her face and stroke the edge of her cheekbone. "I don't know how to control you." The words taste like bitter acid, and I feel the first pulse of fatigue wave through my body.

"Because you can't," she says, matter-of-factly. I know it's true. And the words from my brothers once again invade our space. The bond would never allow the other to want to be away from them. They'd kill each other before wanting to be away. *So why does she fucking fight me?* I feel it. I feel it all. Why the fuck doesn't she?

I want to tell her I am trying to learn not to control her by doing the smaller things. That putting her on my lap in front of an entire school and announcing I could crown her is what that looked like in my head, a way to show her she means more. That she belongs and not for just for a moment. That teaching her to portal, even if we kept failing and fell into my bed, was me trying to learn to trust she won't run. That the thing in the water was a test I thought she could chew and spit but surprised me when it almost had her in tears.

"Come with me to the ball at the week's end," I say instead.

She searches my face with slight suspicion. Smart girl. "You're serious? Why?"

"Because they'll learn you," I say. "The more they see us together, the more they'll understand." I drag my teeth over her cheekbone, circling my hips. "They'll learn to love you as a weapon to use, not one to be afraid of."

"Or maybe I'll just cut you," she says.

I brush my nose against hers. "You already do."

She closes her eyes for a heartbeat. Something fierce settles there.

"Fine," she says. "But if Creed looks at me like a problem, I will become one."

"It's his favorite hobby," I say. "But not at the ball. Save your wrath for another day."

She laughs, short. Punch-drunk. "Deal."

Chapter Eighteen

Haide

The Flying Grounds are nothing like the rest of Rathe U. There are no polished stone walkways or pristine enchanted gardens meant to impress visiting royals. No ancient sculpture or scripture meant to make one gifted feel more inferior than the other. No distinction based on where they came from, the family names that built their realm, or the ones who merely exist within it. I may be from the island, but even there it was easy to see the hierarchies in the world of magic.

There is a food chain in every area: animal, human, and gifted alike.

Out here, the land is raw and sprawling, a wide circular basin carved into the hillside with cliffs rising on all sides.

High enough for a dragon to launch. Low enough for a Fae to fall without dying when they're still learning how to use their wings. Probably.

The afternoon sun spills through the canopy in fractured beams, catching on the floating practice rings that drift lazily across the field like oversized halos. Grassy patches give way to dark, scorched dirt in places where dragon fire has kissed the ground, leaving spirals of blackened ash curling like old scars. Farther out, massive stone perches jut from the terrain, smooth from centuries of scaled bodies landing and leaping again.

It's huge, open, humming faintly with leftover magic—like every creature that's ever flown here left behind a piece of itself.

I like it.

It feels honest. Untamed.

Not suffocating with rules, etiquette, or all the shit the rest of the university shoves down your throat the second you blink at the wrong noble.

And best of all.

It's empty.

Finally, an entire damn space to myself. No classmates pretending not to stare; no professors watching me like I might sprout fangs and rip someone's spine out. Honestly, I'd be grateful for some fangs right about now. At least that meant there was something under this skin of mine, as Creed so dickishly put it.

I drop into a patch of grass near one of the stone perches and pull out my codex. The leather cover warms instantly under my palm, as if greeting—or warning—me. Or maybe just trying to look impressive so I don't set it on fire like I did the last training dummy.

"Let's see if there's anything worth a damn today," I mutter, flipping it open. The pages flutter on their own, stopping somewhere near the middle where new spells shimmer faintly along the vellum, as if the ink hasn't decided whether it wants to stay or run.

SpellChemy has been…weird.

Useful, sure, but weird.

Every time I leave that class, something inside me rattles loose and the codex shifts to match whatever new knowledge I'm taught. After that first day in SpellChemy, the book had maybe half a dozen spells. Now? It's filling itself faster than I can keep up. Words rearranging, diagrams redrawn, margins scribbling with new instructions that were never there before.

I drag a finger down the latest section.

Binding.

Shielding.

Elemental Manipulation—fire, water, wind, stone.

I pause there, staring at the page.

Fire.

My palm tingles, a phantom echo of the heat that sparked there in class. Warm enough to notice, not enough to understand. I can't decide if I like it or if it unnerves me. Maybe both. A symbol swirls below—a thread of script that curves into something almost serpentine, like flame curling through scales.

It's the first fire-related spell that's appeared since that first day. This one a focusing spell: a way to take raw heat and give it shape. Give it *purpose.*

That…actually makes sense.

The professor's voice nudges the back of my mind: *magic isn't just power, Haide, it's precision.*

A curl of anticipation winds through me, low and warm.

I roll my shoulders back and read the script, slower this time, letting the diagram settle into my mind, feeling for anything inside me that might respond. Nothing dramatic happens. No burst of flame or explosion. But my palms warm just the slightest, a simmer beneath the skin, like something alive is turning over in its sleep and stretching its claws.

"Okay..." I breathe, dragging the heat up toward my fingertips, imagining it shaping into the pattern the spell wants from me. "Let's try—"

A prickle runs down the back of my neck.

I freeze, eyes lifting and flicking across the grounds.

It's empty, but the sensation of being watched doesn't fade. It fucking tightens, circles like a predator's breath against the back of my skull.

I turn slowly, ready to tear someone's face off, but there's no one there. Nothing but the perches and a distant bite of wind.

I shake it off, forcing my shoulders down. "Paranoid much," I mutter, returning to the diagram despite knowing it's pointless.

How can I be precise if I can't give all my focus?

Taking a deep breath, my pulse steadies. The heat flickers again along my palm, climbing toward my knuckles, and I focus on imposing the shape the spell wants on the delicate thread of control that—

A whisper of movement against the floor cuts off my thoughts.

I snap my hand out, fingers hooking as if to catch a throat, but all I come up with is air.

Unease sits in the center of my spine, coiled tight, watching the horizon like something is about to pop out at me. There's a snap above me, and my head tilts up just as a long, curling shadow slips across the leaves overhead in the familiar silhouette of a tail.

My fingertips warm instantly, heat blooming across my palm.

I drop my gaze back to the codex, pretending I'm not suddenly on high alert. My heart tightens in that quiet, coiled way it does when a fight is coming. The words blur, meaningless, because every ounce of my attention is stretched out across the grounds, listening for the wrong breath, the wrong shift of wind.

Slowly, casually, I nudge the codex off my knee.

I bend to pick it up, fingers sinking into the soil. As I rise, I let the book fall from my palm again, and the moment it hits the ground, I whip the fistful of dirt into the space directly in front of me.

It hits something solid. Something *invisible*, wafting out into a cloud that starts to take shape.

The air splits with a surprised cough, and the glamour collapses, peeling back like torn cloth until a gifted girl wearing the same Rathe U uniform I do snaps into view.

I don't give her a second to think. My knee drives up into her gut, folding her in half with a strangled wheeze. My other leg sweeps hers from beneath her, dropping her hard onto her back, and before the breath can even leave her lungs, I'm already straddling her, dagger pressed to the hollow of her throat.

The girl snarls up at me, her lips curling. "Bitch."

"Says the girl on the ground. Bet you've never seen that little dirt trick, have you?" I lean closer, pressing the blade tighter to her throat. "Don't worry, it's something only a poor little giftless would know." I fake pout.

"We know it was you!" she screams. "You're going to pay! You're already screwed and you don't even know it!"

I frown, ready to argue when her eyes begin to glow a deep yellow. I act before whatever magic she has explodes out of her.

I slam my forehead into hers, the crack echoing through the clearing. Her eyes go blank and her body limp. Warm trickles of blood slip down my forehead and across my nose. I shove off her chest, wiping her blood from my brow with the back of my hand, and push to my feet with a sigh.

"Fool," I mutter, brushing dirt from my pants and adjusting the dagger at my boot.

I dust off my codex, and start walking toward my dorm, already annoyed at how fast the peace of the grounds disappeared.

Fuck did she mean I'm already screwed?

I know that I'm stuck here and all, but I am sort of starting to like it. For now. But that's beside the point!

How would she know that?

Am I being played?

"Damn girl, shut the fuck up," I utter to myself. Since when do I go getting all paranoid?

Since when do I give a flying fuck about any of that?

Despite myself, my thoughts continue to run. Now I just want to get fucking punched hard enough so that *I* can take a damn nap.

That girl back there doesn't know how lucky she is, getting her mind to shut up for five minutes. I did her a favor.

Just as I'm about to pass the last stone perch that signals the exit of the Flying Grounds, the shadow reappears. It glides between the trees in a way no person could soundlessly manage.

I pivot hard and throw my dagger. The blade sinks into the dirt with a solid thunk, just where I intended, and something enormous exhales.

The trees shudder, and then he steps out.

Ruby-red scales catching light like molten glass with wings

tucked tight against a body big enough to flatten half the university if he felt dramatic about it. His long neck curves toward me, eyes glowing as bright as the Forbidden Gems back on Exile, a deep, volcanic red.

Dragon, and not even a fully grown one.

"Thank you," I say lightly, like I'm greeting an old friend. "I know that was you, the snap of the branch."

His pupils widen, round and bright, and he lowers his head a fraction, huffing a warm breath across my skin.

"Did you see her?" I wonder.

He snorts, a plume of smoke curling around my knees.

"Smelled her." I nod. "Of course."

A deep rumble vibrates through the air, low and warning. His long neck coils then stretches toward the earth, gaze darting toward the far end of the field.

Slowly, he backs away, the ground trembling with each step, his wings unfurling like a banner of fire and shadow.

I watch him go, a strange sense of satisfaction sweeping through me.

With one last glance back at the Flying Grounds I take off toward the main campus.

When the spires of Rathe University rise into view, I angle toward the eastern promenade, following the path of lanterns suspended in a lazy arc of floating chains. These weren't here on my way out, but it's clearly a path meant to be followed.

Something in my chest pulls tight, like an invisible hand curling inward and urging me elsewhere.

I flip the codex to the map, and ink appears, shifting into lines, the campus sketching itself alive beneath my fingertips. Glowing faintly at the border of the Fae Conservatory is the royal gateway.

Not twenty feet from where I'm standing, and the opposite pathway of the lanterns.

I step off the path and the lanterns flicker and die as I follow where the codex wants to lead—Creed has said that was the whole point of it, right? Like it knows best or some shit.

And there it is. Tucked beyond a curtain of hanging willow branches sits an archway, small enough to miss unless you're looking straight at it. Gods, it's beautiful.

Vines of gold and black curl around its frame like veins beneath translucent skin, pulsing faintly, responding to the magic of the campus like a heartbeat. Flowers shaped like falling stars cling to the arch, their petals luminescent and dripping soft sparks into the grass.

And carved deep into the stone lintel, so delicate it could've been etched by a whisper: Deveraux.

I step closer, breath drawing slow and uneven. Some instinct in me paces against my ribs, urging caution while another thrums with…curiosity.

"Well, well, *King Creed*," I murmur, reaching out. "That's a half a point for you. But let's see if there is a lie in there somewhere."

The moment my fingertips graze the wood, pain snaps up my arm, sharp and electric.

I hiss through my teeth and shake out my hand, then place my palm back against the surface.

This time the burn is instant, searing across my skin like a brand, heat licking up my wrist like molten gold poured beneath the bone, but I don't pull away. I lean in. Dare it.

The fire climbs hotter and I nearly crumble to my knees when it suddenly drops.

Ice floods outward, freezing the surface beneath my palm,

crawling up my veins like frost gripping a windowpane. I gasp and yank back, flexing my fingers as white steam curls from my skin.

"What the fu—"

A whisper cuts across the air, footsteps following.

I focus but don't move, listening.

Three, maybe four, closing in.

One breath.

A second.

I pivot, hands already finding the dagger at my thigh as figures slide from the shadows between the trees. All students here at Rathe U, each one wearing expressions carved from suspicion to hate.

One steps forward, the wind whirling around her wrist.

"There she is," she spits. "The Exile rat."

I raise an eyebrow. "Must've taken all of you to come up with that one. Impressive."

"Shut up." Another steps beside her, crackling flame in his palm. "You couldn't just follow the damn path like a good little *giftless*, could you?"

"Ah, the lanterns." Glad I looked at my damn codex. "That wasn't obvious at all, now, was it?"

The other jerks forward again, lips curled back in a sneer. "If Galley would have done her job, we wouldn't have needed a backup plan."

Galley. The girl from the Flying Grounds.

That's what she meant. She was supposed to somehow lead me right into the palm of their hands.

She picked the wrong fucking place to do it.

"Trail to the dark lands or right here in the heart of campus, it doesn't matter," she continues. "We'll just have to kill you a little more silently than planned."

My head yanks back. "Kill me?"

Angry gifted out for my blood twice in one day?

This place is feeling more like home by the day.

"We know you're behind the murders!" One hisses, light flickering from her fingertips.

"Right," I drawl, sliding my gaze across them, counting angles, advantages, and I'd count weapons but these are gifted kids. Their weapons live inside them. Fuck. "Because when I kill someone, I always leave them in public places for maximum inconvenience."

The girl's face twists. "You killed your partner in combat class—everyone saw it. But he was a Stygian and you didn't have the guts, not with our Kings so close. So, you went after someone you saw as weaker just because she was Argents."

"We know you killed Elena!" another yells.

My jaw ticks. "That's cute. Completely wrong, but cute."

They advance, magic thickening in the air around us.

Double fuck.

I throw the first strike, blade aimed low, not to kill but to disable. I don't miss, drawing a clean line across the calf of the boy on the left. He yells, stumbling, but the girl is already on me, hurling a blast of energy that knocks the wind from my lungs and sends me sliding through the dirt.

I roll, spring back up, only to take a second hit across the ribs.

The force seizes my breath, vision pulsing black at the edges. I slash blindly, catching one across the forearm, and the scent of blood fills the air.

Two down but not enough.

"Whatever enchantment you put on King Legend," the girl

snarls, magic gathering around her like storm clouds, "it'll fade. And when it does, he'll see you for exactly what you are."

I spit blood into the dirt. "Deadly? Gorgeous? Really flexible?"

"*Murderer.*"

Her spell hits like a sledgehammer.

My knees buckle and pain blooms at the base of my skull, jabbing like someone driving spikes through my neck.

A third steps in, voice cold. "You slit her throat so we will slice yours."

"I didn't—"

"You think Argents are weak?" he sneers. "You're not one of us. Not Stygian. Not Argent. Not even Fae. So, what the hell are you?"

His magic wraps around my ribs, squeezing. A bones creaks and my vision fractures.

"Worthless," he finishes. "That's what."

Blood floods my mouth, my skin burning from the inside out, like something deep within me is trying to claw free.

Just as spots appear before my eyes, a roar whips through the air like thunder.

Legend erupts into the clearing, power crackling off his skin, rolling in waves that shove the attackers backward before he even touches them.

The first boy goes flying—spine slamming into a tree so hard the bark cracks. The girl tries to lift her hands in surrender, but Legend twists her wrist, hurling it into the dirt where it detonates in a burst of ash. The last attacker barely opens his mouth to beg for mercy before Legend's fist connects with his jaw, sending him sprawling, unconscious before he hits the ground.

And then he's crouching beside me, strong, solid arms carefully scooping me up, holding me as if my bones might dissolve if he loosens even a fraction.

His chest heaves, his jaw tight, and his eyes—gods. They burn like he wants to raze the whole realm for touching me.

I blink up at him, everything spinning, my blood humming with the echo of that roar. I should want to push him, to deny his careful hands and wordless fear he stares down at me with.

But I...don't want that. Not right now.

Safety wraps around me in the shape of his arms, in the scent of his being...in something I refuse to name.

"It's okay, little monster," Legend purrs. "I've got you." Bending, he kisses my forehead with gentleness that makes me bite my tongue.

I don't like this...this tightness in my chest. The feeling is an odd one, coiling around my ribs like barbed wire, but beneath that sharp tug is warmth. Almost satisfaction, like the part of me I don't recognize feels settled with Legend this close.

Legend turns toward the archway and steps forward, carrying me as if I weigh nothing.

"I can walk," I grumble, even though every inch of me has already relaxed in his hold.

"I know you can, but I'm going to carry you anyway."

I don't respond.

Behind him, fire erupts. His brothers and London have joined us, burning ropes curling around their hands, faces carved with murderous intent as they drag the unconscious students aside.

Legend bites into the thick web of flesh between his thumb and pointer finger and smears it across the carved sigil on the door.

The blood of a royal...

The arch glows, flares, and then splits open. A corridor of light yawns wide, ancient and hungry.

I tilt my head over his shoulder just long enough to meet Creed's stare.

His eyes narrow, following Legend's every step as he carries me through the Royal Gateway.

Our gazes only break when the portal closes, sealing him on the other side.

Chapter Nineteen

Haide

"Seriously, Legend," I protest. "You can put me down, you know. My legs work."

His grip tightens, his chest rumbling. "No."

"You're annoying," I mutter, but the word comes out softer than intended. My body has apparently decided his chest is the most comfortable place it's ever been. I blame the lack of airflow to my brain in the moments before he appeared.

His room is all shadowed stone walls broken by narrow windows. Weapons hang from the far wall—swords, axes, blades shaped like they were made for tearing souls instead of skin. Above the bed, a map of Rathe burns softly with shifting lines of light, alive with movement I don't understand.

"Why do you have weapons if you don't fight with your hands?" I ask, almost sighing as he lowers me onto a bed of feathers, black silk surrounding me from head to toe.

He handles me with care that would be insulting if my ribs didn't still feel like they'd been kicked in by a particularly enthusiastic dragon.

"Just because you've never seen me feed my fist to a man in full combat doesn't mean I'm not well-versed," he boasts. "You think otherwise, but I could very easily hold my own to you, little monster."

A bratty hum leaves me because no—I do not believe him. I would kick his royal ass in a magicless fight.

Legend smirks and shifts closer, so I push up on my elbows.

"Okay, we had our little kidnapping adventure, fun times, now take me back."

"Later." He straightens, eyes sweeping over me, cataloguing every injury and place another's magic touched my skin. He hates it. His jaw flexes. "You're bleeding."

"I've bled worse," I say, but my voice comes out a little thinner than I'd like. The room tilts sideways when I try to sit up.

His hand lands flat on my sternum, gentle but unmovable, pressing me back into the mattress. "You're staying here until you rest."

I glare up at him. "You don't get to decide that."

"I get to decide everything," he counters. "I'm your King."

"I'm going to slap you."

Legend chuckles, but goes silent a moment later, eyes not leaving my face. "Lie down, Haide."

Something in his tone, low and edged, slides along a part of me that isn't interested in arguing.. I sink back, hissing when a bruised patch along my spine protests, and he curses under his breath.

"Stay," he orders, like I'm a particularly troublesome dragon pup.

"Not a pet," I grumble.

A basin full of steaming water magically appears. The surface shimmers with the telltale sheen of a healer's magic.

A bitterness coats my tongue.

If I were a real gifted, I would heal on my own with time.

Legend wrings out a cloth and climbs onto the bed with focus that screams I'm currently the center of his kingdom. I swear I can *feel* the satisfaction rolling off him and into me. Not because I'm "hurt," but because he gets to heal me.

It's way too fucking much.

"Legend," I warn as he braces one knee by my hip.

"Relax," he murmurs, leaning over me. "I'm just cleaning you up. No big scheme here."

The cloth touches my cheek, cool against skin that feels too hot. His hand cups the side of my face, thumb stroking once, slow and soothing, as if he's taming a skittish creature instead of a girl who can kill like a beast.

"I am not a weak doll that needs caring for. I don't need you."

"*I* need to do this; and you're going to let me," he says quietly.

The words land with more weight than they should, and my throat tightens.

He must be bewitching me or something. Slipped some herbal drug into that water or the air because this girl who lies back and lets someone else in—she's not me.

She can't be me.

To want is to lose, Haide. To need is to die.

He works in silence, wiping away blood and dirt, following the line of my jaw to my neck, my collarbone, and the exposed stretch of my stomach where my shirt has ridden up.

“Your eyes are turning white,” I mutter, and those eyes, swimming with royal magic, snap up to mine, sending a jolt straight down my spine.

“My mate is in my hands,” he says simply.

“You’re delusional.”

“And you’re beautiful.” He says it with the same quiet certainty he uses when issuing orders, as if it’s an undeniable fact of the universe. As if the sky is violet, dragons breathe fire, and I am beautiful.

Beauty has never meant a damn thing to me. I’d never even seen myself outside of a reflection in the water or a puddle of rain until he locked me up in Rathe. I liked what I saw, but beauty?

Not sure I understand what that is.

He cocks his head. “You don’t believe me?”

“I mean, I’d fuck me.”

Legend throws his head back with a laugh, and my muscles relax instantly.

He finishes with the cloth and tosses it aside, fingers lingering at the edge of my shirt. “Lift.”

I arch a brow. “Did that sound like an invitation?” It totally can be, but I might need the gash on my neck healed first. Could make a real mess if things get too fun.

“Your ribs,” he reminds me, though his mouth curves. “Let me see.”

Rolling my eyes for show, I help him peel the fabric up. Dark bruises bloom across my side, ugly and impressive. I’m not sure I realized magic could even do that.

Legend's expression goes thunderous at the sight.

"I will kill them," he says softly, like he's discussing the change in tide. "Slowly. Painfully. *Publicly.*"

"Already unconscious, mighty king. Don't go pissing off more people because of me. I do that enough on my own without your help."

"It's non-negotiable, little monster. They will die, but I hear you. I'll find other ways to make them regret what they've done, and just when they start to feel safe again, I will end them. Slowly." He drags his knuckles lightly along an unmarked patch of skin as if that can erase what's beneath.

The touch is featherlight, but everything in me goes tight, breath locking in my chest. His eyes catch mine, and something heavy settles between us. It's thick, electric. It's familiar.

The thing that might be between us—that pull I refuse to dignify by calling it anything else—flares, hot and bright, threading from my chest to his. My fingers curl into the sheets to keep from reaching for him first.

"Legend."

"Yes?" His hand slides higher, palm flattening just beneath my ribs, pinning me with no effort at all.

"This doesn't feel very 'rest and recover.'"

"Disagree." His mouth lowers, brushing the corner of mine. "You relax best when you're beneath me."

"Cocky," I breathe, but my lips are already tilting toward his.

"Confident." His smile ghosts against my mouth. "Let me take care of you," he repeats. Something inside me that's been braced for impact since the moment I arrived in Rathe…eases.

I let him.

He kisses me slow, nothing like the frantic, teeth-and-claw kind of contact we've had before. His tongue traces the cut on my lip as if trying to soothe it from the inside. His hand slides to cradle the back of my head, holding me in place like I'm something precious instead of a weapon that keeps accidentally going off. When I sigh into him, the sound is embarrassingly soft, and he swallows it like it's his favorite thing he's ever been given.

His weight settles more fully over mine, careful not to crush, but solid enough that I can feel every inch of him. He's all heat and strength. His pulse beats against me like a wild drum. My fingers find his shoulders, then his hair, dragging him closer.

"Tell me if it's too much. Tell me if—"

"Shut up," I mutter, dragging him back down. "If you stop now, I'll stab you."

He laughs into the kiss, the sound low and unrestrained, and then there's nothing but dizzying pleasure that has my body forgetting any pain. He removes my knife from my boot. I wait for my defenses to kick in and demand I fight back. Protect myself.

It never comes.

My chin lifts and my limbs spread wide of their own accord. He doesn't hesitate, chest rumbling as he slices his way up through my clothes, leaving them to fall open around us.

My boots stay on and nothing else.

The weight of him settles fully between my thighs, and I inhale sharply, hips lifting before I can stop myself. His answering groan vibrates against my lips, rough and hungry. He kisses down my jaw, the scrape of his teeth dragging a shiver straight through me.

"I should have been there," he rasps, his cock sliding deep

inside me. "You shouldn't have been alone." He pulls out, pushing in again, even slower this time.

My back bows and he leans down, licking across my chest.

"I can't stand being away from you, little monster." His hips roll and my nails dig into his back. "You're mine, Haide. Mine to protect, and I failed you tonight."

"Legend," I warn, body already trembling.

Why does the tone he's using make me ache?

This is supposed to be sex. Raw.

Reckless.

It's...I don't know what it is but I need it to stop.

I need it to stop, yet my fingers curl into his shoulders, drawing him closer, guiding without words. And the second I do, his mouth crashes into mine again in a kiss that's sure to split my lip back open. His hands slide under me, lifting my hips into his, and the soft drag of friction steals every coherent thought I have left. Still, he fucks me slow and steady, and it's the sweetest fucking torture.

"I'm going to come inside you now," he whispers, lips lifting when he feels my pulse start to pulse. "And you're going to come all over my cock at the same time, ain't that right, baby?"

"Shut up."

"Come."

It's like he's speaking in command and my body decides to obey.

I come hard. Long, and his eyes eat up the sight.

After a few minutes, he pulls out and falls onto the bed beside me.

I pull in a deep breath, letting it out slowly. Sweat cools my skin, my muscles now loose in that rare, floating way that only comes from a good orgasm.

Guess Legend was right.

My head lolls to the side, spotting the faint smear of blood on his lip where I bit him a little harder than necessary.

"Oops," I say, not sorry at all.

His thumb swipes the red away and he grins in a satisfied way that makes my stomach do something stupid. "My favorite kind of wound."

"Pervert."

"Your perv," he counters, voice already thick with oncoming sleep.

The last thing I remember before the dark takes me is the weight of his arm banded around my waist, the steady rise and fall of his chest at my back, and the strange, terrifying comfort of knowing that if anything tried to touch me in this moment, he'd burn the world for it.

When I wake, the room is dim.

My head feels clearer and my body less like someone's favorite punching bag, though dull aches still whisper from my ribs and shoulders.

Legend is a heavy warmth at my back, his arm still slung over my waist, hand splayed against my stomach. For a second, I let myself stay there, eyes closed, breathing with him.

Eventually, reality slaps me upside the head.

I wriggle carefully out from under his arm, easing his hand onto the mattress. He makes a low sound, a protest threaded with confusion, but doesn't wake fully. I slide off the bed, wincing when my feet hit the cold floor, and steal his shirt off the ground.

Just as I reach for my boots, a rough voice rasps behind me.

"Where do you think you're going, little monster?"

I glance back to find his eyes locked on the hem of his shirt, brushing against my thighs.

He sits up, sheets pooling around his hips, hair a mess and eyes shadowed. He's paler than normal and his under eyes look bruised. They might just be, I didn't exactly see all the damage he did yesterday.

He looks like he's been trampled by a pack of Lycans and then dragged behind for good measure.

"Back," I say, straightening slowly. "To the university. The place where I live now, remember?"

"No." His answer is immediate, flat. "You're staying here."

I cross my arms, ignoring the way the movement tugs at bruises. "I said take me back."

He studies me, gaze moving from the set of my jaw to the stubborn line of my shoulders, and something darker than usual flares in his eyes. "I will burn that place to the ground if anyone even *thinks* about hurting you again," he says, voice low and lethal. "I'll kill every gifted in that place if I have to. Then I'll come back here and kill the ones who gave them their names. That can't happen, so I can't send you back."

"You don't have a choice, Legend," I remind him. "You stood before your people and claimed me as your queen—still fucking ridiculous, by the way. But you did that. That was your premature ass half-cocked decision."

"You are my mate, Haide. That makes you a queen."

"If you don't send me back, you make me look weak." I ignore his statement. "I will look like I'm hiding or afraid. And I will not fucking hide and I am not fucking afraid."

"Haide—"

"I think Creed was right and I might have powers," I cut in, the words tumbling out before I can second-guess them.

That pulls him up short.

"I don't know for sure, or what I could be able to do, but I need to figure it out," I speak slowly but firmly, hoping it'll get through that thick skull. "I can't do that if I'm tucked away here like some little trophy. I'm not, Legend. If those assholes didn't have the jump on me, I could have beat them with my hands alone. Imagine if I could do more."

Slowly, satisfaction curls at the edges of his mouth, tempered by a pride so fierce it steals my breath more than once. He swings his legs over the side of the bed, standing despite the way the motion nearly sways him.

He crosses the space between us, stopping close enough that I have to tip my chin back to keep our eyes locked. His knuckles graze along my cheek so gently it almost undoes me more than anything that happened last night.

"Okay," he says, voice rough but sure. "Okay, little mate, but I will be watching."

The word digs into my chest, sharp and sweet, and I pretend it doesn't.

He takes my wrist and leads me back to The Royal Gateway we entered through.

He reaches for it without hesitation, palm closing around a jagged, golden thorn along the door's frame. It slices deep into the flesh below his thumb. Blood wells, and he drags it across the center of the door in a slow, deliberate line.

The stone shudders.

The sigils flare, lighting up one by one, following the stroke of his hand until the entire surface glows with blinding radiance. A crack splits down the middle, widening, the air rippling with heat and the metallic tang of portal magic.

A gateway opens.

He releases my hand and steps back. "I'll see you soon."

I nod, moving closer, and just before I step through, Legend asks,

"What did you mean when you said you think *Creed* is right? What did he say?"

Shit.

"He said maybe I had real power. That I should behave while I'm here and figure out if I do."

"Is that all my brother said?"

"That's it," I lie.

Legend studies me for a long moment before finally nodding. "Okay."

"Okay." I turn and step through the portal.

If they're going to come at me, let them come.

Chapter Twenty

Haide

Professor Astra's class is officially my favorite, even over Warcraft. Shocking as fuck, honestly. I never expected I'd like *listening* to someone talk more than I would punching their face, but here we are.

That's because you never had the chance to be taught anything real before now.

Might also be the way the room changes with each class in a way that doesn't necessarily reflect the outside world. Storming inside when the courtyard is clear. Or stars burning overhead in the middle of the day. Today, it smells like hot metal and rain, even though it's bone-dry inside. Low clouds churn above us like someone tipped a cauldron of fog upside down and trapped it under glass.

Dozens of students are already seated when I enter. The sound of my boots hitting the stone floor instantly snatches their attention.

They don't bother hiding it anymore.

Whispers stutter and die, eyes following me with open suspicion or even outright hate. I clock every stare, meet a couple dead-on until they flinch, and move toward my usual place at the back. For people who think I'm a murderer, they're awfully fucking brave.

I drop my codex on the desk, the cover vibrating faintly once beneath my palm, like it's happy to be here. Weird little book. I'm going to steal it and take it home with me when I leave.

The thought draws unease through my veins and I grit my teeth. Unease?

I am not uneasy. Nothing has changed. I know exactly what I want in the end.

I just want to do the dance here first. Get some powers and shit.

Rolling my eyes at myself, I throw my boots up on the desk, crossing one over the other and taking up the full space beside me—no one else will sit there anyway.

Professor Astra's back is to us as she stands at the center. Her rolled-up sleeves reveal the silver ink curling over her forearms in intricate, living patterns that shift when she moves. The symbols she traces in the air are not the standard ones from her SpellChemy lessons. They're looser, more fluid lines that look half script and half smoke that glow faintly.

When the bell tolls, she flicks her fingers. One at a time, the symbols grow several sizes, pulsing in the air as they spin in slow, steady circles.

"Today," she says without turning, "we move beyond repetition."

A hush settles over the room, the kind that says even the little noblelings know this is important.

Astra faces us, hair braided tight against her skull, eyes sharp as ever. "You all know how to cast a spell someone else designed for you." *Yeah, exactly one so far, but who's fucking counting?* "When casting, you reproduce the pattern someone else designed and let your magic flow through their structure. That is spellwork."

Her gaze slides over the class, lingering on certain faces—the promising ones with ancient family lines humming in their veins. The ones whose names start with "Lord" or "Noble" or "Prince." When her eyes reach me, they pause for a solid second that snaps my brows together.

"Creative magic," she continues, looking up at the hovering symbols, "is the art of weaving something new."

She snaps her fingers and the room shifts. Threads of light appear in midair, thin as spider silk as they move above us. Some gleam golden and ember red. Others are shadow-black with a blue so soft it almost looks like bottled moonlight. They drift lazily, waiting for her instruction.

"The simplest way to explain creative magic is to focus on the three ideologies," Professor Astra says. "Essence. Emotion. Intention."

She lifts a hand and a strand of pale flame drifts toward her fingers. "Essence is the material you're working with. Fire, water, shadow, bone, blood, time—whatever your principle powers and the realm allow you to touch."

She catches the thread between forefinger and thumb. It

coils there obediently, like a tamed snake.

"Emotion is the current. It motivates and nourishes. Rage, fear, love, desperation. You cannot cast or create without feeling. It is the one and only way. A numb mind is a worthless mind."

The thread shivers brighter, flaring white.

"And intention," she adds quietly, "Intention is the force that emanates from within that completes and creates. It is the difference between a trickle and a flood. Between a healing warmth and a killing burn."

Her earlier words echo in my head. *Magic isn't just about power, Haide. It's about precision.*

Something sparks low in my chest, pushing against my ribs like it doesn't know this body isn't meant for things like that.

If magic is just another kind of knife, I can learn to use it with precision and *intent.*

"Open your codex," she instructs. "Today, you will attempt to design a spell rather than repeat one." She flicks her fingers and dozens of glowing threads drift toward us, hovering at eye level. "Something small and harmless." Her eyes harden. "Relatively."

Nervous laughter trickles through the room. I don't join. My thread is ember-red, warm even before it touches my skin. When I wrap my fingers around it, heat licks along my palm, not burning, but *tasting.* Like it's testing whether I belong to it, or it belongs to me.

"Remember," she says, voice carrying even as she begins to move through the room. "Essence. Emotion. Intention. Pick one thread. Draw on one emotion, not five. And be specific in what you mean to create. A general spell is a sloppy spell. Sloppy spells misfire."

She glances my way again as she says it.

Around me, students close their eyes, faces smoothing as they reach for whatever feelings live in their heads. Some glow faintly, magic answering like a well-trained pet. Others frown, their threads flickering.

I stare at the thread in my hand.

Intention. I huff. I can internally snap someone's neck but it's not something I plan beforehand. It's impulse.

Every move I make is pure impulse. I'm not so sure I know how to think differently. My brain was wired this way—and unless there's some kind of witchery shit for that—then it's probably going to stay that way.

Be careful when calling on fire, Professor Astra had warned.

I release the thread and sit back in my chair, arms crossed. Yeah, not about to go full fucking pyro in here and get accused of escalating to mass murderer. Prickly fucks.

Professor Astra strolls toward me, hands carefully laced behind her back. "Sulking, are we?"

"Nah. Practicing self-control," I tease. "It's a terrible feeling."

Her lips twitch but she shows no other sign of amusement. I think it's safe to say she likes me, but what's not to like? I'm fucking fantastic.

"You think you won't be able to control the essence."

"I bit one of your Kings, while he sat on his throne, in a room full of royal guards because I fucking felt like it."

"That was foolish."

"It was."

"Do you regret it?"

"Not even a little bit."

"Why not?"

"Because I wanted to make him bleed."

She nods, coming to stand in front of me and lowering herself so we're at eye level, and whispers, "*Intent.*"

My eyes narrow, following her as she stands.

"If you were listening, truly listening, then you heard the word I wove into my instruction." Her fingers glide across my codex and it sparks angrily at her touch. "Look around the room, Haide," she calls over her shoulder as she walks away.

I study the gifted in the farthest corner, slowly moving from one student to the next, and with each I pass, my frown deepens.

Everyone's frustrated and annoyed. Some even slumped in their seats like they're just waiting for this to end.

I replay Astra's words.

I straighten in my seat. *Attempt.* That's the word I missed.

Attempt.

My feet fall from the tabletop. A slow smile curves across my lips as I sit up. She doesn't expect anyone to actually succeed. It's an assignment beyond the capabilities of anyone in this room.

Finally, I understand school. Today, the gifted in this room are my fucking equals.

I laugh quietly and reach out for one of Professor Astra's threads. This time, it's light that settles in my palm.

I draw a slow breath through my nose and let my shoulders loosen. I picture the light in my palm, not as a bright full moon over the island, but as something waiting for direction. I feed it a sliver of irritation—at this school, these rumors, the way they attacked me in a group like cowards—and it brightens, intimately pleased.

Intention.

Fuck.

What do I want it to do?

Killing them all is probably not what Astra meant by harmless.

I picture a small blade of light narrowed to a single point. Pale and blinding at its core so it's sharp enough to sting, but not enough to break skin. It appears in my mind as clearly as a knife in my hand. I wrap the intention around the thread, let my anger thread through it like wire.

Heat rolls up my arm, settling in my chest. It pushes against bone as if it wants out, and my heart beats like a wild animal beneath my ribs.

"Come on, Professor Astra," a student begs, "give us something we can actually accomplish. Creative Magic is for fourth years. We haven't even studied ancient symbols. How are we supposed to create our own without learning those first?"

My focus falls and the thread in my palms with it.

Professor Astra smirks at the boy. "Glad someone caught on to the missing piece." She makes her way back to the front of the class. "That was just an example to show you the amount of work needed here at Rathe U. That is, if you wish to get to the point in your journey where magic will answer to your call." She snaps her fingers and the room grows brighter. "Open your codex. Today is day one of ancient symbols."

The sounds of bending leather and turning paper fill the space as the class obeys. A slow grin curls across my face.

So, none of us should be able to create new magic.

Pretty fucking sure I almost did.

"Professor?" I ask.

Her eyes lift to mine, hand freezing mid-write. "Yes?"

"If emotion is the current and intention is the shape," I say slowly, "what happens if the only thing you intend is to make someone or something stop existing?"

Every head in the room snaps toward me. Fair enough. The question is sort of general, a workaround really for any and all "intents."

Professor Astra goes very, very still. "We have moved on, Haide. Your codex."

"Come on," I coax, a bit mockingly. "We don't get to learn this for four whole ass years." I hold her gaze. "Humor me."

"That," she says finally, voice softer but no less sharp, "is not a spell you are ready to design."

"That's not what I asked."

A muscle jumps in her jaw. Around us, someone hisses under their breath while another mutters, "Of course she'd ask that," like I'm not three feet away.

Professor Astra steps forward, lowering her tone so it doesn't carry as far, but I know everyone is straining to hear anyway. "In theory," she says, "if you only gave the magic the command to unmake…it would look for the most direct path. It would not be quick. Or clean. It would strip away everything that makes a person *them* before it touched the flesh. It would be—"

"Cruel," a boy at the front blurts, unable to keep quiet.

"Precise," Astra corrects, gaze never leaving mine. "But unpredictable. Wild. Because the caster did not bother to define what 'existing' means. Body? Memory? Bond?" Her eyes narrow suspiciously. "A spell like that doesn't care about consent or collateral." She lets that sink in and then adds, pointedly, "It is the kind of magic that has gotten entire bloodlines erased from Rathe and only one in a million gifted could even attempt to create."

The room chills.

I hold her stare, something cold and stubborn setting behind my ribs. "So, the problem isn't the spell," I say. "It's the caster being lazy."

For a heartbeat I think she might actually smile. Then it's gone. "Class dismissed," she snaps, breaking whatever strange current spun out between us.

Chairs scrape and the dome overhead clears to pale daylight as everyone begins to file out. They give me a wide berth, like they're not sure if I might gut them right here and now in front of everyone.

But only a few faces look wise enough to fear me. The rest? Pissy little fucks I'll need to watch out for.

Professor Astra calls another student over with a question, but her gaze tracks me as I move toward the door, unreadable. My smirk is full force as I curve out into the hall. I'm going to the Flying Grounds and I dare someone to track me this time. I'll be fucking ready and they will be dead. Then they can call me a murderer and it will be true. I mean, I am already if you really think about it. But I didn't earn the title the way they're accusing.

My good mood evaporates with a groan as soon as I spot someone blocking the exit of the building.

Creed.

He fills the doorway like it was carved to fit him, one hand braced against the stone above his head, the other buried in his pocket. He's opted for a more casual style today, wearing his training clothes. Everything else is the same. All sharp lines and unbothered violence that is definitely directed at me.

I stop a few feet away, shifting my weight onto one hip. "Oh, mighty big King. To what do I owe this absolute fucking travesty?" I drawl. "Or did you get lost? The self-righteous prick convention is down the hall to the left."

He doesn't smirk. His gaze flicks once to the hand I used for the spell, then to my face again. It's like he knows what no one in that class figured out. "Enjoying your lessons on building prettier ways to kill?"

"I'm a quick study," I say. And yeah, he knows because it's all I can think about. Doesn't have to dig real hard into my mind to see it. "Why, you nervous?"

"I'm never nervous," Creed replies, and I almost believe him. "I'm…evaluating." His eyes narrow, something like disdain and grim respect mixing in equal measure. "You keep asking questions like that, brat, and even the ones who don't already want you dead are going to start wondering if they should."

"Let them wonder," I say. "Better than thinking I'm weak."

He huffs a humorless breath. "You are many things. Weak isn't one of them. Reckless? Absolutely. Unwanted? Couldn't make that more obvious if I tried."

"Is this the part where you threaten me again?"

"Not yet." He straightens away from the doorframe, stepping just close enough that I have to tip my chin to keep our eyes level. Power hums off him in a quiet, suffocating wave, but I refuse to step back. "This is the part where I remind you that my brother is hanging on by threads I'm barely keeping intact."

My stomach flicks, a quick, defensive twist. "You're the one who keeps saying the bond isn't real," I say. "So why do you care what questions I ask?" And I never said I was asking because of any bond…

Not going to clear that up, though.

His jaw tenses at my mention of the bond, but he's quick to smooth his features once more. "Because I see what you're doing to him, Haide. And I will not allow it."

"Not really your sole decision, is it?" I challenge. "If it were, I wouldn't be here at all."

His mouth curves. "Is that what you think?" He approaches, voice lowering to a whisper. "He may have brought you here, girl, but I am the one allowing your stay. See, sending you back now wouldn't serve me. There are things I am trying to figure out. Something has been torn and I will find where the other half lies. Even if I have to drain you drop by drop myself."

"But, Captain-Control-Issues," I drawl sarcastically, "I have done as you asked. I've behaved like a good little girl. I know why you're here and honestly, it's embarrassing that you don't just outright say what you came to say."

His lips pull back in a snarl. "And what do you think that is?"

"I was at the Royal Gateway. I watched Legend open it with the blood of his palm. I know now that what you said was real and I should be, I don't know, grateful that you're not just a liar or some shit. Or maybe you're concerned things have changed because when I stepped through that thing in your brother's arms, it wasn't sand I found on the other side and now you're afraid things have changed."

"Have things changed?"

I mask my surprise. Honestly, I didn't expect him to just come out and, well, not admit, but def thought he would deny or feed me some royal riddle shit.

"If they had." I cock my head, watching him closely. "Wouldn't you already know...*mind* man?"

He's silent for several seconds, but when I try to sidestep him he moves with me, his features blank.

"Be careful, Haide," he says slowly. "Knives are useful. But the sharper they are, the easier they cut the hand that holds them."

“That’s what gloves are for.”

Creed studies me for a long moment before he finally steps aside so I can pass through the doorway. Still, his attention—heavy and assessing—stays pinned on me as I pass. Like I’m a spark in a room full of explosives.

“My brother is a smart man, Haide,” he calls at my back, but I keep walking. “Eventually, he will see you for what you really are, and when he does, he will turn against you.”

I look over my shoulder because I can’t stop myself, frowning at the certainty in his eyes. He smiles then, a full curve of his lips that sends a shiver down my spine.

“Legend will destroy you from the inside out and I can’t fucking wait to watch.”

I start walking again, giving him nothing and believing not a damn word.

Legend would never turn against me.

Right?

Chapter Twenty-One

Legend

The door swings open before I can even reach for it.

Haide stands at the threshold, arms folded and a fucking grin spread on her face. I love to fucking see it. Especially when I know she's been sleeping with one eye open since our own fucking people tried to attack her seven moons ago, if we're tracking in giftless time.

They might have been Argent-born, but they still belong to us. We— *I* am still their fucking King and she is mine. They don't know it yet, but I have their parents in the cellar back in Rathe—the one and only reason I allowed her to walk through the Gateway and back to campus alone. I might free them one day, but the jury's still out.

Pushing closer to her, my nostrils flare, and I swipe my bottom lip. "You smell of Fae juice. I take it you met Emmie?"

She steps aside and I kick the door closed, waiting for it to seal and vanish before crowding her again.

"Mmhmm." She ties her hair back, the little jewels embedded in her temples gleaming when she turns to me. "You're lucky I didn't kill her the moment she knocked on my door. Smooth, by the way, and brave of her. Sending her to me before I could change my mind about your little 'ball.' Not that I still can't."

"But you won't. You want to walk in there on my arm."

She remains silent for several seconds as she watches me. Finally, she says, "She smelled like you."

Her tone isn't that snappy, bratty, kiss-my-ass-or-don't she usually uses with me. It's soft and, dare I say, hesitant.

I *love* her attitude and crave the way she fights me. But right now the bond pulses wildly in response to her reaction; and I swear the thread between us grows a tiny bit stronger.

"I'm yours, little mate," I say, the words an unintended whisper.

I wait while she studies me. Maybe this is the moment she caves. That grabs hold of that feeling she must have inside her and refuses to ever let it go.

The only reason my scent was on another woman was because I hand chose the dresses she brought down for Haide. Still, I fucking *love* her jealousy.

She looks away with a blink. I guess today isn't the day she gives in. Maybe I was too soft with her the other night and she's still unsure about it. She enjoys me wild. But where my mate is concerned, I will always reserve a separate part for times that she needs it.

And she needed it then, even if she didn't realize it.

Haide shrugs, definitely a bit buzzed. "I like her."

"Shocking," I mock, grinning in hopes to hide the heavy. "She help you pick a dress for the ball?"

Haide kicks up from the dresser. "She did, but you can't see it yet."

"I see." I push closer and her chest inflates, her eyes not trusting my approach.

So off-balance, my mate.

It's clear something's changed between us, but she still refuses to admit it. That's okay though.

It's not lost on me that the Royal Gateway spat her out back here, at Rathe U. The place she didn't want to be instead of her island.

This is your home now, Little Mate. Can you see it?

I sense fire and I spin just as the door reveals itself. I yank the door open, ready to rip someone's main artery out, when it opens onto Creed.

His hands fly up in surrender, but there is a tension in his expression I don't fucking like. Last I saw him, he was spewing lies about her, as if he knew what it felt like to want someone so fucking bad you'd tear your own skin off just to feel her closer.

"Brother," he says, tone flat and expression blank.

I haven't had a chance to ask him what he told her during their last conversation about magic, but that will fucking come. Soon.

"What do you want?"

His dark brow raises. "Can I not come in?"

I step aside and check the hall. Empty. Good.

"What is it?" I ask, backing up against the door to close it.

He takes in the room, Haide has changed into one of my shirts that hangs right to the top of her knees, and put her hair up in that curl shit that girls do.

Her eyes bounce between my brother and me. "What?" It's no secret the two of them hate each other, but at least in Haide's defense, it's valid.

Creed's mouth flatlines. "We have another...*issue*. Vicente needs us immediately."

Fuck. Not good.

"And he couldn't come tell me himself?" I grind out. Not trusting my brother when it comes to my time with my mate.

The man's got a serious issue with her that needs to be dealt with and fast.

Creed shrugs, eyes sliding to Haide. "I was closer, so he probably thought it'd be quicker."

I don't give a fuck about what he says, because Haide just bent over to pick a pair of black panties off the floor. Now, all I think about is wearing her hair as a bracelet while I fuck her hard. Matter of fact—what *is* she wearing under that if she's holding her panties?

My head tilts. Suddenly I don't give a fuck about what Vicente has to say. Or that Creed is in the room. All I want is to bury myself in Haide and not come up for fucking weeks.

Before I realize it, I've crossed the room and my arms are around her back, locking her in place. Daring her to move and have me carve my fucking name over her forehead. See if that shit matches the color of her dress.

I lower my lips to hers, brushing them way gentler than I want. She wriggles away and my other hand lands on her throat with enough force I have to physically stop myself from not tearing the damn thing out.

Fuck you if you think you're running from me right now.

I need this. Need her.

She tenses for a moment before her hand sprawls over my chest to push me away, but my tongue laps the outline of her lips, and her body unravels in my hand when she opens for me.

I know she's close to feeling it. To believing every time I've told her she's my mate.

Told her she's mine.

I know she's starting to feel that live wire that's knotted between us. Now, I just need her to pet it. Fucking use the rope to choke me with it , I couldn't care.

"Mine." My lips curve over hers without breaking the kiss. *"For-fucking-ever."* It's low and intimate, but no doubt Creed is listening. Good. As much as he'd think this was a show for him, me making a statement and flipping him and his theories the middle finger, the second Haide's in the room nothing else exists.

No one else exists.

Her fingers crawl up my chest, leaving fire in their wake. These are the moments I want, where her lips meet mine, not in war, not in spite, but in actual fucking surrender. It's enough to fucking undo me.

I've been starving. Literally starving. My power playing tricks on me because it needs her—that is the only way to explain the strange strain on my gift I've felt lately. The bond has been clawing at my insides, at my magic, because it fucking wants her more. It wants her to acknowledge that she's mine.

But these moments where she yields, where it feels like she's marking me back the same way I do her…

Dare a motherfucker to stand between that.

My fingers knead into the plastic things in her hair, holding her in place. She tastes like magic and defiance and mine, mine, mine.

Power crashes through me in waves, raw and vicious, settling in my bones like liquid fire. The bond doesn't purr—it roars, searching for something it can't seem to find.

Every instinct I've been leashing snaps free at once. I want to bite her throat until she bleeds. I want to pin her down and make her say my name until her voice breaks. I want to mark every inch of her skin so thoroughly that no one else will ever dare touch what belongs to me.

She groans into the kiss and heat waves twist through the cages in my chest.

The kiss turns savage, all teeth and claim, the hunger being satiated. I've always secretly dreamed of my mate, wishing to find her for as long as I've understood what it meant to have one. No one knows this, but it's true.

And now she's here and she's not just kissing me back—she's fighting me for control, and *fuck*—that makes it so much better. If the Gods gave me a docile doll as a mate, I'd tear her apart within seconds. They knew I needed this. A fucking warrior. On the battlefield, in the War Room, and on my fucking dick.

"You guys done?" Creed's voice has her pulling away just enough to break the kiss.

He's been doing a great fucking job at pissing me off lately. I turn over my shoulder, enough so he can see a hint of my grin. "You think I won't fuck her with you in the room?"

Creed scoffs. "I know you would, but the question is, would you share—"

I'm in his face in an instant. "For that," I whisper, plucking his shirt. "You can watch."

"Legend," Creed warns, his tone dipping to one of warning. "You're going to make it worse."

I don't know what he's talking about and I don't care.

I defy him by grabbing Haide by the throat and forcing her lips back onto mine. Her hesitation vibrates over my palm, but I force her back against the wall without breaking the kiss. Every lick over her tongue, every moan that escapes.

I catch each one.

"Lege—"

"You gonna tell me no?" My forehead rests on hers, our breathing on some fucked-up collaborative pulse. "Hmm? Like you don't want it..."

Her eyes turn to slits, the challenge set. Fingers curl around the back of my neck as her thigh finds a place against my hip. "Okay then, Royal. Fuck me—"

I don't let her finish the sentence. I pick her up from the backs of her thighs, my mouth crushing hers as I lift her body and drop her onto the dresser. Her body is the kind that deserves to be worshipped, but all she's getting from me tonight is being torn apart.

She chuckles, her back arching as I tear off her shirt while yanking her farther into me. I need her every-fucking-where. It's too much. As if the mere thought of not having her beneath me is poison.

Using her hands, she pushes herself up and wraps her legs around my waist, locking me in place. The thought is clear: We're both too desperate for each other to give a fuck about anything else. Her hand's down my jeans, tearing them loose, and when she opens her mouth again, my tongue tingles as a smirk touches my lips and words fail.

Her playful smirk drops to a glare. The fact that Creed's in here is saving her ass from not being made a meal right now. It's only out of pure selfishness and the refusal of gifting my brother a speck of a view.

Still, I reach between her thighs, cupping her warmth. And drop forward to catch her mouth with my teeth. Wet and needy, like I knew she would be.

I drag my tongue across the bottom of her lip, imagining the circles I'd carve over her clit. My chest caves in around me as our breathing becomes deeper. Her hand wraps around my length, using the cushion of her thumb to clean me off before bringing it to her lips.

Falling deeper and deeper, I push myself down and as soon as I feel her wet against me, I fucking lose it. She swallows me with a grip tight enough that I could fucking pass out.

"Fuck," I growl against her throat, teeth scraping skin.

Her nails rake down my back, hard enough to leave marks. Good. I want everyone to know what happened here. Want the evidence carved into my skin.

"Harder," she breathes, and the word shoots straight to my cock. "You know I can take it."

I pull back just enough to see her face. Eyes half-lidded, lips swollen from my mouth, cheeks flushed with want. She's wrecked and we've barely started.

"You sure about that?" I thrust hard, the dresser slamming against the wall. She arches, a broken moan spilling from her lips.

"Is that all you've got, Royal?"

The challenge in her voice makes something feral snap loose in my chest. I grab her hips, fingers digging in hard enough to bruise, and set a rhythm that's all possession and no mercy. Each stroke claims her deeper, marks her as mine from the inside out.

She meets every thrust, demanding more, taking everything I give and still hungry. Her magic sparks against my skin where we're connected, little bolts of power that make my vision blur.

"Creed's still watching," I rasp against her ear, not slowing down. "Want me to stop?"

Her laugh is breathless, wicked. "Let him learn something."

Christ. She's going to kill me.

I shift the angle, hitting that spot that makes her cry out, and her legs tighten around my waist like she's trying to crawl inside my skin. The bond between us fires its approval, satisfied. What I'm not sure she realizes yet, what my brother absolutely *does*, is that each time I take her, the bond strengthens.

She gasps, desperate for me to what—stop?

Like I could stop. Like anything in this fucked-up world could make me stop when she's falling apart in my arms. When every sound she makes rewrites something fundamental in my DNA.

The dresser rocks with each thrust, sending items crashing to the floor, and I don't give a shit about any of it. All that matters is the way she feels around me. The way she says my name like a prayer and a curse rolled into one.

"Legend," she breathes, and the word breaks something open in my chest. "I'm close."

"Good," I growl, fingers wrapping tight around her throat, pressing into the skin with every intention of leaving a pretty little necklace behind. "Come for me. Let him hear you."

Her body goes tight. Magic crackles through the air like lightning, sparking from my palm and burning into the skin of her neck. She shatters around me with a cry that's pure music. The sound of it, the feel of her clenching around my cock, the way her power floods the room—it's enough to drag me over with her.

I bury myself deep and let go, marking her from the inside

while her name falls from my lips like a fucking curse.

When the world stops spinning, she's still wrapped around me, breathing hard against my neck. The room smells like sex, magic, and us.

"Well," Creed says from somewhere behind us, voice thick with amusement. "That was a bad idea."

Something shifts between her and me, whether it's from the bond or not, it's…different. For a fucking moment, I want to reach forward and swallow her whole yet at the same time I need to take her again. That wasn't nearly enough.

Fuck. I need to get rid of fucking Creed. Fuck up her hair enough for this ball.

Her cheeks flush as she tucks her hair behind her ear, and the movement fractures my chest. As if in this moment, I cracked through a smidge of the hard shell she's cemented in place to protect herself. A tiny hint of vulnerability that only I'll ever see.

Fuck. She's never leaving my fucking bed.

Creed gestures to the door. "Vicente is waiting."

Fucking Vicente and his shit timing.

"Go," she tells me. "I have class to get to anyway. Wouldn't want big brother to spank me for being late."

His lip curls. "You wish."

Haide winks and I'm out the door.

Every step away from her feels like tearing muscle from bone. The bond below screams in protest like never before, a physical ache that starts in my chest and spreads like poison through my veins. By the time I reach the corridor, my hands are shaking with the effort of not turning back.

Soon, little mate. I'll be back soon.

Chapter Twenty-Two

Haide

The hallway dims as I leave class, draping me in that creepy darkness the walls of this place love to trap you in. My codex is in hand and my jacket dangles from my satchel instead of on my shoulders where the instructors insist it belongs. It's too stiff, too polished, too *Rathe*. Right now, the only thing I care about is the warm line of blood sliding from the gashes along my forearm, dripping past my wrist like it has somewhere urgent to be.

Warcraft games. I won. Mostly.

The other guy had to be portalled out, so I'm calling that even.

A smirk forms at my lips as I catch a familiar sight.

London LeCroix—or maybe it's Deveraux now—leans against the stone wall, and the sight of her stops me for half a breath before I force my feet to keep moving.

White hair spills down her back, sleek as satin, eyes already flicking black as her Ethos comes to the surface, likely searching for a threat in me.

I saved her ass when I knew nothing about her, the reason she stands here at all, but I get it.

Bros before hos and all that.

She clocks the steady flow of blood running down my arm, her gaze dragging from my face to the mess dripping down my wrist, then back up again. The look she gives me is a sharp mix of frustration, annoyance…and something that feels too much like concern to sit right in my chest.

I hate that it reaches a small, stupid corner of me. I also hate that she's the only person besides Legend who bothers to track me this closely.

"Well, well," I drawl as she pushes off the wall with a lazy grace I will never have. "Look who it is. The newest queen of Rathe. How's it feel to be the only queen in a pile of kings?"

She lifts a brow. "Missed you too, Haids." Her eyes soften—barely—but it's enough to sting my ego. "Got a bad habit of bleeding."

Course she heard about the bullshit from the other day. "Yeah, well at least this time it was fair."

"Come on." She sighs. "Let's go see Silver. Let him fix you up."

"I'm fine." I slide the jacket onto my arm, covering the blood like that solves anything. The warm liquid instantly seeps into the fabric.

London hums, unimpressed. "I'll feed you after."

That earns the smallest twitch at the corner of my mouth. "Lead the way then, your highness."

She laughs once, half-annoyed and half-amused, and we fall into step together, trading light conversation that feels almost... normal. If anything in Rathe could be considered that.

Silver's infirmary is half clinic and half battlefield. He's already bent over someone when we step inside.

London presses closer first, looking over the male.

Her mouth falls open. "What the hell happened to him?"

The gifted glances toward us. Those yellow eyes linger on me; and he smirks like getting disemboweled is flirtation. "Exile girl."

"Lycan boy." I smirk right back, taking in the blood painted across his body like modern art. His clothes are a shredded pile sitting in a pool of blood by his feet. "You look like you got dragged backward through a war."

"Felt like that too." He chuckles. "I'm all fixed up now."

"Shame," I say sweetly. "I was hoping the eye that was hanging out when they carted you off like a baby would become your new jewelry piece. You know, the start of a new fashion trend."

His laugh is deep and unbothered. "We can't all have pretty little stable pieces on our bodies." His gaze lifts pointedly to the jewels embedded in my temples.

I tap one with a finger. "Hey, I was born with mine. Or so I was told."

"Well, just know, you have an open invitation after that performance. You can kick my ass anytime you want."

"You say that like you crave the pain."

"I'm a Lycan, little warrior. My skin was made to tear." He rises from the table, moving toward us, and London hits him with a snap of magic—an invisible command that slams through the air like a leash.

"Down, Stygian," she warns. "This one's temporarily claimed by a royal. Wait your turn."

Temporarily.

The word punches something low in my ribs, sharp and involuntary. I don't like how it feels. I don't like that I feel anything at all.

This place is poison to the heart and mind. I need to do better at remembering as much.

The Lycan lifts his hands and offers a small, respectful bow before silently stepping away. The evidence of his presence vanishes the moment he crosses over the illuminated markings that surround Silver's work table. The floor returns to a polished marble, not a spec of red in sight.

Silver flicks a glance at me, then pats the table. "Hop up, Haide."

I obey, mostly because I was promised food and partially because I like him. He's steady in a way nobody else here is. Like he isn't run by anger or resentment.

"You look a lot better than he did," he says, nodding toward the Lycan sulking near the wall.

I smirk. "That's the thing, doc. You all grew up with hovering bottles and little glass vials that do half the work for you. All I've ever had at the tips of my fingers are sharp nails and endless free time. Oh, and glitter bombs." I flick my fingers around and little trickles of glitter rain down. "Absolutely worthless but fun to blow in people's faces when they're about to kill you for the tenth time."

He chuckles under his breath and pulls my jacket sleeve down.

I swing my legs where I sit on the table, heel knocking lightly against the metal frame. Silver's quiet. Too quiet. When I glance up, a small frown creases the skin between his brows.

"What?"

He doesn't answer. He lifts his hand over my arm, a soft glow blooming beneath his palm, and a shiver runs over my skin as his magic pets me. The dried blood melts away in a ripple of magic, sliding off my skin like ink pulled into water.

And left behind is...nothing.

Just smooth flesh, faint sheen of newness where there should be carnage.

Silver's eyes flick up to mine, and there's something new there—interest, uncertainty, *calculation.*

Behind him, London steps closer, her voice low. "Not even a scar..."

Silver glances her way, jaw tight.

"There were multiple," she murmurs, staring at my arm. "And bone-deep. I wouldn't have bothered to bring her here for anything less."

"Huh," I say, staring at the smooth skin where carnage should be. "Looks like I do the whole self-cauterizing thing now. That's fucking cool."

I expect some form of response. A joke. Or an eye roll. But all she does is stare at my arm like it's a ticking time bomb. Something unreadable flickers across her features.

I shrug, pulling my jacket back on and tapping my nails on my codex. "Maybe Creed was right and I have some power in me after all."

I hop off the table and start toward the door, only to realize London isn't next to me.

She's still by Silver, the two staring at each other with

conflicting expressions.

"Well," I call and she snaps her head toward me like she forgot I existed. I gesture down the hall. "Feed me."

With one last look at Silver, London leads me out of Silver's sanctuary. We walk through the middle of the school, and it's kind of hilarious how everyone dips their heads when she walks by.

The girl's got mad aura, and I don't think it's *only* because she's currently the only queen they've got.

Maybe it's the freaky white hair and the way her eyes flash black when the demon that is literally inside her gets triggered.

I wonder how that works?

Like, does it talk? Is it like a Lycan's beast—a second being inside them who has a mind of its own? Or is it simply an extension of London herself?

She wasn't born with it. According to all the shit I've been reading in my codex from Professor Astra, it's a result of being fated to a Royal. A gift from the gods.

Wait...if it's "fate," then maybe she *was* born with it?

A huff leaves me, and I feel her look at me from the corner of her eye.

I need to have a little chat with that professor. Probably need to bring my knives 'cause every time someone asks about royal bonds, she shuts the conversation down like it's some coveted shit no one else should know about. Lame. And apparently everyone is waiting and hoping to be matched with one of the Deveraux brothers around here, so this shit is like a daily topic at this point.

Not that I think I'm mated to Legend or anything...

Yeah. Okay, Haide.

Fuck.

London leads us to a place called The Cauldron House. It's a creepy, cool place that sits high in the hills behind Rathe U, tucked so deep into the stone and steam that most students don't bother climbing this far unless they're starving or hiding.

Blackwood trees crowd the edges, their branches twisted like they're reaching for the heat that rolls out of the open-air kitchen. The whole place smells like charred herbs and roasted meat and magic—old magic, the kind grown from bone broth and cauldrons that have boiled for decades. Probably gifted bones.

London keeps glancing back at me like she thinks I'm going to cut into the trees and run. It annoys me enough that I dig my boots harder into the incline just so I can pass her at the last second and claim the shadowy table tucked beneath an overhang.

The moment we sit, someone drops a plate piled with meat in front of me. Perfect. I tear into it with my hands because utensils are slow and unnecessary—and because London looks faintly horrified when I do it. Always a plus.

For a while we eat in silence, just the low hum of the cauldron bubbling behind us and the soft scrape of London's fork against her plate. It's almost peaceful.

Then London ruins it.

"So," she says casually, like she's commenting on the weather and not about to stab me sideways. "You're Legend's mate, hm?"

I freeze mid-bite, hand still suspended in the air, grease slicking my fingers. It takes a moment to recover from the sudden question, and I search her face—trying to decide if she's joking, prying, or trying to start a fight. I'll lose if she uses her magic on me, literal demon inside her and all.

"So he says," I manage around the mouthful.

London tilts her head. "But you don't think so."

My jaw works once, swallowing hard.

The thing behind my bones flares like someone dragged claws across the inside of me. It's been doing that more and more lately—every time I see him, or smell him, or hear someone say his name. Even thinking about him lights some stupid ember low in my stomach, a heat I can't control and don't understand.

It just keeps getting worse, a constant tug beneath my ribs that gets more unbearable each time I try to ignore it.

Ugh. Damn it.

I wipe my fingers on the edge of my jacket and lean back. "Bonds are new to me," I say. "On the island, the only people who talked about mates were the ones who'd already lost themselves, claiming they had someone back in Rathe. But no one ever explained more than that, and you don't ask fucked-up people any real questions. They just lie." I suck the sauce off my pointer finger and thumb. "I figured it was…I don't know. Someone you like to fuck. You know, 'mate,' so you basically imprison them."

London's brows shoot up. "Imprison them?"

I shrug one shoulder. "I mean, that's what I would do. You know. Just in case. So no one else could have them."

A small laugh leaves her, soft and almost genuine, but her features tighten again almost immediately.

"Haide," she begins. "Do you feel Legend on the inside? Here?" She watches me closely, tapping two fingers against her sternum.

I feel him everywhere. In my pulse, in my teeth, in the back of my throat. In the way my breath changes when he walks into a room. But I'm also prone to obsession, and that king is good with his hands. And his dick. So…who the hell knows?

I don't answer.

Her eyes narrow with interest, but her expression softens. "When my and Knight's bond first presented," she begins, voice low, "it was instant chaos. Pure destruction. I was drawn to him instantly…and he wanted to ruin me because he felt the same and he hated it." She smiles lightly.

Her gaze drifts out toward the violet fog hanging over the hills, but she keeps talking, words rolling like she's reliving it rather than recounting it.

"It was a pull that never stopped," she says. "A hunger. A certainty. It didn't matter how much we fought, something in me kept dragging me toward him. And him toward me. Like gravity. Like fate had a hand around my throat. I guess it did."

My lungs tighten one slow notch at a time.

Because that's exactly what Legend feels like to me.

Chaos. Pull. Hunger. Certainty.

Even when I don't want it. Especially then.

London goes on. "And the dreams started almost overnight."

That snaps me out of whatever soft, dangerous place I'd slipped into.

"Dreams?" I echo, maybe too fast.

London's eyes lift back to mine, studying every twitch in my face. "Oh, yeah. The dreams are the most important part," she says. "That's how you really know. It's one of the steps in completing the bond."

A cold, heavy dread sinks into my gut like a stone dragged down to the bottom of a deep, dark well. I hate it. I hate it because I don't have dreams, and I loathe it because what the fuck?

It's not like I *want* to be his…fated mate, right?

I don't want to want or need something or someone.

But I do want *Legend and I like the thought that I'm here for a reason. That I'm not just a forsaken child of a damned isle.*

The admission slams into me without permission. So hard I choke on nothing but my own spit.

No. No, no I don't *want* Legend.

I want his dick.

There is most definitely a damn difference.

Right?

Holy shit, maybe I'm a power bank and sex is what fuels whatever powers I may—or may not—have.

I've been having sex with Legend and today, my body healed itself.

I need to fuck him again and maybe then I'll be able to portal!

That would explain everything.

It would explain why he's always on my mind, his scent tickling the tip of my tongue.

His voice in my ear.

Maybe I should find a way to imprison him…just until I'm sick of him or whatever.

London watches me closely, and just as she makes to speak, something buzzes from inside her pocket. She pulls out a small square, lifting it to her ear as she climbs from the branch seats. "Be right back." She wanders a few feet away, keeping her back to me as she faces out the cauldron house window, voice dropping low as she answers.

Flames crackle from the open-air kitchen behind us, mixing with the wind carrying Blackwood spice and steam across the hilltop. I keep eating, tearing through my food with my hands and letting the warmth settle in my chest while London murmurs a string of *hmms* and *okays*.

Then something brushes the inside of my ear.

It's a soft rush, like water being pulled overhead, followed by a low, rolling hush. It fills my skull in a slow, sweeping tide—and then it clears. Like the waves withdraw, taking with them everything the land had held, leaving nothing but smooth sand in its wake.

Only, as it clears, a voice appears in its place.

"Come to me, baby. We're still in the archives room and I'm going fucking insane."

I pause, meat halfway to my mouth.

Knight. His voice cuts straight through my head.

I blink and exhale, nostrils flaring just as he speaks again.

"We've been here for a full moon and still not even a mention of a possessed flower that can kill our kind. The closest we've found is something called the Silkvien. But it says they attack the senses, which doesn't feel right."

"Yeah, there was too much blood for that," London whispers, but she may as well be screaming with how loudly I can hear her inside my head.

"Exactly, and they're solid white, not red with black thorns."

I perk up. Hold up. Possessed flower? Red with black thorns?

My smile is instant.

"Great, so what now?" London mumbles.

"Creed sent for the mage before we found this so she should arrive soon. If this poison has a source, she should know which scripture we'll find answers in."

I scoff, muttering under my breath, "Well, that's a waste of time."

The air around London shifts, her shoulders stiffen. Her

whispered conversation falters as she spins to face me, eyes narrowed.

"What?"

Slowly, she comes toward me again. "Knight?" she calls, but only to get him to answer.

"Mate?"

I roll my eyes and hers narrow further.

"You can hear him." It's not a question.

I lift a shoulder, stuffing a small potato into my mouth. "He speaks loudly."

"No. He doesn't."

"What the hell is going on, mate? Is that Haide? Where are you?"

"Quiet," she tells him, gaze pinned on me. "Haide, what do you mean 'it's a waste of time?'"

I wipe grease from my fingers, still focused on my plate. "I mean your books won't help."

"Explain."

I huff out a breath that would be a laugh if I weren't so tired. "I literally just did. You won't find answers in your little Rathe books."

The frown forming between London's brows is sharp enough to cut. "How do you know this?"

"Because I discovered them."

Her face falls.

"Discovered them...where?" Knight asks after a beat of silence.

I don't know why he asks. His tone says it all.

He already knows.

I meet London's stare without a grin. "On Exile."

Silence buckles among all of us—thick, heavy, a held breath

before a blade drops.

Then another voice snaps through, colder and far more final:

"Bring her here. Now."

Creed.

London straightens, her expression shifting into something clipped and formal—the Queen of Rathe again, not the girl who ate lunch with me a few minutes ago.

I drag my hand through my hair and stand, brushing crumbs from my blood-soaked jacket. "Great," I mutter, stepping past her. "Bossy older brother. My favorite."

London doesn't smile this time. "Haide," she says slowly, "they're going to want every detail and they will make you give it to them."

"Oh, I'm happy to." I lick one last trace of grease from my thumb, smirking as I push ahead. "So long as I get something in return..."

Chapter Twenty-Three

Haide

"Absolutely fucking *not*!" Creed screams like a loud voice means a damn thing to me.

There's a woman on Exile Island who literally lets out bloodcurdling screams every 4 and a half seconds. Every day. All fucking day, as if cursed to never stop. So Creed yelling? Yeah.

Not impressive.

I shrug. "Then I'm not telling you shit."

The reaction is immediate. He steps into my space so fast the air gets shoved aside, his palm braced on the stone beside my head as he cages me in. His lips peel back in that regal snarl he favors, eyes whitening at the edges as his gifts rise, sharp and bright.

"You will do as you're told, little girl," he grinds out, voice so low it almost vibrates against my skin, "or I will make you."

I let my gaze drag lazily over his expression, over the rigid line of his jaw, over the fury coiled behind his teeth.

"You can try," I murmur, my voice rolling slow and warm, because I know it irritates him more than shouting ever could. "But before you start fantasizing about your big intimidating moment, maybe remember who you're talking to. I've lived through torture since the day I was born, oh mighty king man. There isn't a single thing you could dream up that hasn't already been done to me twice over."

His nostrils flare. Knight shifts a step behind him, tension rolling off him like storm air before lightning hits. London looks caught between yanking us apart and stepping back so she doesn't get hit by shrapnel if we start breaking things.

I uncross and recross my arms, tapping one finger against my elbow. "Where's Legend? Because I'm not talking to you."

Creed presses forward, speaking low. "I can see right through you, you know. I will not allow this to continue. You are *done* manipulating my brother. Those pretty little claws you've got sunk into his flesh? I'm going to cut them at the knuckle."

White-hot anger flashes through me at an alarming rate, his words detonating inside me in a way that feels like a direct threat to my life.

Shut him up.

Gut him.

End him.

Those words whirl through my mind, and heat burns at my fingertips, my limbs shaking.

It's a bit of an irrational response, but it's strong.

Just as my conscience decides to listen to the foreign whispers in my mind, Knight's words reach through the noise, and I tense.

"Speak of the devil," he mumbles like he's bored.

My brows furrow and I follow his gaze toward the door.

Legend strides toward us like he owns each bit of space between his steps, shoulders loose, expression cut from the same cool arrogance he wears like a weapon.

But something is wrong.

He closes the distance, stopping in front of me, close enough that the room tilts a little with how solid he stands. His shadow falls over mine the same way it always does, swallowing the light between us, but it's like stepping toward a fire only to find the heat missing.

"Hello, little monster," he purrs, but it doesn't feel like a basilisk's tongue tasting my spine like I've gotten used to.

I narrow my eyes the tiniest bit. "What's wrong with you?"

His head tilts, a faint rise in one brow, and a ghost of amusement curves his mouth. "I haven't touched you in too long, that's all," he says softly. "Come here," he says, even though he is already right in front of me.

My eyes narrow further.

He reaches out, thumb tracing the edge of my mouth in a slow, claiming sweep. He leans closer, breath touching my cheek. "You feel that?" he whispers. "Our bond is starved, mate. I need you."

His mouth dips toward mine, slow and deliberate, as if expecting me to break open with longing.

And I let him.

I tilt my face up, letting him close the last inch, letting my lips brush his, soft at first. A sigh slips from me despite the simmer under my skin that has nothing to do with desire and everything to do with the violence humming quietly in my blood. I can almost taste his surprise when I press a little closer, as if I'm giving in, as if I'm falling for it.

Then he stills.

A sudden, jarring stillness, like every part of him just froze mid-step.

His eyes open slowly in a flicker of disbelief, then widen with recognition, but it's the faint shiver that betrays him.

He looks down.

I follow his gaze.

A knife hangs in the air between us—my knife—hovering at his throat, the tip pressed just enough to break skin. A bead of crimson gathers, then slides down the sharp line of his neck.

Except…I didn't call it.

I didn't reach for it.

I didn't even think the command.

My eyes shoot wide and the blade drops, metal clattering sharply against the stone floor.

And the face in front of me—Legend's face—begins to melt.

It ripples like heated glass, dissolving, as bones rearrange under skin.

In the blink of an eye, Sinner stands before me, wearing a grin that is all teeth and wicked.

"Well," he drawls, wiping the streak of blood from his throat with two fingers, his tongue flicking across them leisurely. "Someone has a little magic in her after all."

He studies me slowly, cataloging every twitch of shock I haven't recovered from yet.

He leans in just enough that I feel the heat of him at my jaw. "Good girl," he murmurs, voice like silk wrapped around something sharp. "Can't wait to find out what else you're hiding, you little liar."

I open my mouth to respond—something sharp, something that will definitely earn me a threat or twelve—but the air behind him shifts.

A pull. Low. Hot.

Irritatingly familiar.

My chest tightens and loosens all at once, like invisible fingers just curled around the inside of my ribs and dragged. My eyes are lifting before I can stop them.

And there's *my* Legend.

The thought slams into me, rogue and stupid and completely uninvited, and I want to claw it out of my own skull. But it still blooms behind my ribs, warm and reckless.

Son of a bitch, I think he is mine.

But is he my favorite toy or my…fated mate?

Legend strides into the room. His hair is a mess, his jaw shadowed with exhaustion, darkness bruising the skin beneath his eyes like he hasn't slept in a century. He looks dangerous in that lazy, lethal way only he can manage. Like he just rolled out of bed and murdered someone on the way over.

His gaze scans the room once, landing on the expressions of his brothers, then snapping to me.

"Why does everyone look like they just saw our mother?" he asks, voice low, roughened, dragging over my nerves like smoke.

He doesn't break stride. He hooks two fingers into the front of my jacket and tugs, pulling me into the line of his body. His scent puts a thorn through whatever argument I had been piecing together.

London exhales sharply, stepping toward us. "Haide is… developing," she says, flicking a glance at her brothers. "Her senses sharpened and she reacted to a perceived threat. A knife appeared at Sinner's throat."

"Wow, London. If I didn't know any better, I'd say you were being a snitch right now."

"It's not personal, Haide." She shakes her head, and her tone tells me she's not having fun, but it is what it is. "They're my family now."

Family.

The word sends a sharp ache through my chest, but I push it down.

To want is to lose. Stop forgetting that.

"We sure developing is the right word?" Sinner raises a brow. "Seemed pretty effortless to me."

Legend's arm goes instantly rigid around me. His muscles coil beneath my palms as he shifts me partially behind him in one smooth motion, barricading me.

It's…hot, his show of possessiveness.

Insanely hot.

And also dramatically unnecessary.

"What did you do?" Legend demands.

"I might have played a little game," Sinner drawls.

Legend's jaw flexes but doesn't even turn his head. "You lost." Legend's words are a statement, not a question. His certainty warms a part of me that I try to ignore.

"I did," Sinner acknowledges without shame. "Not entirely, though. Now we know she's got more skill than she pretends."

I snort. "If I could call a knife without meaning to, you'd have figured it out by now. I probably would've sliced Creed into pretty little pieces ages ago."

Creed surges forward, eyes flashing. "This isn't a fucking joke, you lying, siphoning little bit—"

Legend starts to growl but Knight steps between the two,

cutting Creed off with a single, razor-edged look.

"We can deal with this shit later. Let's not forget why we're here." His attention snaps to me, steady and unblinking. "Talk, wannabe demon," Knight says, voice a quiet command, not to be argued with. "Tell us about the black-thorned flower."

"It's called the Isle's Kiss."

London pulls herself up onto the bar top, crossing one leg over the other. "You said you discovered it on the island. How?"

"How does anyone discover anything? I found it when I was walking through the old caverns."

Creed crosses his arms. "And?"

"And went to find the witch."

"What witch?"

"I don't know, royal. We just call her *the witch* because she is "the witch." She's like the eyes and ears of the island. If I missed something, she saw it. If something was lost, she found it. If there was something you needed to know, she had the answers. Sure, you had to solve stupid riddles to figure them out but still. Answers."

Knight and Creed share a look while Legend's fingers dig into my hips, his free hand coming up, knuckles pressing beneath my chin. Our eyes meet and he smirks.

"We need to know what you know, my little monster. What did they deny you?" His long fingers wrap around my throat, squeezing slightly.

The second his fingers tighten, something inside me kicks awake—hot, reckless, a creature digging its hooks into my ribs as if it's been waiting for him. I press into his palm and his pupils flare.

"I'll give you what you want, baby. Always." Those blue eyes are on fire, and it spreads through me. "I don't give a fuck what you ask for, it's yours. So tell them, if only to get your way."

My way?

If I had it my way, I'd be impaling myself on his cock right now 'cause fuck *me*. No literally, fuck me.

Please.

Legend's smirk is knowing, his chuckle sending a shiver down my spine. "Let me give you what you want." He leans closer, whispering in my ear. "*Both* the things you want."

"I want to help find your murderer."

Legend's features shift fast. His smirk is swiped away, a deep-rooted glare in its place.

Sinner chuckles somewhere in the room. "Changed your tune real quick there, brother."

"Mind your fucking business." Legend's jaw ticks, his eyes locked on mine. "Fine. I'll take you."

"The hell you will."

"Absolutely fucking not."

"Fool."

Knight. Creed. Sinner. Their responses pop off at once and I couldn't hold in my smile if I tried.

London sighs, sliding off the counter with all the grace of someone who's used to cleaning up Deveraux disasters. "You're all wasting time," she says, dusting her hands. "If Haide has information, then we move. Now."

Creed snaps his glare to her. "She's unstable."

"So are you," London fires back. "Difference is she's actually useful right now."

"Yes. Because she is the only common denominator here. Everything that is happening started when *she* came back," he argues. "Just look at Legend! She's sucking the life out of him!"

Wait, what?

My head yanks toward the man in question, but he only shakes his head, exhaustion written all over him.

"Legend?"

"Enough." Knight's fingers drum once against the table before he pushes to his feet, voice dropping into that cold, decisive authority that ends arguments. "We take her to the scene, let her look around. If her information is useful, she can help. If not—"

Legend growls, low and lethal. "Finish that sentence, and we'll have another body to investigate."

Legend's growl hangs in the air like a threat, venomous and absolutely meant, and his family must know it. Not one says a word, just staring at him with varying expressions.

"We leave in five," Legend informs, leaving no room for argument.

Sinner rolls his shoulders like he's bored, but his eyes flick once to the blood on his fingers, then to me. I can practically hear the thoughts he doesn't say out loud. Creed's stare stays on Legend. It's easy to see he is pealing past his damn skull and into his mind—or trying to at least, can't say for sure.

London mutters something about getting supplies and disappears before anyone can drag her into the next argument.

Just like that, the room fractures into motion.

Everyone has somewhere to go, something to do, or a role to play. For a second, I'm standing there with my codex tucked under my arm and my pulse still thrumming from the knife that appeared without my permission. And the way Legend looked at me like I'm both a weapon and a treasure.

Then his hand finds my wrist. He doesn't say a word as he pulls me through the corridor that leads away from the room. The second a new door shuts behind us, the silence swells, thick and private, and it does something strange to my ribs.

Legend stops, his hand going to his face.

He doesn't turn me toward him right away, just stands there for a moment with his head angled slightly down. His shoulders rise and fall with a single deep breath.

When he finally looks at me, there's still that familiar lazy dominance. That infuriating calm he wears like armor—but this time there's a crack in it, thin as a razor's edge, and it shows what sits underneath.

Concern.

Real, raw, vicious *concern.* Unease settles beneath my breastbone

"I don't want to do this," he says, voice quiet enough that I almost think he didn't mean to say it, but then he continues. "Take you toward potential danger."

I huff a laugh, head shaking. "You don't get to decide what I can handle."

"I know." His eyes drag over my face. "That's not what I'm saying."

The playful arrogance he lives in seems to have evaporated completely.

"What are you saying, then?" I ask, because I can feel the argument sharpening on my tongue, but there's something else there, too. It's a strange sensation, almost like an itch in my mind needing to be soothed.

I don't like it. Mostly because where I come from, voices in your head are a very *bad* thing. I open my mouth to argue, but Legend's thumb rises and presses gently to my lower lip.

It's a command to shut the fuck up. Without the cruelty, sure, but a command nonetheless.

"Quiet," he murmurs, and the word should make me

bristle...but it doesn't. It settles over me like a hand on the back of my neck, steadying. "You're still getting your way. I'd give you anything you could ever want and more, and you know it. Even if you deny it, you know."

My mouth parts on instinct—half to argue, half because his thumb is warm and my nerves are traitors—and his gaze drops to it like he feels every millimeter of surrender.

"But this is a risk," he continues, "and I don't know how to accept that when it comes to you."

The words settle into my bones like a stone dropped into dark water.

A risk, as if I matter. As if I'm not just some Exile stray they dragged into their realm to interrogate and contain, but something he's trying to... keep.

As if all he's been saying this whole time is true.

That I'm his.

I swallow, my throat tight. My gaze drifts away for one stupid second because it's easier to stare at the wall than the way he's looking at me.

He doesn't let me ignore him, though. Because this is *Legend,* and Legend can never be ignored.

His other hand slides to my jaw, tilting my face back without force but with certainty, like he knows I'll comply even if I don't understand why.

I hate that my breath catches. I hate the warmth spreading under my skin. I hate the way my body seems to recognize him before my mind can decide what to do with it.

"You're spinning out," he says, almost amused, almost *gentle*.

"I don't do gentle," I mutter.

"No," he agrees softly. "You don't."

His thumb shifts, dragging along my lip again, and something in me pulses—hot, reckless, familiar in the way it shouldn't be. Like a thing inside my chest perks up and leans toward him, hungry and pleased to be noticed.

My eyes lower to his hand before I can stop myself, to the thumb still there, and that small patch of skin that made my thoughts scatter like frightened prey.

A stupid impulse rises, something that feels like curiosity wearing a crown, so I give in just enough to prove to myself I'm still in control.

I lean forward and press my lips to his thumb in a small kiss. It's barely a touch and should feel like nothing, but it feels like *everything.*

Legend goes still, his throat working, and the satisfaction that flickers in his eyes makes my stomach dip.

I do it again, only slower this time, more deliberate. I let my mouth linger, my lips softening around the edge of him as if I'm tasting the boundary of what I'm allowed to want. Before I can think too hard, I suck his thumb into my mouth, tongue swirling and bursting at the taste of this man.

I give him a good nip.

A warning bite.

A promise?

Legend's breath punches out of him in a low, rough sound. His head dips as if he's fighting the urge to drag me closer and devour me the way I know he wants to.

"Haide," he rasps, and it isn't a reprimand. It's a plea with teeth.

There's a dangerous kind of delight flickering in me because, for once, I'm the one holding the reins.

"For someone so concerned about danger," I murmur, voice

soft and wicked, "you make it really hard to listen."

His eyes flare white at the edges, like his power is answering mine without permission. His thumb slips free from my lips as his hand slides down to my throat, not squeezing or threatening, but holding. Claiming and possessive in a way that makes my skin hum.

"Later," he says, and there's a hard edge to it now, a restraint that looks painful. "When we return, I'll give you whatever you want."

I should scoff.

I should tell him I don't want anything.

Instead, the words drag themselves out of me, breathy and honest before I can stab them. "I'm going to hold you to that."

He locks on my mouth like he's memorizing it before he sighs and steps back. "Come on. Let's wait for them in the courtyard. They should be ready soon."

With that we head out, a nervous excitement swimming through my veins.

Because if what they've described really is Isles royals' Kiss, these royals have a lot bigger problems than little old me on their hands.

I just have to figure out what it is and what it means.

The only thing coming to mind?

Not fucking good.

Chapter Twenty-Four

Legend

She's under the oak like a weapon someone dropped and forgot about. My brothers are taking a lot longer than the five fucking minute countdown I gave them.

I think it's messing with her mind.

I stop at the field's edge, watching her rip grass from the earth in violent little fistfuls. Each blade she destroys makes my chest tighten—not because I give a fuck about the landscaping, but because she's this close to detonating and I'm not the target.

That bothers me more than it should.

Her head snaps up, those green eyes finding me through thirty yards of space like she can smell my thoughts. The hostility in her face shifts to something worse—resignation.

Like she's too exhausted to fight me right now.

Good. I'm too exhausted to fight her either.

I cross the field and drop beside her without invitation, my shoulder brushing hers as I stretch out on the grass. She doesn't move away. Doesn't move closer either, but the fact that she's not currently trying to stab me counts as progress. Maybe, for once, our little conversation from a few minutes ago will actually hold after the moment ended.

"Don't let Creed get to you." The words come out before I can stop them.

"Why? Because you're the only one allowed to fuck with my head?"

"Because he doesn't understand you."

"And you do?"

"No." I turn my head to look at her profile—sharp jaw, sharper tongue, sharpest edges I've ever wanted to cut myself on. "But I'm trying to."

Something in her face cracks. Not much, just a hairline fracture in all that armor, but then—fuck me—she smiles. Not her usual smile that promises violence and tastes like blood. This one's soft. *Real*. Small enough that if I blinked I'd miss it.

It destroys me.

The smile vanishes as fast as it came, but the damage is done. My ribs feel too small for what's expanding in my chest—this vicious, consuming need to stand between her and anything that might dim that expression. To hunt down whatever made her learn to hide softness like a fucking shame.

She's a pain in the ass in the best and worst ways, giving me a little and taking it back. Only to give a little more the next time. She's creaking, and each time she does, that gap fills with a little more of me.

I want her to break open until half of me makes up the other half of her.

"What?" She's studying me now, and I realize I've been staring.

"Nothing." It's anything but nothing.

"Bullshit. You look like someone just told you your favorite torture device got discontinued."

"Maybe they did." I reach over and pluck a blade of grass from her hair. She goes still, not even breathing as my fingers brush her temple. "Maybe you're it."

"Your favorite torture device?" She lifts one perfect brow.

I shrug. "The only one that works anymore."

She turns to face me fully, and we're close enough that I can see the color of nature in all that green. "That's either the worst pickup line I've ever heard, or you're having a stroke."

"Can't it be both?"

Another smile threatens the corner of her mouth. "You're genuinely disturbed, you know that?"

"Says the girl who killed someone with their own finger last week," I tease.

"Allegedly."

"We all saw it, didn't we?" Because she didn't necessarily hide it.

She holds my eyes. "Prove it."

This. This is what makes her, her. The way she can discuss murder like foreplay, violence like vocabulary, and still somehow make me want to burn down the world just to see her laugh. Not smile—laugh.

"You're thinking too loud," she says, lying back on the grass beside me. Our arms touch from shoulder to elbow, and neither of us moves away.

"You're not thinking loud enough," I whisper, annoyed with how tight my throat feels.

"Trust me, Royal, you don't want to know what I'm thinking right now."

I prop myself up on one elbow, looking down at her. "Try me."

She meets my eyes, and for one second, all her walls drop. What I see there—the exhaustion, the loneliness, the rage that mirrors mine so perfectly it hurts—makes me want to kill everyone who's ever made her feel less than fucking extraordinary. Because that's what she is, and not even the fucking Four Horsemen of the Apocalypse could take her from me.

"I'm thinking," she says slowly, "that your brothers are right about me."

"My brothers are idiots."

She sighs. "They're trying to protect you."

"I don't need protection." I lean closer until I can feel her breath on my face. "Especially not from you."

"You should." Her hand comes up, fingers tracing the edge of my jaw with surprising gentleness. "I ruin everything I touch."

"Perfect." I catch her wrist, pressing her palm flat against my chest where my heart is trying to punch through bone. "I'm already ruined."

She laughs and I swear my fucking heart flatlines. Why can't shit be simple? She feels like home. No, that isn't right. She feels like coming home to your house on fire, but being fine with living in the debris because having her in little, fucked-up pieces is better than not having her at all.

"You're completely fucked-up," she says, but her fingers curl into my shirt, holding on.

"So are you." My lips brush hers, because if I don't feel her on me I'm gonna kill something.

So what if your mate is more like mutual destruction?

The need to protect her hasn't lessened. If anything, it's grown a taste for blood. But now I understand it better.

I don't want to protect her from everything.

I want to protect her right to destroy it whenever she wants to.

"Legend?" Her voice is smaller than I've ever heard it.

"Yeah?"

"Your brothers are going to try to separate us."

"Let them try." I lower myself back down, pulling her against my side. She doesn't resist, just fits herself into the space like she was carved for it. "I'll kill them all before I let them take you."

"You don't mean that."

"Want to bet?"

She's quiet for a long moment, then, "I'm a little scared."

I freeze on her words.

She continues. "Of what I might become with you."

"And what's that?"

"Worse than I am now."

The smile I give her probably looks like a threat to anyone watching. Good. Let them watch. Let them see what happens when you give a monster his favorite snack.

She kisses me, and it's nothing like the violence we trade in daylight. Her mouth is soft, searching, and I let her take what she wants even as my hand finds the back of her neck, fingers threading through her hair. She tastes like a battlefield, and when her tongue slides against mine, my grip tightens.

She makes a sound—fuck, a tiny broken sound—and I

swallow it whole, pulling her closer until there's no space left between us.

My other hand spans her waist, feeling the way her breathing hitches when I angle her head back, when I take control of what she started.

When she pulls back, we're both breathing hard through swollen lips.

"Your brothers are right about one thing," she says against my mouth with a smirk, and I feel the words more than hear them.

"What's that?"

"I'm going to destroy you."

I grin. "Can't wait."

• • •

Haide

He's ridiculous and completely serious. His next words prove it when he reaches out, his knuckles gliding along the slope of my breast.

"Fuck the little flower quest," he purrs. "Let's stay here instead," he purrs, pressing closer.

"Don't push your luck," I whisper, but my voice is already betraying me.

"Worth a shot." He smiles, slow and pleased. Two fingers press lightly over my sternum, where that strange pull always seems to live when he's near and where my body reacts in ways my mind doesn't understand.

"Are you mine, monster?" he asks, voice low and gravelly.

"Can you feel me here?"

My breath catches hard at his question. They're words I've heard from him before, asked or said in different ways, but still familiar from his lips.

This time, though, anxiety curls through me, tight and bright.

Excitement.

Fear.

Hope, which is the most disgusting of all.

Because the answer is complicated, and I don't have language for it. Admitting anything feels like handing someone a blade and turning my back. Never in my life would I have ever thought such a thing would sound appealing, yet my fingers twitch to do just that. To take the blade from my sheath and place it in his palm, if only to see what he'd really do.

To prove to myself what I already know?

I swallow.

I don't answer, but step in to him instead.

I rise on my toes and kiss him. Not the rough kind of kiss that I now see as *ours,* that dirty, frantic territorial kind of kiss that tastes like violence and hunger. I've become obsessed with the way his lips devour mine. Maybe even obsessed, but this… shit.

He's kissed me like I was breakable before. Once. But only a fool would pretend that this one right here isn't something brand fucking new.

It is.

It's a kiss I've never given anyone because I didn't know I could and I never had the urge to.

Legend makes a sound that vibrates into my mouth, and his hands find me like they've been searching for permission—

one sliding to my waist, the other cupping the back of my head, holding me with a careful reverence that makes my throat ache.

Like he's terrified of breaking me.

Like he's more terrified of losing me.

My fingers curl into his shirt, pulling him closer, and the heat between us rises fast, thickening the air, turning the space into something private and dangerous. Legend deepens the kiss with slow patience and time we don't have, like he's trying to brand the moment into both of us before the world drags us back into blood, questions, and death.

When he finally pulls back, his forehead presses to mine.

His breath is warm against my lips.

His voice is rough.

"There," he murmurs. "That. That's why I don't know how to accept the risk."

My chest tightens, and I hate the softness clawing its way up my spine.

I try to cover it with sharpness. "You're dramatic."

"I'm honest," he corrects, and his mouth brushes mine again, quick and controlled, a promise clipped short by restraint. "And you're walking into something that I don't know how to control. What if it reaches for you?"

My jaw ticks. "Let it reach."

His grip on me tightens just slightly. "If you get hurt," he says, quieter now, more lethal, "I will turn Rathe inside out."

I should tell him I don't need saving, remind him who I am, and what I survived. But the truth is, the idea of him being that furious on my behalf does something wicked to me. It makes me feel...chosen.

And that is its own kind of danger, because to want is to lose.

Maybe, for once, it doesn't have to be?

I don't know the answer, but it's as if something inside me does.

I give him a small, infuriating smirk. "Then don't let me get hurt."

Legend's mouth curves, fierce and satisfied, and for a second I see the possibility of *us*. How ridiculous it is that I can stand here and let him touch me without immediately reaching for a blade.

Legend kisses my forehead and steps back with clear reluctance.

"After," he repeats, eyes burning.

"After," I agree again, and the way his pupils flare tells me he's filing that word away like a vow.

Then he turns, and the moment shifts.

The noise of his family floods in the second he opens the door. I follow him inside with my chin high, heart racing, and that single word still lodged in my mouth like a promise.

After.

Chapter Twenty-Five

Haide

Knight looks across his family, slowly settling his attention on me. "Let's move."

Legend doesn't waste a second. His arm snakes around my waist and he pulls me with him like the decision was already made the moment I opened my mouth and asked for this, making that wild thing in my chest burrow deeper.

"Come on, little monster," he mutters against my temple, voice a dark promise. "Show us what the Exile taught you."

I grin, sharp and pleased. "Oh, I will." I glance over my shoulder to see Creed still standing there with his arms crossed, eyes cutting straight through me. "Try to keep up, Royal."

He bristles.

Good.

"Open the gates, Legend." Creed orders.

But nothing happens.

Legend frowns at the space in front of him, his hand pushing out, but his limbs start to shake. Unease slips into my bones. He evades my attempts at catching his gaze as he runs his fingers through his dark hair. Slowly, his head swivels to Sinner.

A silent conversation takes place between them before Sinner *tsks* and waves his hand.

A tear in the air rips open as a portal appears, Rathe humming behind it. Lightning sparks not in warning, but in welcome. The realm instantly recognizes the blood of its Kings—and Queen. Singular.

Knight and London step through first, followed by the rest of us, and the portal closes the moment Creed's feet hit the soil.

The scent shifts—metallic smoke, iron-rich air, magic old enough to bite in an intoxicating way. My skin prickles, every instinct purring like it finally has room to breathe again after being suffocated in the mortal world.

Weird, considering my entire life was spent on an island that is literally located on Earth. Here, in the real realm of Rathe, everything is wild.

The air itself thickens, heavies, leaving no question or uncertainty—but making it undeniably clear that these lands are wild and you are at their will.

It's untamed.

Unmatched.

"What do you know of the weapon? How does it work?" Knight pushes without meeting my gaze, his eyes focused and scanning for a threat in the distance, just like his brothers.

"You were right before," I tell him. "Isle's Kiss doesn't

attack the senses. It eats the soul."

Everyone jerks their heads my way.

"You're sure?" Legend asks, a curiosity in his gaze rather than the acidic looks I'm getting from his brothers that say they think I'm full of shit.

"As sure as Creed is an asshole." Creed scoffs, but I press on. "On the isle, some called it the island's gift. The one and only mercy it gave the discarded."

"Mercy?" London peers at me.

"Yep." I nod, climbing the hillside and turning toward the sound of howling coming from the forest surrounding us. "The island is intended to torture. It's a free-for-all of chaos; and my people don't hate that. They crave it, but sometimes even the damned get tired and when they do...Isle's Kiss is the answer. It kills slowly. Painfully. It's the only way of death on the island that leaves you dead long enough for them to rest."

"What do you mean?" London asks. "Is it a false death?"

I shake my head. "Everything is a false death on the island, remember? You die; you come back. And eventually, you die again. Wash, rinse, repeat. Day after day, year after year."

Creed glares. "No one here will pity you, so stop trying."

I roll my eyes. "Oh, fuck off."

A low wind sweeps up the ridge, dragging a coil of gray fog with it, thick enough that it swallows my boots halfway to my knees. Something pale juts through the mist a few strides ahead—long, curved, too smooth to be stone. Bone. Lots of it. A whole stretch of the hillside littered with half-buried remains, some small, some the size of overturned canoes, but all pointed downhill like they crawled here to die.

"Where are we going?"

"Keep walking and keep talking," Creed demands. "How

does it work?"

I fight a smirk and nod. "It's not poison, or maybe it is, essentially, but its very soil is cursed. The seed grows of that curse, and the flowers grow of those seeds. Basically it enters the system and eats the gifted from the inside out."

"Eats?" Sinner grins, hands in his pockets.

"It doesn't just kill," I nod, stepping over a jagged chunk of bone half sunk in the hillside. "It eats. Slow. Methodical. First it slips into the veins, threads itself through every pathway it finds, like it's mapping you. Then it starts digging deeper, past the blood, past the marrow. It goes after whatever makes you… you." I tap my sternum once. "Your spark. Your core. Aka…"

"Your soul," Legend completes, reaching out and pushing my hair from my face as he continues to walk beside me.

"Exactly."

"Soul-eating is a fairy tale, even for the gifted." Knight frowns. "There is no such thing. If there were, if *anyone* knew about it, it would be us. Not some outsider."

An outsider who saved your sorry ass once upon a time.

"Why, because you're big bad royals?" I look across them. "I'd bet there is a lot more out there than your little golden crested realm shows you. You're *gifted.* Royals, at that. You have powers, and a being that lives inside you. The possibilities are likely endless. For you more than any… But you're closed off because you sit on your pretty velvet chairs and boss people around. So how could you possibly learn more, *become* more, if you just keep doing the same shit the Kings before you did?"

"Our father was a great king," Sinner snaps.

"I'm sure he was, but I wouldn't know, now, would I?"

Creed glares, but his head jerks toward Legend when he starts to stagger.

My arms shoot out to steady him, but Sinner gets there first.

Legend's eyes close and he accepts his brother's offered shoulder, pulling in a long breath.

"What the fuck is wrong with you?" Sinner beats me to the question.

Legend just shakes his head, a low, brittle laugh leaving him as he pushes off and shuffles to his own two feet again. "Nothing. I'm fine." His ocean blue eyes find mine and he offers a small smile. "Keep going, monster."

My eyes narrow but he tips his chin at me. "Isle's Kiss," he presses.

Right.

"Once the 'poison' finds what it's looking for, it starts pulling." I drag my fingers through the air, mimicking the motion. "One vein at a time, like it's unraveling you from the inside out. You don't notice at first—just a heaviness in your limbs, a little heat under the skin. But then it's like a pack of wolves are born inside you and they're gnawing and clawing their way out. Your veins are ripped open on the inside and the blood starts leaking. First from the nose, then the eyes, then the mouth. Eventually, it pushes out everything it can reach. Even between the legs." I smirk. "Not pretty. But satisfying to watch."

All but Legend stare at me like I've sprouted a second head.

"What?" I shrug. "People killed me every day for sport. You get bored. You pick favorites. And when Isle's Kiss took root in someone, it dragged on for hours. Plenty of time to watch them scream."

Creed's jaw locks. "How do you fight against it?"

"You run as fast as you fucking can and hope it didn't already wrap its thorns around your heart. Because if it did…

it's lights out."

He keeps running his mouth. "If it can be created, it can be destroyed."

"Of course it can. The island's enemy is its counterpart." When they don't guess, I give them the answer. "Fire." I push forward, and their footsteps follow.

I almost trip on a root reaching out of the ground but catch myself before anyone sees.

"Why wouldn't you just open one of your fancy portals here again?" I complain, stepping away from the living tree, shaking what looks like soot from my fingers. "You dragged me halfway across your little kingdom this morning. Seems like a waste of legs."

Legend's laugh is low and amused, and before I can dodge, he nips the top of my shoulder, his teeth greedy. Heat flares across my skin and I've got the sudden urge to tell him to *bite*.

I want to feel his teeth sink into my flesh, I want him to claim me and—

Shit. This thing between us. It has a fucking heartbeat.

"We walk because..." he murmurs against my ear as his hands slide to my hips, lifting me over the shimmering sludge like I weigh nothing. "Portals disturb here. Their young are among these lands, and their mothers are very, very protective. A portal has a certain scent marker, and it smells like a threat to them. If you walk their lands, letting them scent you, they trust in your intent. If you pop in, what is to stop you from taking their little ones and popping out?" Another nip. "Assuming you can escape before they get to you. And if they see you as a threat anyway, well...it's bone to ash, baby."

"That's comforting," I mutter as my feet touch solid ground again.

He smirks down at me, hugging me to him before stepping away.

"Fool," Creed grumbles behind us.

"Jealous?" Legend fires back.

"Disgusted."

"Same thing, brother."

Knight glares. "Focus."

Right. Flowers. Murder. *Death.*

I turn toward the scorched rock face ahead. The wind shifts, carrying a faint metallic sweetness I remember too vividly—the scent that drifted through the caverns on Exile, clinging to my hair, my clothes, my nightmares.

"Dragons?" I guess, voice low as a rush of something I can't name washes over me.

"Dragons." Legend confirms. "Welcome to the Darkadia, home of the dragons."

"Maybe we can say hi to Benny boy while we're here." Sinner jokes, and London slams him with a wave of magic, knocking him to his feet with a laugh.

"Leave my best friend alone," she pouts. "He's adapting."

My feet carry me up the final hillside even faster, excitement coursing through my veins.

A few more miles and then I see it. My lungs open up as a sense of calm washes over me.

I've never seen this side of Rathe before, having only entered near the royal estate, and the sight before me is…wow.

Darkadia is like nothing I've seen before yet somehow feels familiar.

Black cliffs jut up like broken fangs, steam curling from the cracks where the underground fires breathe. The sky itself feels different here—darker, sharper, threaded with old magic that doesn't exist on Earth's polite little campus.

And gods help me…it feels like home.

A weird comfort crawls up my spine, settling behind my ribs like it recognizes the chaos in the landscape. Strange, because this is the place where they claim they saw the Isle's Kiss.

Even fucking weirder, because the flowers shouldn't exist here at all.

My boot sinks into something soft and warm.

I look down.

A slick, iridescent film coats the ground, the colors shifting like oil in water—greens bleeding into glittery violets, violets twisting to black. It pulses once beneath my heel, like it's breathing. Like it's…reaching for me.

"What the hell is this?" I mutter.

Knight stops beside me. "Evidence, and you're ruining it."

London comes around, studying the puddle at my feet. "Vicente froze the residual magical so we can try to track its source."

"She doesn't need to know all the details," Creed snips. "Not when she has given us crumbs of information and still gotten her way."

I think I'll start calling him crybaby Creed because *damn.*

Legend's fingers brush my palms, sending a spark through my fingertips.

"Lift your foot and hold it still until the magic falls," he tells me.

I follow his instructions, only the magic doesn't fall. It wraps around my boots, seeping beyond the material until I'm staring at nothing but smooth, black leather. My head snaps up to his but he's facing forward, so I just stretch past the puddle.

I take another step and nearly slide, planting my hand

against a charred tree trunk to catch myself. The bark shivers beneath my palm, shedding sparks of blue flame.

I jerk back. "Okay, that's new."

"It's threatening you." Sinner whistles behind me. "Don't touch anything in the Dragon Lands unless you want an arm ripped off."

"Dragons love me," I say, inspecting my hand further because it didn't feel like it came from the threat of the tree. That I also felt...but the flame, it felt like the warning I tossed back.

"These ones won't." Sinner seems so certain that determination burns hotter than the flame still warming my hand.

Bet.

I walk a little faster, and the others push ahead of me.

The path narrows, funneling us between two slabs of jagged stones. A low rumble shivers through the ground, faint at first, then pulsing again as we push deeper. The smell shifts, too, less forest and more rot. So thick it sinks into your tongue and coats the back of your teeth.

Knight lifts a hand, signaling for us to move in a tighter formation, and the others press ahead, bodies angled like they're bracing for something. I slow instead, letting my fingers trail over the stone. It's warm and slick in places, like the rock is sweating.

Makes sense, being in the Dragon Lands. They breathe fire, after all.

"So how many bodies were found here?" I ask.

"You tell us," Creed mumbles.

Sinner chuckles, but I roll my eyes.

"These were found the day after your roommate," Creed answers reluctantly. "Two Ordinaries, Stygian born, and both part of the young ordered to report to Rathe. They didn't listen."

Sinner shrugs. "So it's almost like someone did us a favor, cause we would have had to punish them anyway."

Creed scowls. "Shut up, Sinner. An authorized murder of our people is an act of disrespect. They test us. *Question* us."

"Or maybe they're just fucked-up and like to kill people." I shrug. "It's honestly kind of fun to try new ways to slaughter and see what works faster."

Again, several narrowed sets of eyes lock on me. "Don't judge! It was a sport at home. Like, we held actual competitions and shit." I grin, pushing my hair over my shoulder so it hangs down my back. "Guess who is the reigning winner."

Legend chuckles, and it's a deep, appreciative sound that licks along my spine.

"I don't know why we are taking her to the murder site," Creed complains some more. "We have what we need. Time to get back to debrief Vicente and the others. Send teams across Rathe, leave no stone left unturned until we find the cursed soil and destroy it."

"Are you being dumb on purpose or..."

"If you have something to say, say it." Creed glares and, honestly, it should just be his permanent face at this point.

I scoff. "You know what? Never mind. Go ahead, send your little wasted search parties. What do I care?"

Sinner lifts a brow. "Just fucking spit it out. What makes you think we won't find the source?"

"Because it's not a fucking garden that can be planted wherever one chooses."

"What does that mean?" Knight presses.

What are they not understanding?

"I told you guys the curse is in the soil. That soil is cursed because of what it hides, and those flowers were born of the curse as a way of protection. They were created by nature itself."

"So, nature could have felt it needed protection and bloomed them at our site."

"Wrong." I shake my head. "They exist only as a form of defense. They protect the forbidden gems. It's the only reason it exists. It's why you have no knowledge or history or proof of its existence."

Creed's expression begins to fall. If I didn't know better, I'd say that was concern in his eyes. He turns to Legend. "And where are these *gems*?"

"I got a feeling we're not gonna like what she's about to say," Sinner begins, a grin on his lips. "But go on, chaos queen–"

"Do not call her queen." Creed snaps.

"Speak, Haide," Knight commands.

I glare at him, something sizzling beneath my skin, but then Legend's knuckles find my chin and he tips my head up. Blue eyes lock with mine and my limbs settle.

"Where are the gems, little monster?"

"Where they were born. On Exile Island."

Chapter Twenty-Six

Haide

Complete and total *silence.*

Creed's magic presses against my forehead as he seeks entry, searching for the truth that he clearly finds. "What exactly are you trying to say?"

"That you've got a problem."

He gets in my face. "You are my fucking problem, little girl," he hisses so only I can hear. "And he will see the truth soon."

"And if he doesn't?"

"I will *make* him."

Anger, hot and swift, sweeps through me, and I'm five seconds from seeing if that little knife trick will work again.

Only this time, I'll take the handle in my palm and drive it through this asshole's neck.

But before I can try, the cavern opens abruptly, a hollow pocket carved into the hillside. The scent shifts; the rot is still there but it's mixed with a metallic tang. Only that's not all. There is something beneath it. something that doesn't fit but is distinctly familiar. Threading through the stench like a whisper of salt.

Ocean water.

I close my eyes and it's as if I'm back on the island. My breath snags at the thought, chest locking for a beat.

An unexpected panic slices through me—because what the hell?

Since when did the idea of going back become a feeling of dread?

It's not like I want to stay here.

Right?

A narrow opening yawns to the left, barely wide enough for one person at a time.

Knight ducks inside first, leading the group, and I go to follow when I realize Legend isn't at my side anymore.

He stands several paces back, leaning against the stone wall, head down, his breath leaving him in heavy spurts.

"You good?" I ask, unease sweeping low in my stomach.

Worry.

That's worry I'm feeling.

Why? I don't…care about things. Especially not people.

Legend lifts his eyes, lids low but pupils wide. "Just tired," he murmurs, pushing off the wall with a lazy, unfocused shove. "A little out of it, but nothing for you to worry about, little monster."

My stomach curls tighter, because somehow, and without a shadow of a doubt, I know he's full of shit. Something *is* wrong.

I take a step toward him, but Creed's voice echoes behind me. "Move your ass, brat!"

Sighing, I let my shoulders fall. Legend grins, leaning in and sliding his lips across mine before tugging me along.

But his lips are…wrong. Warm instead of molten.

"Come on, mate."

It's on the tip of my tongue to argue, to *deny* that word but…something keeps my lips pressed shut and I don't want to think about what it is.

We push into the "murder zone." I take in everything in my line of sight, which isn't much at first glance, only small, glowing circles.

Sinner sees me looking and steps closer. "Magical markers Vicente placed when the bodies were discovered. They mark where the evidence once was or collected from."

I nod, and I can feel my senses sharpen like they're not my own as I study the place the hunter the island made of me.

Claw marks decorate every surface, but they're not defensive and they didn't come from a dragon. The gaps between are too narrow and there are five, like the hand of a gifted after a shift. What it shifted into, I can't say for sure.

The marks run vertically and horizontally. Crisscrossed. They're upward and downward and across every surface with zero finesse. This isn't outrage, not in the literal sense anyway.

"He's trying to get someone's attention," I mutter.

"He?" London looks my way, tossing a piece of broken brick to the side. "What makes you say 'he'?"

I shake my head, a frown forming. "I don't know." But I'm sure of it.

I can almost *feel* the turmoil coming off the surface in a thick, invisible fog. A fog that seems to be washing over only me and not the others, both weighing me down and stroking along my spine like the touch of a lover.

My toes tingle in my boots and I fold them over in my socks, trying to make sense of the strange pull in my chest that I'm not so sure belongs to me.

A pull to what, though? Because I can't grasp onto anything else on the other end. It's like it's torn or missing something and it longs to get it back.

The thought makes me frown, and I can sense the watchful eyes of the others, so I scowl my expression as best as I can and turn to take in the other side, telling myself I'm just tripping out. That I've been around dragons all my life, so maybe I'm just more in tune with the place they call home than the royals are.

Yeah, because that explains the shitstorm in your head, Haide. Focus.

Thick black tar ribbons down the wall behind Legend. It moves, slow and deliberate, like it's alive. Like something beneath the stone is flushing it outward.

Desperation claws at my insides, its source unknown. Those ribbons run fast; they tie and tangle. The lines crawl across the rock, twisting, linking, until they settle into a shape. No, not a shape, but words.

No, not words…a message.

I'm getting impatient, Hellpet.

A shiver runs down my spine.

I step closer and reach out.

A hand clamps around my wrist, taking me to the side until I'm face-to-face with Creed.

"What the fuck did you just do?" he seethes, grip tightening.

"What?"

His hand jerks to the wall, his gaze even more accusing. "That! How the fuck are you doing that?!"

My brows jump and I look back at the words, only they're gone. Nothing but the black veins slithering angrily along the stone.

Creed yanks me harder and their speed increases.

"I don't think it likes when you touch me."

"What—" He grips me with both hands now, his hold punishing but just as quickly, it goes lax. A sharp line forms between his brows. His head yanks toward his brothers, and his face morphs into horror.

Sinner grips his head. Knight struggles to hold on to London.

"Oh no," I mutter, running to Legend, who looks even worse than he already did.

"Creed," I breathe, leaning to Legend's side. "The flowers. You removed them, right? Locked them away somewhere, at least? You know, with the bodies?"

"What do you mean?" Knight demands, even his voice sounds distant, fading at the edges.

"I mean…" I take a step toward them. "They were removed, *right*?"

"Haide." London's voice cracks. "What was the first symptom again?"

I don't have to say it. They're figuring it out now.

Her eyes widen. "But no one touched anything."

I wince. "Yeeah… Did I forget to mention you don't have to *touch* them for them to infect you? That's why they're called the Isle's Kiss. They infect the very air, just like the scent of salt water."

"No," Creed denies, but he's already struggling to stay on his feet. "Our men were here. They came and took the bodies. Mental memories were created and stored for extraction. They all walked out just fine."

"Because they were full." They just keep staring. "Oh my gods. *Listen* Royals, they are soul *eaters*. They *eat* souls. They had already eaten when they came to get the bodies, but now—"

"They're hungry," Creed mutters, head snapping toward the exit. "We have to move."

All at once, everyone runs, but they make it only a few feet before they start to crumble.

"Fuck. A portal," Sinner panics.

"But you said the dragons—"

"Shut the fuck up." He throws his hands out but nothing happens, his eyes blowing wide. "Knight!"

Knight lurches forward with a sound torn straight from his diaphragm. With one hand braced against the wall, he uses the other to try to carve a portal. His magic fizzles uselessly at his fingertips, sparks scattering and dying before they even form.

London staggers next, her breath catching mid-step. Her pupils flare black, drowning in ink, then flicker back to normal in a frantic pulse that screams *loss of control*. She reaches for Sinner but her fingers barely graze him before her knees give out.

Sinner tries to pull her upright, only to choke on air so heavy it seems to clot in his throat. His hand clamps around her arm but there's no strength behind it—not enough to hold her, barely enough to hold himself.

Creed lasts seconds longer, shoving past them all in a last attempt at the exit. He manages two steps before his shoulders lock, his spine seizing, and he slams a palm against the cavern wall to keep from collapsing entirely. His head whips toward his brothers in clear panic.

"Move!" he rasps. "Everyone move."

But no one is moving.

Not anymore.

The poison is in them.

Every breath dragging it deeper.

That's when Legend drops.

He goes down like the world just cut the strings holding him up—legs folding, palms striking stone, breath tearing out of him in a harsh, fractured gasp. His hand flies to his throat, fingers pressing deep enough to whiten the knuckles as he fights just to draw in another lungful.

His body lurches, shoulders trembling violently. His head tilts toward me in a desperate, blurry attempt at focus, but his eyes are glassy. Unanchored.

Something detonates in my chest.

It's dark.

Possessive. A single, primal command claws up my spine:

Get to him.

Now.

Yours.

The cavern seems to narrow, collapsing inward until the only thing that exists is the distance between us and the sound of him trying, and failing, to breathe.

I push off the stone, stumbling closer to him. The poison thickens, slowing everything, weighing down my limbs like they're filling with wet sand. But the instinct dragging me toward him is stronger. It tears through the resistance, ripping me forward until I crash down beside him, catching his weight before his head hits the ground.

His breath shudders against my neck, broken and uneven. A low, animalistic sound tears from me, protective to the point of violence.

Behind us, the others collapse fully.

Knight's back hits the dirt.

London slumps sideways, hands twitching weakly.

Sinner falls to one knee, then both.

Creed makes one final attempt to stand, growling through gritted teeth, before his legs give out from under him.

They're drowning in it.

Suffocating.

Legend's fingers curl into my jacket, knuckles trembling.

"Mate—" he chokes, barely a sound at all.

That's what breaks whatever thin border existed between me and the creature pacing under my skin.

Heat slams through me, stealing my breath for a heartbeat before releasing it in a surge that feels like the world is exhaling *with me.* The cavern trembles, the stone beneath us vibrating, dust falling in thin sheets from the ceiling. The air thickens again, but this time it's not poison.

It's me.

The poison should be winning.

I can feel it trying to. The way it thickens the air until it feels like I'm breathing wet wool. The way my arms want to turn to stone and my thoughts want to scatter like frightened birds. But something in me refuses to let it take a single inch more.

The cavern doesn't just hold the rot but is part of it, soaked in it, fed by it. And now that it knows the Kings are failing, it leans in—greedy.

The ground trembles beneath my knees. Not from my magic. From the land.

A low groan rolls through the rock like a throat clearing, ancient and annoyed. The black tar on the wall begins to move again, and faster this time.

The ribbons unwind and unspool across the cavern walls in a frantic crawl, branching into thin tendrils that stretch toward the bodies on the ground as if tasting them, choosing them. One curls around Sinner's ankle, slick and quiet. The second it touches him, he jerks like he's been struck, a choked curse torn from his lips before his jaw locks and the sound dies in his throat.

London tries to lift her hand, tries to summon the ink-black blade of her power, but the poison steals it from her mid-thought. Her fingers twitch, useless. Knight's arm shakes so badly it looks like his bones might rattle free of his skin. Creed's attempt to bark an order only results in a raw rasp.

The tendrils slip closer, dragging across the stone with a soft, wet sound that makes my stomach twist. One threads up Knight's boot, another snakes over Creed's palm. When Creed tries to rip it away, it clings harder—like it's delighted he noticed.

I search for the source. For the *thing* behind the thing, and the moment I do, the air shifts.

A shadow moves deeper in the cavern. It slips past the evidence markers, past the claw marks and the dark that isn't dark but the absence of light entirely. The shape presses into the stone like a stain, and my pulse pounds heavily.

My stomach turns over as I wait for it to reveal itself, but then Legend's breath stutters in my arms. His fingers dig into my jacket like he can anchor himself in me if he holds on hard enough. His head lolls toward my shoulder and his mouth opens on a sound that isn't a word—just instinct and need and that horrible, failing pull.

And the moment I feel him slip, something in me snaps.

It's like a chain going taut, like a door being kicked in, like my blood remembers it's been waiting to spill into a flame.

I don't think. Deep in my marrow, something buried inside me refuses to allow this cavern to take him. I will not let it take *any of them*.

The tar lashes out again, whipping toward my wrist like it wants to wrap me up and mark me.

Magic roars to the surface, feral, wild, and nothing like the clean, sculpted spells they've been teaching me. This is older. Uncontained. A raw, ungoverned force slamming against the cavern walls like it wants to tear them apart. Just like when the knife appeared at Sinner's throat, I don't lift a hand.

I don't draw a symbol.

I don't even fucking speak, yet a portal erupts upward, *forced* into existence by nothing more than the brute strength of whatever lives inside me. It's no ordinary portal.

It's one ringed of fire.

Even through the effects of the poison, their confusion is obvious. Legend tries to lift his head again, brows furrowed, but struggles to maintain his balance. I can't make out whatever words London gasps out as Knight stares through barely open eyes, disbelief mixing with panic. As for Sinner and Creed—the former tries to crawl toward us while Creed fails to move a muscle.

It's a shit show.

I tighten my grip on Legend's waist, dragging him up with me, my pulse thundering in a rhythm that matches the trembling in the air. Then, somehow, I'm carrying them all through.

We hit the floor with a hard bang, and the last thing I hear is Legend's roar echoing inside my skull.

Chapter Twenty-Seven

Legend

Knight's crouched beside me when the world swims back into focus, his palm a hot brand against my shoulder like he's trying to pin me to the floorboards by heat alone.

"What's wrong with him?" he snarls at anyone who'll answer, and the question scrapes along my ribs like a knife hunting bone. "Why are we fine and he's not?"

"Her." Creed's one-word answer has my brows pulling.

Everything hums.

My nose leaks slowly and refuses to stop, the taste of iron and ash now permanent on my tongue. The edges of my vision are fuzzy like burned paper.

"Move," Silver's voice reaches me, clean as a scalpel he'll

never have to hold. The court's golden healer in a shirt that somehow hasn't collected a single wrinkle in this chaos.

He takes Knight's place at my side. His hands hover over my face, the air cools, and light threads from his fingertips. Silver on silver, the kind that usually stitches flesh back into obedience.

It touches me, and my body jerks like I've been nailed to the ground by a predator's fangs.

But that's bullshit, because there is no predator greater than me. Than my brothers.

I grit my teeth, chest convulsing.

The light fizzles, pops, and then dies.

Silver's jaw tightens. He tries again with a different angle, a deeper tone, and a low hum intended to coax my bones to remember they're mine. The magic strokes my broken cartilage. My skin rises against it, fighting back like a beast shackled in fire. The light gutters out, leaving only the ache and a trickle along my lip of something hot that isn't blood and is.

"Gods," Silver breathes. "He's rejecting it. This should work. Legend, can you feel me at all?"

My eyes narrow and he sits back on his haunches, looking over at my brothers.

Sinner's sprawled on a small sofa in the back corner, cigarette smoldering between two lazy fingers, smoke drawing sigils of trouble and invitation. "It's the bond," he says around the drag, voice flat, as if stating the weather while the house is on fire. "He's wired to her and frayed to hell. You can't knit a man back together while someone else is unraveling his thread."

Bond.

Mate.

Haide.

My insides coil, fire molding my organs together in a painful grip, and I jerk in my place on the floor, body rolling onto my side as my arms flop in front of me.

How the fuck did I end up on the floor? How the fuck did I end up here?

London steps in behind Sinner, shoulder to Knight's back, steadying him in the way only she can. Her gaze flicks from my face to Silver's hands to the streak of black on the floor beside me.

"Where is Haide? What happened?"

Everyone ignores me.

Silver drags the back of his wrist across his brow, annoyed at what he does or doesn't find. "I can seal the break in his nose manually, but the system's rejecting healing on a deeper level. This is beyond my ability." He presses two fingers to my throat, counting. "Pulse is…volatile."

I laugh and it fucking hurts.

I close my eyes and, deep in the recesses of my mind, there's a spark. It's sharp and hot and undoubtably *her.*

Rage.

My little monster is angry, claws turned inward. If I had breath to spare, I'd laugh at the recognition. Of course, my mate's fury would taste like the edge of a blade that has learned to love its own bite. My bite.

But why is she angry at me?

I try to stand.

"Legend." Knight's voice gentles without his permission. "Stay down."

"Make me." I plant a hand, then another, and push.

My arms shake like a newborn god trying to stand on legs it hasn't earned yet.

Silver reaches to steady my shoulder but my skin rejects him again. The contact crackles, the healer yanks back, shaking out singed fingers with a stunned laugh. "He is a terrible patient."

"Leave me alone. I'll go to her. She's what I need."

"You will go nowhere," Creed says as if it's final. As if he is any more a King than I am.

"Don't make me gut you, brother."

"You're too weak to even try."

"My mate is waiting for me!" I snarl, chest heaving as I tear free and push to my feet. "You can't keep me from her! You can't—"

"Don't you get it, you blind fucking bastard?" Creed slams me back, eyes white fire, words splitting the room in half. "You don't have a mate, Legend. It isn't fucking real!"

My muscles lock tight and the room grows dead silent.

My knees buckle before I can stop them. One slams the floor hard enough that I feel bone grind. My hands curl into fists against the boards, nails biting through my palms until they drip. The taste of copper floods my mouth.

"You lie, brother." *It has to be a lie.*

Creed's stare never wavers. "You're being fooled. Trapped."

The moment he says it, the bond pulls—hard enough to make my chest ache like it's splitting down the center. He's wrong.

I can *feel* her.

He's fucking wrong.

"She is my mate." My jaw snaps, spit and blood stringing the air.

Creed's gaze dips to the black river running from my nose down my chest. "You're bleeding into a place none of us can reach. That bond is a noose, not a tether. It's tightening and it won't stop until it's drained you dry."

"I will end you if you try to keep me from her." I stagger. My spine groans but I rise, inch by brutal inch, until I'm upright again. My vision blurs, but I don't look away. "She. Is. *Mine*."

"Breathe, Legend." Knight snarls, restraining me, my body thrashing in his grip. His glare cuts to Creed like it could flay him open. "You. Explain. Now before I help him hurt you."

Creed slowly shakes his head. "Knight."

"No," Knight argues back. "I know the feeling of a partial bond. Of thinking my mate is gone or hurt or that someone dared to take her from me. I felt my Ethos rage. My mind slip and body weaken. I know the power of a mating bond. You don't. So start fucking talking, brother, or I'm done hearing about this."

"Too much information might—"

"Say it."

Creed is quiet for too fucking long before he finally speaks.

"Don't forget what I can do." Creed leans forward, bringing himself inches from my face, and speaks slowly. "I've been inside your head, brother. I've dug every corner of your mind since you brought that girl back here. I know where you hide things. I've walked the corridors you're too fucking weak to see right now, but I see. I know. And it is my job to fix this. Fix *you*."

"I am not broken. I am missing half of my god damn soul!" I rage.

"Exactly!" He screams back, shoving to his feet as he looks around. "How do you guys not see it?"

"We can't fucking read minds," Knight snaps, and there's a tremor in it that's part anger and part bone-deep fear. He's up in Creed's face faster than I can blink, like he wants to tear the truth out of him with his bare hands. "Tell us everything."

Creed straightens, eyes glittering. "I will tell you what you need to know," he says, calm as a razor. "Not what you want."

"Fuck that," Sinner spits, the words like a match. He steps forward, yanking London with him. "Shield us."

London's eyes snap to mine before going to her mate's.

Knight gives a curt nod, and then their lips are moving, but their words become wind in my ears.

There is no sound, just the anger on my brothers' faces, and the horror that follows.

Every head snaps in my direction.

London's hand lifts to her mouth, her eyes going wide.

The wind's whistle disappears with the clear sheen that covered my family.

"You're lying," Knight growls, eyes on me.

"I'm not lying." Creed's voice is silk over steel. "I am trying to save him. You saw what she did back there. She is getting stronger while he gets weaker!"

"Really?" I cough a laugh. "She saved our asses and you're blaming her for that?"

Creed crouches before me. "How?" he prompts. "How did she save us? As far as we know, she's not supposed to have any true powers, remember? So if she does, if they manifested or were there from the beginning, she is hiding them. Why would she do that, Legend? Yet you're the one who couldn't even use the ones you were born with the other day. You can't portal. You can hardly fucking stand. Why is that?"

I glare and he comes closer.

"When you brought her back here, how did you do it, Legend?"

"Hitched a ride on good old Benny boy," I mention London's best friend. "Dragons guard that place, you know."

"A place where no one is allowed in or out. Yet *she* can. Think. How else did those soul-eating fucking flowers get here? She brought them. And who knows where else she put them? She was born to exile and when the island lost its anchor, it needed a new one...and then a royal walked its soil for the first time."

"I went to claim what was given to me by the gods."

"No. You took something that was never supposed to leave that place, and it took from you in return. Now we are dealing with the consequences of that. She is playing us. That Isle's Kiss? How else would it have gotten here? Why are these deaths all related to the island...to her?"

"I don't care."

"I do!" Creed rages. "She has found some sort of workaround. I know it. And when I figure out how, I will prove it and I will cut that fake bond from your chest before I let it claim you."

"Watch it."

"You're not yourself, Legend. Just fucking think."

"Stop."

He grips my head. "Dig deeper!"

"I said stop."

He presses tight. "Break past that fucking treachery in your mind!"

"Creed."

"The bond is not real!"

My hands are on Creed's throat before I even know I've moved them, fingers closing like iron traps, nails digging in where the skin is soft under his jaw. He makes a sound halfway between a curse and a laugh, shock sliding off his face, then pain when I clamp down harder.

Creed's eyes flash white for a second, then red with effort. His hands slam at my wrists but they're useless, blunted by a panic I can't deny. Behind me, Knight's voice is a strangled roar; Sinner curses and lunges; and I feel them like weights trying to drag me back from the ledge I'm teetering on. Knight's forearms wrap around my shoulders as Sinner's grip catches at my belt.

"Let him go!" Knight snaps, but my fingers only close tighter, a promise of breaking.

Creed's face goes pale, eyes searching mine for the flicker of the brother he's always known.

"Legend," he starts, but I don't want his words.

I snarl at Creed, struggling, every muscle trembling but refusing to give. "You don't get to stand there with your dead eyes and tell me she isn't mine. I—I *feel* her." *Don't I?* "I taste her in my fucking blood." *Can't I?* "Every moment I'm with her, the bond grows stronger."

"Which is why you need to stay away!"

"Never!"

Silver rushes in, hands lifted, panicked. "Stop this! Shackling him in this state will rip him apart, it won't heal him, it will—"

"Shut up, Silver," we all bite out together, the words lashing like whips, silencing him when he stumbles back.

"You can't take her," I hiss, voice scraping like stone. "You can't have her—"

He coughs, a laugh-rasp. "I'm not trying to have her, Legend. I'm trying to keep you alive."

"Liar," I growl, and the mad white thing behind my eyes flares.

"Knight," Silver warns. "You have to do something—"

"Damn it, Legend!" Knight screams, and then his Ethos,

born of his mating bond, rises. Claws break through his flesh and dig into my palms until sharp talons are seen through the other side of my arm.

Whiter blond hair slips into my view, and I snap my teeth at London.

She signs. "Sorry about this, Ledge."

Her hands swipe before my face, and with each movement it's like a fist to the fucking face, her power slamming into me like a sledgehammer.

It connects with the back of my head, then another blow lands across my temple, a thud that knocks the oxygen out of me. I try to jerk, but the room closes in like a fist, taking all the fight I had left until I'm just a bag of bones.

Creed's face is the last thing I see, close and small and terrible. He watches me with an odd, almost tender amusement, as black spots begin to claim my vision.

"We will find the answer, brother," he whispers, hand finding my shoulder as he bends in front of me. "We will erase her from your mind, I swear it."

Over my dead body…

• • •

"Legend."

My eyes snap open, my heart slamming into my ribs. I drag my head toward the door, catching the black painted fingernails curling along the frame, and vanishing around the corner.

Haide.

Fucking finally.

I stagger to my feet, swaying, the sedation pulling harder

at my veins, dragging me toward that false horizon where she waits.

The hall blurs around me as I stumble forward, bare feet dragging across stone. Sconces flicker dim along the walls, smoke curling like shadows that reach for me as I pass. My hands scrape the plaster, leaving smears of blood where glass had cut me earlier, and I don't care. All I care about is her. Finding her. Holding her.

A flash of movement catches my eye, and my pulse pounds in my temples at the sight. Long black hair my fingers ache to tug on. Leather clinging to her body like armor I want to tear at with teeth. My breath rushes out of me in a broken gasp, and I lurch forward.

"Haide!"

She vanishes, and I chase. Down the stairwell, deeper into the belly of the house, toward the smoking room. My treacherous mother's favorite chamber, once upon a time.

A place where the air tastes of sugared wine and smoldering resin. Warm and intoxicating, but too sweet, too deliberate, as if meant to disguise something darker underneath. Smoke curls in lazy ribbons, coiling around carved beams and golden fucking spears, clinging to my skin like a lover's hands.

The light in here isn't natural, pouring from lanterns that drip with wax, each flame caged in crystal as if even fire bows to the opulence of this house. Velvet drapes sag heavily over the windows, hiding the demonic smoke that protects the outer walls, and trapping the perfume of the space, sealing it until the air itself feels drugged.

Shadows pool in the corners like they're waiting for commands, slick and eager, their silence louder than sound, vibrating with excitement as one of their kings enters the space.

As *I* enter the space.

And in the middle of it all, framed by that suffocating wealth, stands a chair carved from obsidian. Its back rises high, etched in runes that catch the lantern glow and flare like veins of flame. The cushions are blood-red, stuffed so thick they mean to swallow whoever dares sit on them.

That's where I find her.

"Haide." Her name scratches up my throat, and I grip the doorframe to keep from falling to my knees and crawling to my queen.

She sits like she was created for that very spot, draped in leather that clings to every line of her body, black as midnight and twice as dangerous. Tight cloth winds across her curves, and she has one leg hooked over the other.

Her hair spills down her back and over her shoulders, long and black, silk threaded with shadow, glinting where the lantern light dares touch it. It hides half her face until she flicks her head, and eyes like pools of ink stare at me as if they'd cut me open before they'd ever soften.

She doesn't look out of place here. No, it's like the throne was carved for her spine, like the smoke was meant to crown her, like every shadow in this cursed room has bent down in reverence without realizing it.

Because it, too, feels this.

It knows that the fates gifted her to them. That she will be the next Queen to join their Kings.

Blood pounds heavy in my ears, surging through my veins and straight to my cock, swelling painfully in my jeans.

The closer I get, the faster the smoke curls around her body, tracing the line of her throat and making me ache to do the same. Her eyes glint through the haze, hard and defiant, and yet my chest caves like a child's at the sight.

My legs barely hold me, but I stumble forward, my hand reaching before I've even thought it. I touch her face. My thumb drags across her cheekbone, trembling, and her skin quivers beneath the contact.

The world tilts, narrows, until there's only her. All I want is to close the inch between us, to take her mouth with mine, to taste what my dreams have promised me a thousand times. To give her all of me, every rune, every fire, every goddamn piece until there's nothing left to take. My body aches with it, my chest splitting open with the need to claim her, to be claimed back.

But the moment I think it, the moment I envision sinking my teeth into that long, perfect fucking neck, my palm burns with betrayal. Because my body knows, my fucking soul knows, what I'm being blinded to see.

My brows snap together, and my grip on her tightens.

She whimpers, a pretty little sound, and tears spark in the corners of her eyes. The sight rips straight through me, but my fingers tighten anyway, cruel, desperate.

My own eyes sting and I clench my teeth. My eyes and my soul war with each other, but still I push through.

I lean closer, so close her breath shudders against my mouth, and then I do the unthinkable.

I snap her fucking neck.

The sound cracks through the smoke like thunder. Her body falls limp, sliding from the chair to the floor, her head lolling at an angle. No living thing could survive. She hits the ground with a heavy thud, hair fanning across the stone. *Blond fucking hair and a face that isn't hers.*

A heavy sigh sounds behind me. "Told you it wouldn't work."

"It did enough. We just needed to stall him. Won't be much longer now."

Stall me? Longer for what?

I spin, rage bursting through my chest, my claws threatening to tear through my own skin. My brothers stand in the doorway, arms crossed and expressions irritated. "What is this? Where is Haide?!"

Before they can respond, the door creaks, and all of us turn. London slips inside, her dark eyes sweeping the wreckage of the room, landing steadily on her mate.

"What is it?" he asks.

"The mage." She looks to Creed, unease pouring off her in waves. "She's here."

They stiffen and slowly, everyone in the room looks at me.

"Then it's time." Creed mumbles, a crease between his brows.

A chill runs down my spine and I tense.

"Time for fucking *what*?"

Chapter Twenty-Eight

Haide

I jolt awake like someone cut a string.

Darkness crowds the edges of my vision, thick enough that, for a second, I don't know where I am.

And then the memories hit me all at once.

Darkadia. Cavern floors. Poison thick in my lungs. Legend choking on air he couldn't swallow.

The black tar on the walls and the message left behind.

My breath drags in high and sharp. I sit up too fast, palms pressed to my sternum because panic tastes like blood tonight, like something reaching through my ribs.

Legend.

The thought hits me harder than the dream.

My hand drifts higher—hesitant, careful, almost ashamed of the fear simmering beneath my skin—until my fingertips brush the center of my chest. I don't know what I'm looking for. I don't even know what the hell I expect to feel. He keeps saying there's something between us, some bond neither of us can outrun, and maybe I'm an idiot for checking, but—

There.

A pull.

Quiet at first.

Then steady.

Heat weaves through me, a thin gold thread winding tight beneath my bones, tugging low and certain, and it feels... Gods, it feels like relief. Like exhaling after holding my breath for years. Like something inside me whispering, *there you are.*

My lips twitch before I can stop them.

He's alive.

I saved him.

Me.

I did that.

And the realization sends a strange rush through my chest, nervous and hot and a little terrifying because I don't feel things like this. I don't want to think about why I am now.

"Get a grip," I mutter, dragging my hand away as if that can sever whatever just lit up inside me.

Still, the warmth lingers and the tether hums, and gods help me—the feeling settles something in me that has never settled before.

I throw the blanket off and swing my legs out of bed, ready to find him. To see that fire-bright stare for myself, but a slip of black catches my eye.

A folded card rests on the floor just inside my room, placed so perfectly it looks almost ceremonial. My name is slashed across the front in handwriting with sharp, arrogant strokes.

I kneel, pluck it up, and the moment I flip it open, warmth curls low in my stomach.

Little monster,

I won't waste time pretending I'm patient. I cannot wait to set my eyes on you tonight.

Your power is waking like a creature starved, and I will be the one it bends for. Try not to break anything before I see you.

Wear something that will ruin me. I intend to make tonight one you will never forget.

– Your mate

A slow, traitorous smile pricks the corners of my mouth before I can kill it.

"Asshole," I whisper, even though the word tastes nothing like irritation.

I stare at the note for longer than I should, happy to know that he's okay. That he waits for me.

Gods, I sound gross but for the first time…I'm not so sure I care.

A knock shatters the quiet.

I straighten, and the door materializes. Emmie, the girl he sent to me with a million dresses in tow, is on the other side.

"Hello again." She smiles. "Shall we?"

"Shall we…what?"

Her eyes glitter. "It's time to get ready for the ball."

• • •

I stand in front of the tall window overlooking Rathe University's inner quad, arms crossed, trying to ignore the girl behind me tugging at my hair like it personally offended her.

"Almost finished, miss." Her voice is soft. Pleasant. The kind of voice designed not to irritate.

I hate it.

"Don't call me that," I mutter, watching students weave below in their pressed uniforms, all moving with purpose I don't share. "I'm not your miss."

"Of course." A pause. "What should I call you then?"

"I told you before. Haide works fine."

"Haide it is." She threads something through a section of my hair. Pins, maybe. Or tiny weapons. Hard to tell with these people.

I glance back at her. Young face. Maybe mid-twenties. Blond hair pulled into a severe knot that makes her features sharper than they probably are. Her hands move with practiced efficiency, each twist and curl deliberate. Her simple gray dress screams servant, and the sight of it grates.

"You don't have to do this," I say.

"Do what?"

"This." I wave a hand vaguely at the room, at her, at the stupid concept of royalty needing someone to touch their hair. "Play 'yes ma'am' for a bunch of overgrown children with crowns."

Her laugh catches me off guard. Quiet. Genuine. "I know I don't have to."

"Then why??"

"I'm paid. Fed. Protected." Her tone stays even. Factual. "My family's served the Deveraux line for generations; this is the position I wished and worked hard for. It's an honor to be part of the royal staff, not a shackle."

I snort. "That's what they tell you."

"That's what I choose to believe." She meets my eyes in the reflection of the dark glass. "Big difference."

I study her. No fear. No hesitation. Just…calm. Like she's explaining weather patterns.

"You're Argent," I say.

"I am."

"And you serve the people who just murdered your queen and took your throne."

Her hands pause for half a breath. "Magdalena wasn't *my* queen. She was a tyrant who bled our people dry and called it loyalty after the death of our true King and Queen many moons ago." She tugs gently at a curl. "The Deveraux brothers are brutal. Violent. Terrifying on their worst days." A small smile. "But they don't pretend to be anything else. That's refreshing."

I blink. Process. "You've lost it."

"Probably." She grins. "But so have you, or you wouldn't be here."

Fair.

I turn back to the window, letting her work. The silence stretches, not uncomfortable, just present. The kind of quiet I'm not used to with people.

"How long have you worked here?"

"Since I was sixteen. My mother before me. Her mother before that." Her fingers dance through another section. "We're good at what we do."

"Which is?"

"Making Royals look less feral." She laughs again." And occasionally keeping them from killing one another."

I almost smile. Almost. "That happen often?"

"More than you'd think." She secures the last pin. "Legend's the easiest, though."

My spine straightens. I try to make it look natural. "Is he?"

"Absolutely." She steps back, assessing her work. "Creed's too intense. Knight's too quiet, which is worse. Sinner's—" She shudders. "Sinner. But Legend? He's cheeky. Playful. Dangerous, yes, but in a way that feels intentional. Controlled."

Controlled.

The word sits wrong. Legend doesn't control anything. He collides with it. Bends it. Breaks it if it doesn't bend.

"You like him," I say.

"Everyone likes Legend." Emmie circles around to face me, tilting her head. "Even when they shouldn't."

"What's that supposed to mean?"

"Nothing." But her smile says otherwise. "Just that he has a way of making people feel safe when they're around him. Like he's got everything handled even when the world's burning."

My stomach twists. Because I *do* feel that. That stupid, irrational sense of security when he's near. Like I could burn the entire campus down and he'd just laugh and hand me more matches.

"Is that his magic?" I ask. "His Ethos or whatever?"

Emmie's brow furrows. "No. The royal Ethos rises only after a mating bond. It's his principal power, the one he was born with, inherited from Queen Cosimo's bloodline. He can manipulate the mind. His is mind sedation. He can calm, make people feel at ease. But—" She hesitates. "It doesn't work if you don't already trust him on some level. Magic can't force feeling. It can only amplify what's already there."

Fuck.

So it's not just his power. It's *me*. I trust him. On some primal, ridiculous level, I trust Legend Deveraux.

I want to hate that realization.

I don't.

Emmie moves to the vanity, organizing bottles and brushes. "Let me guess. You're trying to figure out if what you feel is real or manufactured."

"I'm not—"

"You are." She doesn't look at me. "Everyone does when they're around the Deveraux brothers. Especially if they're bonded."

My jaw tightens. "I'm not bonded."

"Right." The word drips skepticism. "That's why you smell like him. Why his scent is woven so deep into your skin I could track you across campus blindfolded."

"That's—"

"Denial?" She finally looks at me, eyes sharp. "Look, I don't know what you two are to each other. But whatever it is, it's loud. Everyone can feel it."

I turn back to the window, arms crossing tighter. Below, students mill around the fountain, laughing, shoving, living normal lives where they don't wake up covered in blood or get accused of murder.

And then I see him.

Legend.

Standing near the quad's edge, leaning against the low stone wall like he owns it. Because he does. He owns everything here.

He's talking to someone. A girl.

Tall. Slim. Hair like spun gold catching the fading sunlight. She's wearing a pale blue dress that looks expensive and delicate and everything I'm not. She laughs at something he says, touching his arm.

My hands curl into fists.

"Who is that?" I ask.

Emmie follows my gaze. Her expression shifts. Hardens. "Arabella."

"And?"

"And she's just Arabella." Emmie's voice goes flat. Careful. "Daughter of one of the higher Argent families. Pretty. Ambitious. The kind of girl who thinks proximity to power makes her powerful."

"She's touching him a lot for someone who's just ambitious." I will not show my whole ass and expose my jealousy, but something about Emmie puts me at ease. Or maybe I'm drunk on the air.

Emmie doesn't answer right away. When she does, her tone's measured. "I guess she's trying to secure her position, especially since there are no longer any Argents in any power positions."

"Secure her position?" I blink. "By fucking Legend?"

Her eyes flutter. "I don't think she's fussy with the who, Haide."

Jealousy claws up my throat. Hot. Vicious. Completely irrational. I barely know Legend. Barely trust him. And yet the sight of her hand on his arm makes me want to portal down there and remove that hand at the wrist.

Except I can't fucking portal and, judging by the shoes in Emmie's hands, I won't be able to run in those, either.

"You don't like her," I say.

"I don't trust her." Emmie crosses her arms. "She's too calculating. Too clean. Like she's never gotten her hands dirty and doesn't plan to start."

I watch Legend laugh. He looks relaxed. Easy. The way he does when he's pretending not to be dangerous.

Arabella leans closer.

My vision tunnels.

"Haide."

Emmie's voice pulls me back. I blink, realizing I've stepped toward the window like I'm about to launch through it.

"You're growling," she says.

"I'm not—" I am. Low. Feral. The sound of something territorial and furious.

What the fuck is wrong with me?

I remember the lecture. The one about mating bonds. Multiple stages. Some being recognition. Claiming. Completion. The professor's voice droning on about how mates become obsessive, possessive, even violent when their bond is threatened.

This can't be real.

But the rage burning through my chest says otherwise.

I turn away from the window. Force my hands to unclench. "I need a drink."

Emmie's brow lifts. "It's not even dark yet."

"Don't care." I scan the room, spotting a cluster of bottles near his bed. I cross the room and grab the most expensive looking one. Purple liquid sloshes inside.

"That's Fae Juice," Emmie says. "From the Shadow Hutt at the markets. It's—"

"Strong?"

"Very."

"Expensive?" My brow curves.

She mirrors it. "Very."

"Perfect." I flash the bottle at her, forcing a grin that feels manic. "Drink with me."

"I'm working—"

"You're done with my hair. I can let it all out closer to the time. Now you're off duty." I uncork the bottle and take a swig. It burns like swallowing fire and tastes like blackberries soaked in violence. "Come on. When's the last time you had fun?"

Emmie's gaze flickers between me and the bottle. Something shifts in her expression. A crack in the professional mask. It's exactly what I need. Why couldn't she have been my bunk buddy instead of all the others?

"Fuck it," she says, reaching for the bottle.

I grin. Real this time. "There she is."

We pass the Fae Juice back and forth. It hits fast and hard, warmth spreading through my limbs, dulling the sharp edges of jealousy still scraping at my insides.

"So," Emmie says after her third sip, "you really think you're not his mate?"

It's on the tip of my tongue to deny, but instead I take another drink. "Mates are supposed to...I don't know. Complete each other. We just piss each other off."

"That's not mutually exclusive." She leans against the dresser, studying me. "My parents were mates. They fought constantly. Screamed. Threw things. But they also couldn't exist without each other. That's the bond. It's not about peace. It's about necessity."

I swallow. These are truths I don't want. I want someone to lie to me or tell me that they agree. Roomie would have lied to me. Emmie, I get the feeling, won't.

Emmie smiles, sad and knowing. "You'll figure it out. Or you won't. Either way" —she gestures at the window where Legend and Arabella are still talking—"that feeling? The one making you want to rip her throat out? That's not going away."

"Great." Another sip, and then I pass it to Emmie before I accidentally drown the whole fucking thing and use it as a weapon to slit Arabella's throat.

"Look at it this way." She sips and winces. "At least you're not boring."

I laugh. That's not what I expected her to say, but I'll take it. "Is that what we're calling this? Not boring?"

"Better than the alternative." She pushes off the dresser, steadier than she should be after that much Fae Juice. "Come on. Let me show you the dress."

I freeze. "The what?"

"The dress." She stares at me like I've grown four heads. I turn to the mirror to check. Nope. Still one. Emmie blinks. "For tonight." She crosses to the wardrobe, pulling out a garment bag. "I picked it out myself. Legend just said to get you something that'll make you fit in."

"I'm terrified," I say, and again with the truth because he sent a damn Argent to buy my dress?

"I thought you might be." She unzips the bag slowly. Dramatically. "That's why I picked this."

She pulls it out.

My mouth drops.

The dress is black. Full-length. Lace so intricate it looks like spiderwebs woven by magic. It's tight. Obscene. See-through everywhere except the places that matter—a strategic strip of solid fabric over the titties and another over the kitty. Everything else? Bare skin visible through delicate, deadly patterns.

It's a bomb disguised as clothing.

I love it.

"Damn," I breathe, my face stinging from the smile.

Emmie grins, wicked and bright. "I can't wait to hear Legend's reaction."

I nod, excitement rushing through my veins. "He's going to lose his mind."

"That's the idea." She hangs it carefully on the door. "Honestly, it's something I'd wear if I wasn't—"

Warmth spreads through my chest. Not just from the Fae Juice. From something else. Something that feels uncomfortably close to friendship.

"Come with me," I say. "To the ball."

Emmie's smile fades. "I can't."

"Why not?"

"Because I'm a maiden. We serve. We don't attend." She takes the bottle back." That's the deal."

"Fuck the deal." I step closer. "You just spent an hour making me look like I could murder a room full of royals. Come watch me do it."

"Haide—"

"I'm joking, I won't kill them." I hold her eyes. "Please come."

The word feels foreign. Wrong. I don't beg. But something about Emmie, the way she laughs and the way she doesn't flinch, makes me want her there. Makes me want someone in that crowd who isn't judging. Who isn't waiting for me to fail.

Emmie's eyes soften. "I wish I could. But if I show up, it'll cause problems. For me. For you. For Legend." She squeezes my shoulder. "But I'll be thinking about you. And tomorrow, you'll tell me everything."

I swallow the disappointment. "Deal."

She hands the bottle back. "Finish this. You're going to need it."

I take a long drink, watching the purple liquid disappear. Through the window, Legend's still talking to Arabella. But now he's looking up. At the window. At me.

Our eyes meet.

He's too far from me to feel that ever-present pull, separated by distance and wards, yet I still *feel* him as I think of him. I feel him because he's inside me. In that irrational bond that my body understands even if my brain doesn't.

He smirks. Like he knows exactly what I'm thinking. Like he can taste my jealousy from across the quad.

Bastard.

I raise the bottle in a mock salute.

He laughs. Silent. Visible. Then turns back to Arabella, but her hand drops from where she was touching him.

Good.

Emmie watches the exchange, shaking her head. "You two are going to burn this place down."

"Probably." I drain the last of the Fae Juice. "But at least it'll be entertaining."

She laughs. For a moment, I let myself imagine what it would be like to have this. Real friendship. The kind that isn't built on survival or violence. Or sex.

It feels dangerous.

It feels good.

"All right." Emmie collects the empty bottle. "I need to go before Legend comes back and finds me drunk and alone in a room with you."

"He'd probably laugh." I watch as she plucks discarded trash.

"He'd definitely laugh. But Creed wouldn't." She heads for the door, pausing at the threshold. "Haide?"

"Yeah?"

"For what it's worth?" She glances back. "I think you're exactly what Legend needs. Even if some refuse to believe it."

Before I can respond, she's gone, door clicking shut behind her.

I'm alone.

With a dress that could start a war.

A mate I'm not ready to claim.

And for the first time since I arrived at this cursed university, I let myself feel it. The pull. The need. The terrifying, exhilarating truth that maybe—*maybe*—Legend Deveraux is mine.

And I'm absolutely fucked.

Chapter Twenty-Nine

Legend

Gods, her body is fucking perfection, so soft for such a prickly little thing, my mate.

My Haide.

"He's waking," someone says.

Waking? From what?

I reach for my mate's legs, tugging her closer, but my fist closes around nothing. My eyelids flutter, peeling open to find my brothers standing above me.

The sight of Creed has my teeth clamping until something in my jaw pops. I stare at my oldest brother, wondering if I look hard enough, I'll find the seam where the lie he spoke was stitched into him.

My bond is real.

Sinner bursts through the door, wearing my fucking face. I glare at him, until it morphs back into his own. He looks from me to my brothers. "It's done. She saw me."

A sound in the hall draws all our attention, and Silver rushes in, eyes hard. "She's waiting."

"Let her in," Creed orders.

The room goes thin around the edges as the smell of salt and winter herbs cut through smoke and copper just as the mage appears. She steps over the threshold and stops like she ran face-first into a fate she didn't order.

Her eyes take me in. From my busted nose to the smear of black drying at my mouth and chest. The shake in my wrists I'm pretending isn't there. Something like alarm breaks through her stone-cold expression.

"This is worse than I thought," she says. She drops to her knees beside me. Cold, dry fingers press to my sternum, and every muscle in my body lights like a fuse. My limbs burn, a starved fire racing out to my edges, and then some invisible hook takes my spine and lifts.

My chest rumbles with a deep groan. Every bone aches as I'm held, torso suspended, eye level with the Stygian like the room forgot which way gravity was supposed to go.

Knight swears and steps in, but she flashes him a look that stops him mid-lunge.

"Touch him and you will snap his spine," she warns. "And it seems he's unable to heal so I suggest you stand back. It's weak. Any movement, it tears."

"Tear what?" Sinner asks, voice gone flat.

"The braid," she says. Her palm never leaves my chest. I can feel her power tasting me like a viper's tongue. "Two threads, one knot, and a third, much older, looping the others tight."

"Speak like a person," Knight grinds out.

She ignores him, eyes on me. "Listen, boy," she murmurs, and the word boy should make me laugh, but nothing in me remembers how. "The shore you want will drown you if you go as you are. The moon split its light to keep a tide alive. One part burns in you. The other burns where she's missed."

"Riddles," I breathe, head lolling, fury too tired to lift its fists. "Why are you here, mage?"

"We will end this," Creed says again, steadier now, tasting my glare and not looking away.

"Creed," Knight shakes his head.

"There is no choice. We have to buy time, figure out how to cut her from his core without unraveling the thread that's actually keeping his heart beating."

Knight's jaw clenches so hard I hear it. "We're not—"

"We are," Creed says, not looking away from me.

The mage's hand leaves my chest and the invisible hook lets me drop an inch or two. I sway and Knight lunges to break the fall.

The mage clicks her tongue, and I jerk to a halt like a marionette whose strings were yanked from above.

Creed steps up, decision in his shoulders like armor. "London," he says. "shield the room. No one can know."

"What are you doing, Creed?" I jerk.

Why can't I move?

I open my mouth, but nothing comes out.

Why can't I speak?

"God damn it, do it!" Creed shouts. "Now. Everyone, all at once."

"It's wrong," Knight snaps.

"I said fucking do it!"

"It's forbidden, even to us."

"There is no choice." Sinner.

"Enough! Now! All of you!" my brother screams.

The air goes cold, prickles of ice erupt across my skin, only to burn like fire a moment later.

I think I scream or roar. Hands clamp me from all angles.

My body ceases, chest thrashing with each ragged breath, lungs burning as I try to contain the storm inside. In and fucking out—chaos scratches her razor-sharp claws down the marrow of my bones, leaving splinters of madness in her wake.

Red. Everything is fucking red.

"WHAT THE FUCK!" The roar that leaves my chest is feral. It's years of hunger rolled into one explosive moment, echoing off the walls with enough force the windows rattle.

The door flings open with enough force to crack the wall behind it. The sound barely registers through the searing hot rage, and pain.

Pain.

Aching. Like an open infected wound beneath my skin that will never close and—

"Oh my..." soft. A voice, unfamiliar yet somehow known, pulls me to her. She stands at the threshold, golden waves that curl around her shoulders like silk in the dim light. Her skin, pale and fragile as porcelain, seems to glow from within.

Her eyes lock on mine, and something shifts in the universe.

Red bleeds to a hue I'm unfamiliar with, something warmer, gentler. The rage, for the first time in my memory, submits to something softer, leaving me breathless in its wake...

Her lips part, trembling like she isn't sure if she should speak, but instead of words, it's the faintest smile that curves her mouth. It's…fragile, almost sad, like she walked into the pit on purpose and already knows the monster will eat her alive.

Am I the monster she fears?

No, she should never fear me, she should…

My mind splinters and my teeth snap, jaw aching with the need to tear the softness right off her face.

Her eyes grow glossy and my brows yank together as my chest rattles from the sight, something deep and primal tearing at my insides. It's a vicious demand clawing through me.

Fix it, comfort her, touch her.

It's brutal, the way it tears at me. Like my skull is being split open from the inside, pressure behind my eyes making the room tilt. Making my heart slam too hard against my ribcage.

The girl lowers slowly, almost like she's floating to the floor's surface. Like gravity bends differently for her and is honored to do so. Every inch of her body folds down in front of me, and my anger intensifies.

Why the fuck is she on her knees for me?

I should be the one at her feet. I should be the one begging to—

No.

I growl, shaking my head and rattling the thought from my skull.

No. What the fuck is going on?

I thrash forward, but my body goes nowhere, a sickened snap sounding as fire curses through my veins. My wrist has snapped and my head swings to the side.

My brothers hold me back. One on each arm. Red and black ropes winding around my arms, binding me to them like an animal on a fucking leash.

"Who is this?" My voice cracks across the room, rough,

jagged. “What the fuck are you doing?”

They pull me back harder, an invisible force locking me in like a pathetic little pet, and the rage floods, thick and hot, burning every nerve raw. I thrash, teeth bared, desperate to break free and rip the truth out of them.

And I fucking will.

I’ll tear this entire room apart and I’ll find my—

A whimper, low and devastating, tears the fucking roof off and drops the world flat.

I freeze, every muscle locking like chains just cinched me. The sound rips through me like claws to the spine, sinking deep, tearing everything open. My lungs seize, my chest caves, and I can’t breathe past the punch of it.

I turn toward her on instinct, like every string in my body’s been tied to that sound and yanked tight.

Hold. Touch.

Her tears shine because of me and my rage collapses under it, leaving me choking on the need to put her back together. To drop to my knees and press my hands over the crack I made and swear I’ll never fucking do it again.

Every muscle in me pulls toward her, violent and helpless.

I search her for any injury but I find none visible to the eye, and a small part of me eases.

This girl… She’s gorgeous. The definition of perfection and purity. She looks like something that belongs in a display case, porcelain and untouchable, like a doll.

My little doll…

“No,” I grit, throat raw, tearing the thought apart. “What the fuck is happening? What are you doing?”

Dark hair. Defiant eyes.

Wild and crazy and mine.

My mate.

"It's not working," Knight growls.

"It will," Creed fires back.

"He's losing it," Sinner adds.

"He won't!" Creed barks, his tone then lowering with the command, "Do it. Now!"

No!

I fight against them. Every ounce of energy I have surges, but then something as soft as silk drags across my skin, and the fight drains out of me before I can even claw it back. The sensation carves straight through, splitting me open and stitching me into something else.

My whole body seizes, shudders, spine snapping tight like a bow pulled too far.

It isn't just the touch.

It's the recognition. It's a brand carved, a tether locking into place with the kind of certainty I've never known. The air itself strokes me softly, but beneath it is steel chains, and vows older than time.

My eyes jerk up and slam into hers. The girl.

Her green eyes pierce mine, a calm of emerald, stabbing into me until breathing feels like a crime.

Her other hand joins the first, pressing into the opposite cheek. My power answers instantly, violent and uncontrollable.

Heat explodes from my chest in waves that shake the floor, and my vision sears white.

"Is it working?" someone asks.

"Is it killing him?" Another.

"Quiet," a third voice whispers. "Look at his wounds. They're sealing."

"He's getting stronger."

"He feels the truth now. There is no denying."

Don't know who says what and I do not care. I want them out.

To leave me here alone *with her.*

Because this girl, this perfect little doll on her knees before me, she is all that matters now. When she smiles, my body vibrates in response.

"Hello, my King." Her voice is silk stretched thin over steel, sliding straight into my bones, and I'd give up my crown to keep it there.

"Hello...*mate.*"

Chapter Thirty

Haide

Black lace clings to every curve and I spin in front of the mirror, watching the sequin patterns glisten with different angles of light. Emmie did good. So fucking good.

My thumb brushes over one of the patterns. What even are these?

I tilt my head, studying the lines. That better not be a fucking flower...no. Funny. It almost looks like the angles of live plants that breathe oxygen into the ocean.

My examination continues up my torso, where the top cuts deep, my breasts nearly spilling out, and finally ending on dark black lips. At first, I was hesitant. Who rocks up to a royal ball with black lips? But then I remembered who the fuck I was.

Me. Haide. *I'd* rock up to a royal ball with black fucking lips.

My hair tumbles down my back, as black as the dress, but for the first time ever, this particular chaos is tamed. It no longer rages down my spine in a violent waterfall, but rather glides in sharp, heavy waves.

I look like a Queen.

I look like death.

I look like *his*.

The thought slams into me, unwelcome, and I bare my teeth at my reflection. *Fuck.* When did I start thinking like that? When did I start *wanting* to?

I drag a finger along the edge of the mirror, smudging the silvered glass. The Haide staring back at me isn't the same one he stole many weeks ago. That Haide would've laughed in my face if I told her she'd ever entertain the idea of a *mate*—let alone a fucking *Royal.* That Haide would've gutted me for even suggesting it.

But that Haide didn't know *him.* Not like this.

I spin around, holding my breath with a pressed palm over my belly. Fuck. What have I gotten myself into? This world is so different than the one I came from. It's twisted, and fake, and somewhat manic at times.

My fingers bite into my stomach.

"Pull some shit again, and I'll show you exactly what it means to be mine."

I should've stabbed him all the times he laid claim to me—as if I was some pawn in a game I didn't care to participate in.

I *wanted* to.

But I didn't.

My hands slam onto the vanity, fingers digging into the

wood like I can carve my way out of this mess. That damn bond thrums under my skin—always there, always *pulling*—like some sick joke of a leash tying me to him.

I've fought it. Ignored it. Told myself it was nothing.

But you don't get to lie to wildfire and expect it not to burn you alive.

And Legend? He's not just fire.

He's the goddamn *match*.

I close my eyes but he's there. Memories of him embedded too deep in my brain for me to forget. The way his hands grip, the way his voice drops, the way his eyes go black when he's two seconds from losing control. The way he *looks* at me. Like I'm the only thing in the room worth killing for.

I hate it.

And I *hate* that I don't hate it.

Plain and simple, I crave Legend now. I've become obsessed with that maniacal man and I'm okay with that.

A knock at the door jolts me out of my thoughts. I straighten, my hand instinctively going to the dagger strapped to my thigh beneath the gown. Old habits. Not like they can't see it through the mesh anyway. I wanted it that way. I may be the mate of a royal, with powers I didn't know I had slowly surfacing from deep within, but I'll never be caught without my dagger.

Emmie's head sticks through and I instantly relax. "Emmie, you almost ended up with a six-inch blade between your pretty eyes. Come in."

She flashes a wide smile, closing the door behind her. "Wow, now look at you!"

"I feel weird. Uptight. Fake."

Her hands land on both my shoulders. "You don't look any of those things." She tilts her head, taking in every inch of her fine work. “Are you purposely running late to this ball?”

“I’m late?” I try to find the little bag that she had paired with the dress. Some fucking bag since it has no band or strap.

She flashes me the small black leather—”Here’s your clutch. Do you have everything else you need?”

I pop it open and find the phone. These things would save a lot of walking on Exile Island. “Yes.”

“Good.” She steps back, arms crossing. “Well, off you go then.”

I stare at her, my hand frozen on the clutch. “Portal there?”

“Why not?” She shrugs like it’s the most obvious thing in the world. “The ball’s in the war room. You’ve been there before so you should be able to picture where you intend to go.”

My stomach clenches. “I don’t know. I’ve only ever pulled it off when we were in danger—”

“You do.” Her voice goes softer as she steps close. “You just have to believe enough in yourself, Haide. You are a lot more powerful than you even know.” Her hands land on my shoulders, turning me to the mirror. She holds my eyes. “Try again.”

She’s right about my magic. It’s a constant demand that won’t stop pulling deep in my gut, only over time, it’s spread like a virus, and every day I feel it in a new place.

I close my eyes, reaching for that dark current that’s been building in my chest. It leaps to my call, hungry and immediate, as if it’s been prowling beneath my skin just waiting for me to unlock the cage.

“Just…focus on where you want to go,” Emmie says, her voice drifting in and out. “Picture it.”

The war room materializes behind my eyelids in a pair of massive doors. The bone table in the middle and the way shadows dance across ancient stone. I can almost smell the weight of old magic, the signature scent of a room as old as time.

My power surges, electric and wild, and my fingers tingle as reality begins to bend, space folding in ways that should be impossible.

I crack my eyes open and there it is.

A jagged *wound* in the world, throbbing with the same black fire that's been eating me alive from the inside. Fitting. Of course my portal would look as damaged as me.

It's alive, writhing and blowing heat waves into my face. Embers crackle off the dance of flames that curve, reaching for solid ground. It *stinks* of gasoline and ash, and all the hungry places of the Earth.

And fuck holy shit, the flowers.

Blackened petals, half-rotten, but still clinging to life. Roots twist through the dark vines like veins, pulsing with something that shouldn't be there. Something that refuses to die.

Again, like me.

Emmie's breath hitches beside me, sharp and startled. "Haide—"

I don't answer. Can't. My throat's too tight, my pulse wild. Because this? This isn't just magic.

This is *mine.*

The middle is an open wound, throbbing, weeping... whispering?

"Holy shit." Emmie's voice sounds far away.

My pulse kicks hard, slamming into my ribs. *Me.* I just ripped through space like it was nothing. *My* magic. My hands. My power.

"Go," Emmie whispers. "Before it closes."

I step through, the world lurching sideways as magic carries me across space. My heels click against stone as I stumble out the other side, the portal snapping shut behind me with a sound like crashing waves.

Here I am. Right in front of those damn war room doors—the same ones Legend hauled me through that first night when my whole world flipped upside down.

Some fancy-ass music seeps through the cracks, all prim and proper, the kind that makes my jaw clench. And the voices? Just a bunch of rich people talking over each other; it's a hollow noise that makes me want to punch something.

Only now, this is my life. Only now, this is my future.

I smooth down my dress, checking that my dagger is still secure against my thigh. The blade's weight grounds me, familiar and dangerous. *Mine.*

Through the crack beneath the doors, golden light spills across my feet, the music only just drowning out chatter.

My hand hovers over the door handle. Once I walk through, there's no going back. No pretending this is all some twisted game. No more hiding behind sarcasm and violence. No more pretending I don't feel exactly what Legend has been begging me to feel all this time.

Inside that room, he waits. His brothers wait. His entire world waits to judge whether I'm worthy of standing beside their king and it won't matter, because he chose me. The bond. The Gods. They all chose him to be mine.

And now, I'm finally ready to stake my claim.

I grip the handle, metal cold against my palm, and push the doors open with as little effort as possible.

And fuck…

This isn't the war room I remember. It's like someone cracked the world open and spilled magic everywhere, leaving it to harden into something beautiful and deadly all at once. The ceiling disappears, giving way to a night sky stuffed with stars that shouldn't be there, shining too brightly and way too close. They aren't just tiny dots of light, they dangle like diamond encrusted chandeliers, all fire, silver, and ice.

Ripples spread beneath my boots—not stone, not wood, but something caught between liquid and light, each footfall sending frozen waves through depths that shouldn't exist. The bone table is still there, only...

Its bones ripple like vertebrae when it shifts, the head turning to me. Only it's fucking alive.

Damn. That's cool as shit. Okay, so maybe I jumped to conclusions a little when I first imagined this ball.

Figures glide between floating candles, their flames bleeding colors I've never seen. Violet, poison green, the soft blue that can't decide if it's green. Shadows twist along the pillars, alive, wrapping around carved bone and stone while vines slither upward, unfurling flowers that wither before they hit the ground. A fawn with a woman's face tilts her chin as she passes, hooves clicking against the impossible floor.

What the fuck is she supposed to be? I don't stare long, swiping a drink from a table.

I sip without inspecting the drink, since right now, I'd take anything. I'd take damn Emmie with a bottle of Fae Juice more than this. Where the hell is Legend?

Then everything goes quiet.

Not suddenly, but like someone turned down the volume—conversations trailing off, laughter cutting short, until all that's left is this eerie, half-heard music. Like violins playing from another room.

Heads turn. Eyes snap to me. A few at first. Then the whole damn room.

Some guy's date leans in to whisper, but he doesn't even blink, just keeps staring like I'm something he's been hunting. A woman fidgets with her necklace, fingers shaking, not from the weight of the gems, but from whatever the hell they're picking up from *me*.

Their expressions all seem to shift. Hunger. Greed. The kind of want that strips bones clean.

No in-between. No mercy.

My heart kicks into a sprint. Sweat beads at the back of my neck.

Some look like they could devour me. Others seem to think I'm not worth devouring.

Fuck this. All of it. I should've stayed in my room, claiming sickness, but Emmie was so sure. And I wanted to look good for him. I wanted to prove to him that none of this shit means anything to me and that I'm ready to admit it now.

But I don't see Legend anywhere.

Just faces I don't recognize staring at me like I'm an outcast, which I am. I'd fought hard to keep my place in their uptight world. I failed some classes, but passed others, I haven't killed a single fucking person since I first got here. Yet they still stand here, high on their horses, and look down at me as if I'm lesser.

And Legend wonders why I hate them all.

Where the fuck is he?

I cut through the crowd of Fae with their sharp grins, eyes tracking me like I'm the main course. A cluster of warlocks nearly knocks me over, reeking of burned magic and whoever they took to bed last night. And then there are the giftless, clinging to the walls like they're afraid the floor might swallow them whole, all wide eyes and desperate energy, praying someone notices them.

I feel the weight of stares digging into my back. Hear the whisper of voices that drop to silence when I glance their way. Resent the way the air itself seems to hold its breath, waiting for me to crack.

A laugh bubbles up from somewhere to my left—high, fake, the kind that's meant to be heard. I don't look. My focus narrows, sharpens, slices through the noise like a honed blade.

He's here. He has to be.

The bond wouldn't let him stay away, not when I'm in a room full of predators who'd love nothing more than to see me bleed.

But the seconds stretch. The crowd doesn't part. The bond stays quiet.

And the hollow space in my chest spreads wider with every breath I take.

My fingers tighten around the clutch until the leather creaks. Maybe this was a mistake. Maybe I should've told Emmie to shove the dress and the hope up her—

There.

My breath catches.

Leaning against one of the bone pillars near the far wall, drink in hand, looking like he rolled out of bed and decided indifference was a better outfit than whatever the fuck everyone else is wearing. Dark shirt, sleeves rolled to his elbows. No jacket. No tie. Just Legend being Legend and somehow making everyone else in the room look like they're trying too hard.

Relief floods through me, hot and immediate.

Then dies just as fast.

Because he's not looking at me.

He's staring at his glass like it holds the answers to questions he hasn't asked yet. Swirling the amber liquid. Bored. Distant. Like I'm not even *here.*

What the fuck?

I take a step forward. Then another. The crowd parts without me asking, bodies shifting away like I'm contagious. Fine. Let them. My eyes stay locked on him, waiting for that moment when he'll sense me, when the bond will snap tight and pull his attention where it belongs.

Nothing.

He brings the glass to his lips, drinks, doesn't even glance up.

My stomach twists.

This isn't right. He *always* knows when I'm near. Always. It's like his entire body is tuned to some frequency only I broadcast, and he can't help but lock on.

But now?

Now he's acting like I'm furniture.

I'm five feet away when I stop, suddenly unsure. The music swells around us, all wrong, too loud, filling the space between us with noise that sounds like mockery.

"Legend."

My voice comes out steadier than I feel, but he doesn't move. Just keeps staring at that glass like it's the most interesting thing in the room.

"Legend."

His jaw tightens. That's it. That's the only sign he heard me at all.

Then, slow as fucking death, he lifts his head.

And his eyes…

Cold. Flat. Like looking into the eyes of a stranger who's already decided you're not worth his time.

My heart drops into my stomach.

"You're late." His voice is ice. No heat. No edge. Just…nothing.

I blink, thrown. "I—yeah. Sorry. Emmie was helping me

with—" I gesture vaguely at the dress, at myself, suddenly feeling like an idiot for caring. "I wanted to talk to you."

He rolls his eyes.

Actually fucking *rolls* them. Like I just asked him the dumbest question in the world.

He takes another long pull from his glass.

A slap would've hurt less.

"What the fuck is your problem?"

The words rip out of me before I can stop them, sharp and raw. A few heads turn nearby, curious, hungry for drama. I don't care. Let them watch.

Legend finally looks at me. Really looks. And there's nothing in those eyes. No fire. No possession. No *us*.

Just ice.

"What do you want to say, Haide?"

The way he says my name—flat, clinical, like he's reading it off a list—makes something crack in my chest.

I shake my head, trying to clear whatever weird fog has settled over this entire fucked-up moment. "I'm done fighting it." The words tumble out fast, desperate. "You were right. About the bond. About us. I know you're my mate. I *believe* you now. I—"

Movement to his left cuts me off.

Blond hair catches the light first. Then blue eyes, sharp and assessing, land on me with all the warmth of a blade.

Arabella.

She steps up beside Legend, close enough that her shoulder brushes his arm, and something dark and vicious claws up my throat.

Legend shifts. Not away from her. *Toward* her. His body angling, protective, like he's shielding her from *me*.

"What the fuck is going on?"

My voice cracks on the last word. I hate it. Hate the way it sounds small and broken when I need it to be sharp.

Legend's eyes harden. His free hand moves, settling on Arabella's waist, and the world tilts sideways.

"You don't belong to me."

The words hit like a fist to the gut.

"What?"

"You heard me." His voice drops, cold and final. "You're nothing. A little exile who thought she could worm her way into my life."

The room goes silent. Not just quiet. *Silent.* Like someone hit pause on the entire fucking universe.

People stop mid-conversation. Glasses freeze halfway to mouths. Everyone openly turns toward us, feeding on this moment like it's the best entertainment they've had all year.

Panic claws up my throat. Because if I don't have the protection of the Royals—if I don't have *him*—then I'm just a target. An outsider. Fair game for anyone.

"What do you mean?" My voice sounds far away, like it's coming from someone else. Someone weaker. "Legend, I don't understand. What's—"

"You want me to spell it out?" He cuts me off, stepping forward, and darkness rolls off him in waves I've never seen before. It's wrong. All wrong. Like something crawled inside him and wore his skin.

I flinch.

Actually fucking *flinch*, and I see the exact moment he notices. See something flicker in his eyes—too fast to name—before it's gone again, buried under ice.

"You're a witch," he announces. Loud. Clear. Making sure

every single person in this room hears. "Sent by the island to drain me. To take my power. And you almost succeeded."

My mouth opens. Closes. No words come out.

"She's not my mate." He pulls Arabella forward and takes her hand, bringing it to his lips. Kisses her knuckles while staring straight at me. "Arabella is."

The room erupts.

Voices slam into me from every direction—sharp, accusing, vicious.

"Witch!"

"I knew it!"

"She should be executed!"

"Exile trash—"

"No." The word comes out strangled. Wrong. I shake my head, wishing it could pull me out of this shitshow. "No, you're lying. This isn't—"

I'm about to say Sinner. It has to be Sinner again playing his stupid games, but I feel it. In the bond. In the place where he lives under my ribs, burning and constant.

This *is* Legend.

Not Sinner wearing his face. Not some illusion. Not a trick.

Him.

And he's destroying me.

My eyes snap to Arabella. She's smiling. Small. Victorious. Like she just won a game I didn't know we were playing.

Rage ignites.

I don't think. Don't plan. Just *move.*

My body launches forward, hand already reaching for the dagger strapped to my thigh, aiming straight for that smug fucking face—

Legend catches me mid-lunge.

One second I'm airborne, the next I'm flying backward. My body slams into the far wall with enough force to crack stone. Pain explodes across my spine, skull, and ribs. The air punches out of my lungs.

I hit the ground in a heap, gasping, and the room spins.

Fuck.

Fuck, fuck, fuck.

I try to move. My body won't respond, locked in place like invisible chains just snapped around every limb.

Sinner.

His magic crawls over my skin, holding me down. I feel his lips brush my ear. "You look hot as fuck in that dress." His breath ghosts across my neck. "Shame you're gonna die tonight. Would have loved to take a turn on you."

My heart stops.

Legend steps forward, slow and deliberate, each footfall echoing in the sudden silence. The crowd parts for him like the sea. I can't move, can't breathe, can't do anything but watch as he closes the distance between us.

He crouches down at eye level. Close enough I can see the blackness swirling in his gaze, the cruel twist of his mouth.

"You're nothing," he says again. Quiet. Just for me. "You never were."

Fear. Every inch of insecurity crawls its way over my skin. I shrink inward, my mind collapsing around me.

Then he stands, and walks back to Arabella.

He cups her face. Tilts her chin up. And kisses her.

Gentle. Soft.

Claiming.

The kind of kiss that says *mine* in a language everyone understands.

My vision blurs. Tears? Rage? I can't tell anymore.

The crowd starts moving. Closing in. I catch the glint of steel—knives, swords, magic crackling in too many hands. They're coming for me. All of them. And I can't move. Can't fight. Can't—

My fingers twitch. Just barely. Enough to feel the dagger still strapped to my thigh.

Come on. *Come on.*

Legend pulls back from Arabella, whispers something in her ear that makes her laugh, then glances over his shoulder.

Our eyes meet.

For one heartbeat, something flickers in his gaze. Something that looks like—

It's gone.

He turns away, taking Arabella's hand, leading her toward the doors.

"I'm going to fuck my mate," he announces to the room. Casual. Bored. "Do what you want with the exile."

The crowd surges forward.

Weapons raise.

Magic ignites.

And I'm still pinned, still helpless, watching my death close in from every angle.

My hand finally closes around the hilt of my dagger. I yank it free, the blade singing as it clears the sheath, and I bare my teeth at the first person who gets too close.

"Come on then!" My voice rips out, feral and broken. "Let's see who bleeds first!"

But there are too many. Too many bodies, too many blades, too much magic crackling in the air. I'm one person, held down by invisible chains, with nothing but a knife and rage.

This is it.

This is how I die.

Not on Exile Island. Not in battle. But here, in a glittering ballroom, betrayed by the one person I finally let in.

Movement at the edge of my vision. Legend, still walking away, Arabella on his arm.

He pauses. Just for a second. Glances back over his shoulder.

Our eyes lock one last time.

Then everything goes black.

Chapter Thirty-One

Haide

Darkness clings to me as the portal sucks me dry.

This one isn't like the others. This one *chews*. My bones grind against one another. My skin peels back in strips. My blood boils in my veins before freezing solid. I can *feel* it—the magic isn't just moving me. It's *tasting* me. Savoring the way I scream.

Good, I think, bile burning my throat. *Let it hurt. Let it all fucking hurt.*

Because pain is better than the alternative. Pain means I'm still here. Still *me*. Not some broken, pathetic thing left sobbing on the floor while Legend Deveraux fucks his *real* mate in front of an entire court.

The image sears through me—his hands on *her*, his mouth on *her*, the way he looked at me like I was nothing. Like I was *less* than nothing. A stain. A mistake. A fucking *witch*.

My vision whites out and then I'm falling until my back slams into something hard. Stone. Cold. The impact knocks the breath from my lungs, but I don't gasp.

Laughter rips from my throat, raw, as I cough, hand on my stomach. Motherfucker! Blood. My own. Slips down my throat.

Consciousness drags me up from the black, my face pressing against volcanic rock, and the familiar bite of Exile Island's dust grinding between my teeth.

Home.

The word should bring comfort. Instead, it tastes like betrayal.

Boots come into view first. Leather, dusty and loosely tied to his feet. My eyes move up his body.

Smoke twists around him, thick and black, clinging like it's part of him.

Rusted metal melts over his chest, dripping down his abs in uneven streaks, and I follow it all the way to where it covers his face, leaving his mouth and eyes visible. Red fucking eyes peer at me from above, his mouth twitching in a way that draws my attention to how soft they look against everything else.

That's when I notice them. I suck in a breath. Dark, jagged horns stab up to the sky on each side of his head.

Holy hell, that is fucked up. Who the hell is this?

My throat locks. I force a swallow—fuck, he's huge. *Good. Bigger targets are easier to hit.*

His gaze burns like a brand pressed to my skin. My teeth grind, jaw screaming, but I don't blink. Don't flinch.

I push up. The ground tilts under me like I'm drunk. My

vision swims; stomach lurches.

This fucking dress—the one that made me feel barely enough—hangs off me in rags. Sparkly bits litter the dirt around me, catching the light.

You were never my mate.

Witch.

His words echo in my skull, each syllable a fresh wound. The thing about wounds, though—they're the main source of a pain that I have no problem turning into a fucking war.

For a moment, I believed him. Fucking *believed* him when he said I was his mate, his queen, his everything. Opened myself up like an idiot, let him see the soft parts I didn't even know I carried. He dug that shit up and used it to fucking bury me.

I hate Legend Deveraux.

Laughter breaks through my spiraling thoughts. For a minute, I forget all about the horned beast. Too obsessed with my hatred.

I bare my teeth, straightening my shoulders as if it's gonna do shit up against this giant. "Cute mask," I spit. "Shame it won't stop me from gutting you."

He tilts his head, slow, deliberate, as if bored.

I fucking bore him?

It's fine, every newcomer exiled to this place has to learn theirs at some point. Even demons. How long was I gone for anyway? And this motherfucker thinks he can walk in here and claim what's mine?

No. Absolutely fucking not. Not after I just endured the royal assholes of Rathe.

I move toward him with purpose, blade ready, smirk widening. Every muscle screams in protest. My ribs burn with each breath, probably cracked from where Legend threw me like a discarded toy. The memory hits me harder than the pain—his face, cold and empty, calling me *nothing*.

Calling me *exile*.

Like it was poison on his tongue.

I hesitate.

"Cute dress." His voice is low, yet in a tone I've never heard. Almost as though it echoes itself enough to vibrate through the air. "Would look better on the floor." Those red eyes remain locked on mine.

He steps forward until he's close enough that the curve of his horns nearly graze my hair. Close enough that his heat, or maybe the ocean's, clings to my skin.

My knives don't waver in my grip—muscles screaming to drive steel straight through his ribs. But my fingers lock up.

That broken laugh scrapes out of him again. Like he's the only one who gets the punchline of some cruel joke.

I shove the blade against his throat. Just a little pressure.

It just takes one quick jerk.

His head tilts back, baring his neck. Like he's daring me. Like he *wants* it.

My jaw clenches so hard my teeth ache.

"You think I won't?" My lip curls. "I wouldn't question me today if I were you. I've had about enough of men to last an entire lifetime."

He leans into the blade, bending it toward his own neck. "Do it," he murmurs. Not a dare. An invitation. "Spill me open. See if I bleed for you."

So, he's poetic.

His massive hand clamps around my jaw, rough enough to bruise, and yanks my face toward his. A wet, searing tongue drags across my skin, sending a jolt through me I refuse to name. His breath burns against my ear as he murmurs, low and dark, "Follow me."

Another pulse of pain through my chest, and I reach for it, as if I can pull it out myself. Fuck it. I can't be bothered fighting this asshole right now. Not with possibly four cracked ribs, a sprained ankle, a possible broken finger, and a damaged ego.

I kick off my ragged shoes, the dust and rocks digging into the soles of my feet as I take in a deep inhale of home air. "Fine. But only because I know where I'm going."

Despite the pain, I start following the large—*demon?*—since I need a minute to gather my thoughts.

Silence.

Goosebumps raise across my skin as my senses peak on high alert.

The island has never been silent. Everywhere you go on Exile you hear the cries of death, the screams for help, or the laughter from whoever is causing it.

I slow to a stop. Trees spill out in front of me, the obvious carve from the track that leads you right down to the main road. From up here, you can see the sculpted ragged rocks that make Exile Island. Thank God that hasn't changed since I've been gone. A bitterness I don't expect sweeps over me, and I swallow past the sour feeling sinking in my gut.

Like the spine of a sleeping dragon, each peak of mountain looks like a vertebra carved from black stone and volcanic glass. The cliffs drop in jagged wings, folded against a sleeping dragon's side as if it's been slumbering here for centuries, waiting.

Of course that's not true. Nothing of the sort is ever the size of this island, not even dragons, but that's just how Exile looks. Widow's Peak is a perfect ridge of a long skull and eye sockets dark and hollow, watching over the restless sea with a mouth that opens for the entrance of the caverns where the dragons sleep.

The demon continues walking, his boots crunching against loose shale. Red eyes glance back at me, patient but expectant.

Rolling my eyes, I continue forward, squashing every thought of Legend and his bullshit family that I just discovered.

The forest swallows us whole.

One step past the tree line and the temperature drops. Shadows writhe between twisted trunks and branches reach like skeletal fingers. No birds. No insects. Just the whisper of leaves that shouldn't move in windless air.

My feet crunch over something hard. Probably bone. I don't look down, keeping my focus on the back of this horned beast, just in case he decides to—I don't know—turn around and fucking eat me.

Wouldn't matter, obviously, I'd just come back and return the favor.

I trail my fingers along rough bark as I pass, and the tree shudders. Not in fear—in recognition. Like greeting an old friend. The path opens before me, shadows peeling back to let me through.

You're home, the Island seems to say, *where you belong.*

Unlike the War Room, with its polished floors and crystal chandeliers. Unlike Rathe University, with its marble halls and students who looked at me like I was dirt on their expensive boots.

Unlike anywhere he tried to make me fit.

The dress catches on a branch. I rip it free, relishing the sound of fabric tearing. Let it shred. Let every piece of that night fall away until there's nothing left but me and this goddamn island that never pretends to be anything other than what it is.

Violent. Hungry. Real.

Trees thin ahead, darkness giving way to flickering torchlight.

We emerge onto Main Street, if you can call it that. More like a strip of cottages and caves, each one bleeding firelight from gaps in rotted wood. Music drifts from a lone tavern, all drums and screaming strings. Something's wrong, though.

No one is killing each other. There's no blood splatter being sprayed across my face.

You were never my mate.

I bare my teeth at the memory. Fuck. I'm going to cut him from my brain if it's the last thing I do.

Exiled move across the pathway, between the thick bush that hides the ocean and the dusted path. But they don't act with the careless violence I grew up on. They act with purpose. *Together.* Lashing timbers into frames, tying handmade ropes, and shaping driftwood…into walls?

They're…building.

"What the fuck?" I whisper out loud, forgetting all about the beast ahead of me.

They're building a house. Not just some thrown-together shelter. It's got real structure—actual walls, lifted off the ground like it's meant for something. Or someone.

Exiles—the same bastards who've spent my whole damn life trying to gut one another before breakfast—are working side by side. No screaming. No blood. Just the steady *thunk* of stone meeting wood. Their movements so in sync it's like they've been doing this for years.

What the hell is going on?

Every single head turns at once, and my breath sticks in my throat.

Masks. Smooth, rust gold masks covering every face, identical down to the way they catch the light. Just like the beasts', only theirs have no mouths. Just eyes. Blank staring back at me.

"What the fuck..." I repeat.

And then they move.

As one, they rise to their feet in perfect sync, their bodies rippling like a single creature with a hundred limbs. They make a single step forward, and then another.

"Is there a fucking problem?" I snap, fingers tightening around my knife. "And what the fuck are you guys doing?"

The quiet stretches, thick enough to choke on. My pulse hammers against my ribs, each beat screaming at me to *move*, but I don't. Not yet. The Exiles stand there—dozens of them—shoulder to shoulder, their masked faces tilted toward me like they're waiting for something. For *me*.

No snarls. No knives flashing. No one lunging for my throat.

Just silence.

And then—movement.

They split apart, a clean divide straight down the middle, forming a path so precise it's like they rehearsed it. My grip tightens on the knife. This isn't right. Exiles don't *coordinate*. They don't *share*. They don't do anything but stab first and ask questions while you're bleeding out.

My muscles lock, every instinct screaming *trap*. If they want me on the ground, they'll have to carve me into it.

I drag a second blade free. My knees bend, weight shifting forward, ready to spring. The stones bite into my bare feet, but I don't flinch. Pain's just proof I'm still alive.

"Come and *fucking* get me," I growl, voice raw. I know how I look—half-naked in this ruined dress, hair wild, and skin streaked with dirt and old blood. Pathetic. But they *know* me. Every single one of them has seen what I can do with a blade and a bad mood.

The horned figure—*thing*—lifts his hand.

The Exiles freeze.

My lungs burn. I didn't even realize I'd stopped breathing.

The masked figures drop like stones.

All of them. Every single Exile on this street falls to their knees in perfect unison, heads bowed toward the beast beside me. The sound of bodies hitting dirt echoes through the silence—dozens of thuds that make my skin crawl.

My breath hitches. I step back, blade still raised, but my hand shakes. Not from fear. From something else. Something that tastes like copper and feels like falling.

This isn't possible. Exiles don't bow. We don't kneel. We fight and fuck and die. But we don't *submit*. Not to anyone. Not to anything.

The horned figure turns toward me, slow as honey, deliberate as death. Those red eyes burn through me. I swear I can feel them peeling back layers of skin, muscle, bone—searching for something buried deep inside.

My feet want to carry me backward, but the stones dig into my heels, trapping me in place.

"I'm so glad you finally made it home, Hellpet."

My knife clatters to the ground.

Hellpet.

The name hits like a physical blow, stealing the air from my lungs.

"Sorry about being theatrical with my messages, but you see…"

He moves closer, and I can't breathe. Can't think. Can't

process what's happening.

My legs give out, but he catches me before I can fall, one massive hand wrapping around my waist. His touch burns through the ruined fabric, searing into my skin like a brand.

"I'm a little fucking possessive of my mate."

Don't miss the thrilling conclusion!

MATE
OF A
MONSTER

Doubling the Trees Behind Every Book You Buy.

Because books should leave the world better than they found it—not just in hearts and minds, but in forests and futures.

Through our Read More, Breathe Easier initiative, we're helping reforest the planet, restore ecosystems, and rethink what sustainable publishing can be.

Track the impact of your read at:

Connect with us online!

@Entangled_Publishing

@EntangledPublishing

@ EntangledPub

Join the Entangled Insiders for early access to ARCs, exclusive content, and insider news!

Scan the QR code to become part of the ultimate reader community.